C000141229

Christine Campbell

Family Matters

Christine Campbell was brought up in Gourock on the Firth of Clyde and now lives in a village near Edinburgh with her husband and youngest daughter, who was home-schooled until the age of sixteen. Christine also has four married children, and ten grandchildren.

Family Matters

Christine Campbell

The characters and events in this book are entirely fictional.
No reference to any person, living or dead,
Is intended or should be inferred.

Published in 2008 by YouWriteOn.com

Copyright © Text Christine Campbell

First Edition

The author asserts the right under the Copyright, Designs and Patents act, 1988 to be identified as the author of this work.

All rights reserved. No part of this publication may be reproduced, stored in a retrieval system, or transmitted, in any form or by any means without the prior written consent of the author, nor be otherwise circulated in any form of binding or cover other than that in which it is published and without a similar condition being imposed on the subsequent purchaser.

Published by YouWriteOn.com

My grateful thanks to my son, Andy, for the cover photo of a sunrise at Embo, and to Veronica Shoffstall who kindly gave permission for verses of her poem to be used in this book as occasional chapter headings.
Thanks also to the good friends and writing buddies who have critiqued, advised and generally encouraged me in my writing. And, most of all, to my dear husband, who has always been a tremendous source of encouragement and help.

Chapter 1

Tom,
I have to inform you that David died, suddenly, ten days ago.
As his father, you probably have the right to know.
Sarah.

Kate frowned as she handed back the letter. "For heaven's sake, Mum. Is that it? Is that all you're going to say?"

"It's more than he deserves!" A small tabby cat wound its body round her legs, pausing to look up at the unusual chill in Sarah's voice.

"Come on, Mum! Now's not the time for bitterness. David's dead. Surely Dad should know about it?"

Sarah folded the letter and stuffed it into an envelope. "I'm telling him." She punched on a stamp.

"You know what I mean. Shouldn't you tell Dad how David died? When the funeral is? Things like that?"

Sarah turned to her. "Listen Kate. When your father walked out on us he forfeited his right to know anything about this family." She slapped the letter down on the kitchen worktop. "I've only written at all because you nagged me."

Dragging out a chair, she bent to pick up the cat and settle it on her lap, allowing the soft warmth of its body to calm her. The cat began to purr softly in response to her gentle caress. "Why on earth, after all these years, did David want to find your father?" She smoothed her palm across the cool pine surface of the table, tracing the grain, feeling the occasional indentation of wear and tear, the faint imprints of heavy-handed homework.

Kate shrugged. "He just did, I suppose." She too sat down at the kitchen table with her cup of coffee, its freshly percolated aroma filling the bright little kitchen, wisps of steam catching the morning light.

"But he never said. I had no idea."

9

"Well, he wouldn't say, would he?"

"Why not?"

Kate shifted uncomfortably, stirring her coffee, watching it swirl round the cup. "Well... you know," she said.

"No, I don't know. That's why I'm asking."

Kate pulled a face. "He probably thought you'd be angry."

"Well, of course I'm angry!" Sarah was up again, the cat leaping from her lap as she rose. She started pacing the room, the usually adequately sized kitchen feeling suddenly cell-like, moving chairs, wiping surfaces with her hand. She picked up a cloth and started to wipe the shining, clean table. "Why should he want to find him?" Her body wound like a spring, her too-thin frame jutting at awkward angles from her newly-loose clothing. "What's he ever done for him? For either of you? He made no attempt to see you. No Birthday cards, no Christmas cards. Nothing."

Sarah closed her eyes, trying to shut out the picture of David as a little, dark-haired boy, standing for hours looking out of the window, waiting for his daddy to come home. She'd put her hand on his shoulder, her heart contracting, adding his pain to hers. She would try to find the right thing to say, the words of comfort or hope that would help him, but there were no words. Only the empty pain.

'It's all right, Mummy,' he'd lie. 'I was just wondering if Martin was coming out to play.' And he'd turn away from the window and go back to his book or the telly, making no effort, having no real desire to call for Martin, his friend.

"And you wonder why I get angry!" She banged her fist on the table, startling the cat and spilling the coffee. "The damage your father did when he left us!" She mopped up the spill with a swipe of the cloth she'd been holding and walked across to facilitate the cat's escape out of the back door.

"It wasn't just me he left. He left you and David. He walked out on his children! I don't know how anyone could do that! All the love and attention he'd given you for years thrown away!" She threw the cloth. It hit the water in the sink, sending a fine spray over the work surface. She neither noticed nor cared. "Thrown away like so much garbage. And for what?" she demanded of the air, her hands outstretched, "For what?" Fire seemed to spring from her auburn hair into the depths of her hazel eyes.

'Time for bed, son,' she'd say. He just nodded and turned from the window following her meekly up the stairs. No tears, no arguments. Just the sadness in his eyes, the mention in his prayers, 'Please look after Daddy. Please let him come home soon.'

Sarah covered her face with her hands, hiding from the images, biting on her anger, tasting its bitterness.

Kate watched in silence as her mother paced about the spring-coloured kitchen, its lemony brightness at odds with her dark mood as she twitched a gingham curtain here, tidied the pot plants there, releasing their herby fragrance into the air.

"He left. Just left! " Sarah snatched up the wet dishcloth, squeezing the water out with a furious energy. "Didn't come home one night!" She frantically scrubbed at the work surface, over and over the same spot, over and over the same wound.

" *'A short haul this time,'* he said, blowing me a kiss. He blew me a kiss! I can hardly believe the nerve of the man! He blew me a kiss!" She wrung the cloth out yet again with even more feeling. "A short haul! A short haul!" Sarah's voice had risen almost to a scream. "Eleven years!" Her face contorted as the near hysteria gave way again to pain and her body crumpled over the sink. She let the cloth fall to the floor and slumped into a chair, her hands covering her face, her anger finally doused by despair.

Kate knelt beside the chair and stroked her mother's hair.

Sarah held her close. "I'm so sorry, Kate," she said, taking her daughter's face in her hands, looking into the deep brown eyes. "I'm not angry with you. I don't mean to snap at you, my darling."

"I know, Mum. I know."

"Oh, we'll get through this, won't we?" She sighed. "It's just… I can't believe David's gone too. That he's not going to walk through that door," she nodded in the direction of the back door, where the cat peeped round, cautiously checking to see if things had quietened down somewhat.

"And throw his coat at the chair on his way through the kitchen."

"Always missed." Sarah sighed. "Never picked it up."

"He knew you would!" Kate sat back on her heels, laughing at the memory of her untidy brother and her mother's happy acceptance of it.

"You weren't much tidier!"

"True."

"He didn't want to talk much," Sarah said. "Just go to his room with the telly, his music. I thought he was happy. Quiet, but he was always quiet. I thought he was happy enough."

"I suppose he just never stopped loving Dad. He was such a little boy when he went, only what? Seven? He only remembered the good times, the fun Dad was, the toys he brought home, the jaunts we'd go. David never knew about the rest. I didn't know about the other side of Dad till you told me a few days ago."

"I didn't want you to think badly of him."

"You protected us, cushioned us from the pain of the truth."

"I don't know if I was right."

"Of course you were right!" Kate squeezed her mother's hand. "We were only kids. We didn't question where the toys and things came from, how we could afford holidays. Kids don't. Question, I mean."

Kate was still kneeling beside her mother's chair and she stayed like that, her head resting against Sarah's arm, the cat pushing its nose against her, trying to find its favourite spot on Sarah's warm lap.

The kitchen clock whirred and ticked, the fridge hummed and buzzed: soothing murmurs of comfort in the clamour of distress.

"So d'you think David saw your Dad?"

Kate straightened up, shrugged her shoulders, tucking an auburn curl behind her ear. "I don't know."

"But what d'you think?" Sarah persisted.

"I just don't know, but I keep wondering," Kate continued, getting up from her squatting position, flexing her stiff muscles, rubbing feeling into her numb legs, her hands warming with the friction from her jeans. "It's hard to believe that Dad was here, in Edinburgh, all this time and we didn't know."

"If he was."

"Yeah. I s'pose he might not have been. Could have just moved back."

"Certainly didn't announce it!"

"But once David found out he was here, he must have tried to see him, I'd imagine." She leant against the worktop. "And yet," she shook her head. "I'm sure he would have told me if he had. He told me most things. Mind you, I didn't know he had an address for Dad till we found it the other night. I was looking for his ring. You know? The one we bought him? I noticed he didn't have it on when, after..." Kate swallowed hard and tried to continue. "Anyway, it wasn't there. Neither was his watch."

"Right, Kate. Let's get on." Sarah walked across to the unit. "We've things to do. We mustn't give up. We've got to keep going. I'll pop round and post this letter," she said as she picked it up, "And then I'll get us something nice for lunch."

"Don't you think...? Can't you say a bit more Mum?"

"Let's not start again Kate. The letter's sealed. I've said all I'm going to say. I have no intention of telling your Dad how David died. We don't know how David died!"

"The coroner said..."

"Yes, yes. I know what the coroner said, but there has to be more to it. Someone, something happened, and I intend to find out what." Fire sparked in her eyes as she turned to face her daughter. "And until I do, there has to be no talk of telling your father anything. It's none of his business."

Kate stood tall, taller than her mother, stretching her back, pushing her chin out defiantly. "I don't suppose I'll get the chance, if you're not even going to let him know when the funeral is!"

"Anyway, we can't know for sure this is his address."

"I'm fairly sure."

"How? How can you know?" Sarah challenged her daughter. "Just because it was scribbled on a bit of paper in David's drawer?"

"Under the heading: 'Dad's address'!"

"So? David may not have..."

"Mum! I checked it out. Well, not me personally. I got a friend to check it out. It's Dad's address."

"But are you sure?"

"I gave Mike a photo of Dad. He says he's hardly changed."

"Mike?"

"A friend," Kate waved a dismissive hand. "Just a reliable friend."

"But how did he…?"

"Mum! It doesn't matter. All that matters is that this is Dad's address," she emphasised her point by waving the piece of paper in front of Sarah, "and you are, quite properly, writing to let him know his son has died."

"Not because I want to."

"I know, Mum. I know. Believe me. This is hard for me too, but we must do what's right."

"He didn't." Sarah muttered.

Writing the letter to Tom had put some fire in her for a while, but it had gone out now, smothered by the dross of her bitterness.

But, later, when she posted the letter, she impulsively scribbled the funeral time and place on the back of the envelope. She didn't suppose he'd bother to come.

Chapter 2

The funeral was the ordeal Sarah had dreaded it would be.

The minister, his voice pious and pompous, having never met David, sounded insincere and unsympathetic.

A few friends from David's schooldays stood, looking awkward and uncomfortable in their best clothes, feeling awkward and uncomfortable in this house of mourning, muttering their condolences, eager to leave death behind and get on with their lives.

She looked around. Had he no friends from work? She felt the turn of the knife again. How had she not seen what was so plain to her now?

There were some of Kate's friends and some of her own from work, concerned faces topping sombre coats, unsure what to say, playing safe and saying little. What comfort could they offer, after all? It was enough that they came.

Neighbours, snuffling noisily into crumpled tissues, pretending a fondness she knew they could hardly feel for a boy they seldom saw and never spoke to. Why were they here? To stare with barely concealed smugness that it was her boy, and not their own, who lay in the bevelled box, whose life had ended in such a tragic way?

But she knew she was being unkind. Mrs Bailey, next door, had laid on refreshments for everyone for later. When Sarah had demurred, 'No more than you did for me when my Bert died,' Mrs B had assured her.

And so little family: only herself and Kate.

It had seemed better not to write to her brother till it was too late for him to fly over for the funeral. She had not wanted him to come all the way from Canada for such a sad and futile reason; there was nothing he could do, no comfort that he could offer that couldn't be offered by letter or telephone. He would come soon, she knew, to help her mourn her loss and investigate its cause, but she didn't want him to drop everything and come at her beckoning.

She had made no attempt to contact her father. He had been no part of David's life, even less so than Tom. Why should he care about his death? Announcement of David's birth had drawn no response from her long-estranged father, information of his death seem superfluous.

Sad that the children had grown up without loving grandparents. Without grandparents at all, effectively.

Tom's parents had always been a bit of a mystery. She had never met them. Tom never spoke of them, never seemed to want any contact with them. 'Good riddance,' was how he viewed them, though she had been unable to fathom why, assuming only that they must not have 'got on '. He claimed no brothers or sisters.

So, here they were, a small group of mourners indeed.

The chapel: cold and featureless; grey brick walls unadorned, harsh, offering no comfort; the organ wheezing, mournful, no solace there. And then the coffin, carried by stiff-backed black coats, their steps measured, practised; a plain coffin, all that they could afford, the meaningless box hiding the remains of a meaningful life.

This is all so hard. Going into his room, wondering why he hadn't woken, gently shaking his shoulder, feeling the coldness of death instead of the warmth of sleep. The doctor coming, telling her what she knew already. Your son is dead!

Oh, God, can there be words more feared, more hated?

Police coming. Undertakers. All of them invading his room, examining him, touching his things. Worst of all, taking him from her, leaving the cold, empty bed, the imprint of his life still upon it.

How could she have slept while her son's life ended?

And now he was here in this cold, hard, wooden cradle... but not here, not here at all.

If only, if only... Sarah felt laughter rising in her throat. It tasted like honey. It was all a mistake. She stepped forward. Her hand reaching out, the pew before her melting away. She saw herself wiping the flowers off the coffin, no screws or nails impeding her hand as she lifted the lid. *My son, my son.*

"It's okay, Mum." But it was Katie's voice that answered the longing in her heart, Katie's arms around her.

David is dead. There'd been an enquiry, a verdict, an official interpretation of why her son no longer walked and breathed and laughed and loved.

" 'For the living know that they shall die: but the dead know not any thing,'" the minister intoned, "'"Neither have they any more a reward: for the memory of them is forgotten. Also their love, and their hatred, and their envy, is now perished; neither have they any more a portion for ever in any thing that is done under the sun. Whatsoever thy hand findeth to do, do it with thy might; for there is no work, nor device, nor knowledge, nor wisdom, in the grave, whither thou goest.' Ecclesiastes nine. Our friend, David, is at peace."

They had looked for a reason for his death. A note, a clue. Instead, Kate found Tom's address among David's things.

Oh, God... Perhaps it had been Tom he'd cried out for, Tom he wanted at the end. Oh, God, no. I couldn't bear that, if he'd wanted Tom, not me.

It had been almost unbearable to see the coffin borne into the crematorium; it was worse leaving it there when she was led out.

Someone tried to show her into a car, Maggie, her friend from work, but she pulled away, shaking off the caring hands. She wasn't ready yet to leave this place, to leave her boy, her David.

The chill of the grey, stone walls made her shudder so she moved out into the sunshine leaving Kate to be helped to the car by a friend, aware her daughter needed comfort but glad it was being offered by someone else.

She had found the atmosphere in the small cloister chapel suffocating. She couldn't breathe there or grieve there. She had longed to shout at them all, the gathered, black-coated crows, 'What is it to you, that my son has died? What do you really care? Why have you come?' But she knew it was just the rising hysteria inside her. They had come out of kindness: the neighbours, the

17

friends. But she could not share her pain with them. They had no part of it.

Her tears were coming now as she sat alone in a corner of the crematorium gardens, unable to go further away, her whole being craving to stay near her child. He had lived within her body, his heart beating deep inside her being.

There was a scream in her head, tearing through her heart. The scream of a mother as her infant is pushed from her womb with a searing pain, forced from her body by its own contractions, her belly left slack and empty, the life within it expelled, its pulsing, writhing warmth wrenched from her.

The years of his life condensed into a moment as she felt again the crescendo of his birth in the abyss of his death.

But this time, the scream went on and on. This time, there was no suckling at her breast, no nurturing her child. This time, he was dead. *I want my baby. Oh dear God, I want my baby.*

She had lain across his body when she had found him, willing the life inside her to give him life again. She had held him, stiff and cold in her arms, his unyielding body proclaiming him long dead, but she could not accept it, would not accept it. She had begged that her life might be given for his. But he was dead, and, in his dying, a brutal, tearing pain was born in her body. She clutched her belly and let the scream rage silently through her as she sat here, in the summer sunshine of this garden, waiting to join her son.

David would have liked it here.

Amazed that there could still be beauty in the world, surprised that she could recognise it, she wept softly as she looked around at the well-kept crematorium gardens.

She didn't know that Tom was there, watching from a distance, waiting until she composed herself and rose from the long bench, ready at last to leave this place.

"Hello Sarah," he said quietly as he approached.

Eleven years fell from her grasp and smashed around her like a crystal vase, icy shards piercing her.

She doubled over, clutching her chest, gasping in pain. "Get away from me," she spat through gritted teeth, falling back onto the bench.

He halted, his hand offered in help, his other raised defensively. "Sorry. I know it must be a shock."

"Shock?" she whispered as she fought to steady her breathing.

"I didn't mean to frighten you."

Waves of blackness crossed her vision. She closed her eyes, listening to the sound of eleven years crashing in her ears. "I didn't believe it was your address."

He ventured a step closer.

"No!" The scream was strangled but fierce. "Get away from me."

But, as he turned to walk away, she was seized by an anger so strong, it propelled her from her seat. She launched herself at his back, striking him, punching his arms, his head; clawing at his jacket, all restraint lost like water spilled from the broken vase. "It should be you in there. It should be you!"

Tom was a tall man, strongly built; he was able to stand the blows. He didn't dodge them, but turned into them, waiting till her energy was spent, then held her to him, letting her cry.

"I thought you were dead," she sobbed. "I thought you were dead."

Oh, God, It hurts so much.

"I'm sorry, Sarah."

She had often wondered how she would feel if he walked back into her life, long ago decided she would show disdain, though she had loved him once. But now he had caught her off guard, vulnerable.

He was David's father, after all.

She had planned over the years that she would walk straight past him, preferring not to recognise him, but now that he was here, she couldn't.

She certainly had never imagined that she would allow him to enfold her in his arms, to stroke her hair, to comfort her, yet that is exactly what was happening now as they stood crying, clinging together.

19

He had shared, as best he could, her childbirth pains, stayed with her during the sweat and the tears, the agony of each contraction. He had laughed with her when their son was born, breathed their shared relief that he was alive and well. She let him weep with her now that their joy was dead.

"Sarah," Tom began hoarsely.

But she shook her head, as she pushed him from her and walked away.

It was too soon for words. Perhaps it would never be the time for explanations. The years were lost, as dead as her son. They could be buried with him for all she cared. All she knew just now was the terrible emptiness that was left. All she needed from Tom was the comfort of his presence as they said goodbye to the son they had welcomed together eighteen years ago.

Truly, the gardens were very beautiful, with the perfume of the wallflowers enveloping them and only the distant sound of cars coming and going, their silent occupants filing into and out of their memorial services.

And gradually the anger and the pain subsided a little. Enough to let her breathing become less searing, enough to let her heart unclench... a little. Too soon yet to feel any healing, only a numbing of the pain for a while, her body's defences anaesthetising her till she could regroup for the next onslaught, the next cruel, empty contraction.

She drew in a long, shuddering breath of the soft life that was continuing unconcerned around her, pressing in on her, making her heart go on beating, her lungs keep filling with air, forcing her to continue her existence, to notice the sun still shining, the bees still humming, the flowers still dressed in their summer best.

"David would have liked these gardens."

Tom smiled his encouragement.

"He was a quiet boy; liked the things of nature. We used to visit the botanical gardens when he was younger. It was one of the outings we could afford."

His smile slipped a little.

"He liked books too. All kinds of books. He had some about flowers, birds, things like that. As a boy, he would pore over them for hours," Sarah's voice softened. "He would stretch out on the rug in front of the fire, calling me or Katie over to share some of his favourite pictures. When we used to go for walks, anywhere, the gardens, the park, sometimes we even wandered the hills, he could tell us all the names of the trees and flowers, and the birds," she laughed. "He could even put a name to the bugs he caught in his insect jar."

They had stopped beside one of the flowerbeds. "He'd have known what they were called. Those lovely pink flowers."

Tom picked her one. "Dahlias, I think."

Sarah allowed him to put the bloom in her hand and walked on. "It doesn't seem important now." She discarded the flower in a bin she passed.

Tom caught up with her easily and matched his step to hers as they continued along in silence.

"It was David who learned to look after our garden at home after you left. He cut the grass and tidied the flower-beds. He even learned how to plant potatoes and other vegetables."

Tom cleared his throat. "I..."

"He loved it. He knew it helped. Not just the work, the veg as well. We didn't have much."

"Sarah, I..."

She raised her hand to stop him speaking.

In the distant car park, neighbours and friends had long since driven away and she was vaguely aware that no-one had thanked them for coming. Well, it had been their choice. There had been no invite. They had just taken it upon themselves to come.

Like Tom.

He had come.

"I didn't see you inside."

"I was at the back. I didn't think I had the right..."

"No."

"You look good, Sarah."

She accepted the lie, knowing her face was gaunt and colourless through lack of sleep and lack of food, her eyes red and puffy from weeks of tears, too weary to argue.

"And you," she said instead. He did look good. Still handsome, still tall and straight, still charming. Still Tom. She sighed and looked around at the garden. "Yes, he would have liked it here."

"Sarah…"

"I did my best, Tom. After you left."

"I don't doubt it."

"I had to work. I tried to be around when they needed me, but I had to work."

Tom cleared his throat. "Of course."

"Children need food, clothes. I had no choice."

"I know."

She took a tissue from her pocket and blew her nose, turning, as she did, to look squarely into his face. "Do you, Tom?"

Tom shook his head. "I just meant…"

"What does it matter now? What does any of it matter?" Sarah sighed, putting the crumpled tissue back in her pocket.

Again, they walked on.

"It was a nice funeral." Tom ventured after a while.

"Nice?"

"Well. You know."

"Not really."

"Well. It was … nice."

"Yes."

"Sarah. I wanted to say…"

Sarah stopped walking and turned to look at him. "Best not, Tom. Not here. Not now."

"But…"

She shook her head and walked on.

Tom touched her arm. "Won't you sit for a while?" He nodded towards a nearby bench.

"What do you want from me, Tom?"

He shrugged. "Nothing. Just to talk a little."

"You've nothing I want to hear." But she sat down anyway.

"What happened, Sarah?"

"I thought that's what you might want to tell me!"

"I mean David. What happened to David?"

22

Sarah got up from the bench and started back down the path they had come along. "He died."

"But how?"

"I want to go to the car now, Tom. I'm tired. I'm not ready to talk about this yet."

He put his hand under her elbow. "Of course. I'll walk over with you."

Sarah drew away from him. "No. Please. I'd rather we said goodbye here."

"Whatever." He shrugged again. "Thank you for walking a little with me, Sarah. And thank you for telling me a bit about my son."

"Yes." And, surprising herself, she smiled.

Kate and her friend had waited quietly in the car until, long after everybody else had gone home, Sarah came to her alone.

"Let's go home, Katie."

They sat silently in the back of the car: Kate, exhausted by grief; Sarah, almost in shock. Trying to unravel her feelings. Trying to understand why. Why she had allowed, almost welcomed, Tom's presence and his comfort.

She had tutored herself to hate him but her heart was an unruly pupil.

By the time Tom's letter arrived, Sarah had brought her heart well under control. But not her anger.

Chapter 3

"How dare he?" Sarah fumed. "How dare he?" She waved the letter about as she paced the room. "Who does he think he is? I want nothing from him! Does he think he can just walk back into my life and take up where he left off? How dare he?"

"How dare he what, mother?" Kate asked for the third time.

"Read this! Just read it! The cheek of the man!" Sarah thrust the letter at Kate.

Taking the letter, Kate sat down and began to read, *"My dearest Sarah,"*

Her eyes flashing, Sarah snatched the letter from her daughter's hand,

"Never mind all the rubbish about how much he's missed us and how he's longed to see us." She screwed up the first page of the letter and threw it from her in disgust, heedless of where it landed in her tidy living-room. "Nobody ever stopped him!" she said, pushing the second page into Kate's hand. "Look at this bit." She pointed to a line a little way down.

Kate took the page and began to read, *"I know that I can't make up for all the years of neglect..."*

"Damn right he can't!" interrupted Sarah.

"...but I'd like to help you if I can."

"Bit late for that now," she muttered.

"Mother! Let me read it!"

"Go on then, go on," Sarah subsided into a chair.

Kate continued to read, *"I've got a few bob stashed away, all legal and proper, I hasten to add. I'm a reformed character, everything above board."*

"Huh!"

"Mother!"

"Hmm…"

"At forty-eight, I'm getting too old to be fiddling things, dicing with the law. I run a clean business now. Second-hand furniture. No trouble. You wouldn't have to worry where the money came from, like the old days. So, I've enclosed a cheque to help you with the funeral expenses. Please…"

"The cheek of the man!"

"Mother!"

"Well! Who does he think he is?"

"Let me finish reading."

Sarah pursed her lips and closed her eyes, deeply offended both by Tom's letter and by Kate's reprimand.

"Please accept the money. I know funerals don't come cheap and, as I say, I'd like to help. I hope to call in and see you soon, if I may.

Yours, Tom."

"Have you finished?"

Kate nodded.

"Then perhaps you'll agree. He has a damn cheek! How dare he?"

"So you keep asking, Mother. But why? Dad's only trying to make amends," Kate said, as she lifted the cheque from the floor, where Sarah had thrown it. "This is a sizeable cheque. You should be grateful. How else will you manage to pay for the funeral?"

"I'll manage! Like I've always managed! I want nothing from your father. I did without his help for eleven years. I don't want it now. When your father walked out that door he left us with nothing, but we got by. It was damn hard work, but we got by. He needn't think he can waltz back in, throwing his dirty money about."

"But he says he's changed, gone straight. He said he's got a second-hand furniture business," Kate reasoned.

Sarah jumped up from the chair and paced the room again. "He says… he says!" She threw up her hands. "He always was a smooth talker. Could talk his way out of any trouble and, heaven knows, he got into plenty!"

"Maybe he really has changed this time."

"Grow up, Kate! This is not some fairy tale where the hero comes dashing back to save the day. It's Tom Reed we're talking about. He's no good. Never was. Never will be."

"You don't know that."

"Of course I know that. Look, I'm sorry Katie. I know he's your Dad, and you want to believe the best, but believe me. I know Tom. He won't have changed."

"You just don't want him to have changed," Kate muttered.

"There's no need to be sullen with me. It's not my fault he can't be trusted." She leant over the back of a chair, reaching for a cushion, which she punched into shape. "So when d'you suppose this amazing change would have taken place? Last week?" The cushion was thrown at the chair. "Yesterday?" picked up "Last year?" and punched again. "When, Katie?"

"I don't know."

"No, you don't!" Sarah discarded the cushion. "Because he hasn't changed. If he had, why did he not get in touch? Where's he been? If he'd nothing to hide, nothing he was hiding from, why wait till your son dies before letting your family know you're alive?"

"I don't know. I just think you should give him a chance."

"A chance for what?" Sarah spread her hands. "To make amends? Hardly! Too late for that now. Too many boats under the bridge. "

"Water. Too much water," Kate corrected her mother automatically.

"What?"

"Nothing. I just think you should let him help. It's not like we couldn't do with it."

"We manage."

"Yeah," Kate sighed. "Whatever."

Sarah lowered her head, frustration and anger ebbing away as weariness crept around her. "Oh, damn the man, damn him!" she cried as she bent, leaning over the back of the sofa. "I thought he must be dead. Couldn't believe that he'd really left me."

"Oh, Mum."

She stroked the material of the couch, watching how the colour changed as she stroked it one way then the other. The cat thought she wanted to play and started chasing her hand, paws swatting at the movement.

"Tom knew how to make me laugh... and love." She bent to kiss the cat's head, "I loved the damn man. Tried to stop after he'd been gone a while," then gently pushed past Kate as she strode across the room, remembering again how long it had taken her to get over her abandonment.

"I missed him too. Loved him too."

"What fools he's made of us."

But Katie was only half listening. "I'm sorry I didn't see Dad at the funeral," she confessed. "I didn't know he was there."

"He stood at the back."

"I'd like to see him, Mum" She looked at Sarah, sadness in her eyes.

With a sigh, Sarah covered her own feelings with the mantel of her motherhood. "I know, I know." She drew her daughter into her arms.

Shrugging out of the embrace, Kate continued. "I went to the cemetery once, you know. When I was fourteen. Skipped school for the day. I pretended it was Dad's funeral," she sighed.

"Oh, Katie."

"I wore your black dress. You know, the 'wee cocktail number' you used to call it. With your black velvet jacket. Very 'eighties'!" She modelled the remembered dress, parading the catwalk behind the couch.

"And I bought a black pillbox hat in a charity shop. It had a net that I could draw down over my face." And she demonstrated how she had done just that, her brown eyes peeping sadly through the imagined curtain. "I felt very sophisticated. Sobbed softly when the coffin was lowered into the grave, howled out when they started throwing in the earth. Even threw a rose onto the coffin."

Sarah's hand was over her mouth, stifling the cry in her heart.

Kate smiled through her tears. "It must have been a real puzzle to the grieving family," she said, remembering the day, remembering the feelings. "Someone tried to speak to me but I ran away, crying very dramatically. It was like being in a play on telly." She shook her head. "I can hardly believe I did it. But I was only fourteen, a very dramatic age. Over the top."

"Oh you poor, poor thing."

"I needed to grieve."

"Did it help?" Sarah asked, amazed that her daughter could have done such a thing, that she had had the courage and the sense of drama.

"Yes," Kate said. "I think it was crucial. I had convinced myself he had died. I mean, he had to have died, didn't he? There was just no other acceptable reason why he would stay away so long. So I needed a funeral. Some way of saying 'Goodbye'. So," she shrugged. "I borrowed one! It seemed the thing to do. My father was dead. I went to his funeral."

"I had no idea."

"No."

"And David?"

"David wouldn't believe Dad was dead. Got really angry with me if I suggested it, so I didn't invite him along. In fact, I didn't tell anyone about it."

Sarah had turned where she sat, her hand resting along the back of the chair.

Kate bent and kissed her mother's hand. "It was okay," she assured her. "It lent the proceedings even more drama, I suppose. Suited me at the time," she shrugged. "Suited the way I was feeling."

She walked across the room, back to the here and now. "But there... he isn't dead after all!" Katie blew her nose noisily. "I'd like to see him, Mum. Would you mind?"

Sarah leant back wearily. "Oh Katie, Katie. Whether I mind or not isn't the point. It's whether it's wise."

"How d'you mean?"

"I think you'll get hurt."

Kate turned, looking puzzled. "But he's my Dad!"

"Yeah! He's your Dad, but where's he been for the past eleven years?"

"I don't think it matters."

Sarah gasped. "You don't think it matters!" Forgetting the cat on her lap, she jumped to her feet. "Katie, wherever he was, he wasn't on the moon! He could have been in touch! He left us here, not knowing whether he was alive or dead, worried sick, broken hearted."

"I don't care."

Sarah threw her hands in the air. "But don't you see? He could do the same thing again! He could wait till you get to know him, then, whoosh... he's off!"

"I don't care. I still want to see him, Mum. He's family. He's my Dad," she shrugged.

Chapter 4

It was a beautiful, cloudless, summer day when they met, by appointment, in the botanical gardens. Kate had chosen the venue because it was always a favourite place of hers and David's. They used to meet here sometimes at lunchtime, when she could get away from work at the same time as he did. David always said that this is where he'd like to meet Dad, given the chance.

'Do you remember the time he brought us here when we were supposed to be at the dentist?' he'd reminisced.

'No wonder! You'd cried so much just at the thought of the dentist, the poor man couldn't bring himself to take us into the surgery!' and they had laughed at the memory.

Kate had no fear of unfriendly ghosts in choosing to meet Tom here today; all the memories held here were happy ones, some of her childhood, some more recent.

She had made sure that she arrived first, wanting to study her father as he approached, knowing that she would recognise him instantly and guessing that it would be different for him. Where he, as an adult, would not have changed so very much, she, on the other hand, had grown from a plump, befreckled little girl into a tall, slim woman. She still had the freckles, but they were no longer the most noticeable thing about her oval face. The warm brown eyes and the ready smile were the dominant features now. The straggly pig-tails had given way to a chic, short, curly, auburn bob, better suited to her twenty-one years.

She had always liked to swim and walk, so her figure was pleasing... not overly curvy, she thought dismally sometimes, but pleasing enough she supposed.

She had dressed with great care, and much deliberation for this meeting, having tried on, and discarded, practically everything in her own wardrobe... and some from Sarah's. She finally decided on her prettiest, most 'daughterly', floral print dress, knowing that its autumnal colours suited her well, and she was ready.

She knew him straight away, recognising the long, striding walk, the dark, good looks. No, he hadn't changed much at all. She remembered him well but was surprised to see his instant smile of recognition as he caught sight of her.

"I didn't think you'd know me," she laughed as he stood, saying nothing, looking at her, smiling at her.

"How could I not have known you, Katie, when you're your mother over again? Just a little taller, the hair a little shorter, a little darker, I think? But the same beauty."

"Flatterer!" she teased.

"Besides, I cheated!" he added. "I saw you at the funeral."

"Of course." A cloud passed over her face. "I forgot."

"Let's not be sad today, though," her father said, lifting her chin to look into her eyes. "There will be plenty times to talk and lots of sad things to talk about. But, today, let's just get to know one another again."

And that's what they did. They spoke of the years they had shared, the good times remembered, the hardships forgotten. They laughed at the fun they'd had and avoided the pain that lay heavily in their hearts.

Tom wanted to know everything about the Katie he'd missed. The teenager, the young woman: her dreams, her plans, her hopes, her fears. He was greedy to hear it all.

Kate could almost believe he honestly had missed them. But where had he been? Why had he made no contact in eleven years? If he had missed them so much, why had he made no attempt to see them? He had known where they were. But when she asked where he had been, he skilfully headed off her questions with more of his own. He supplied no information in return for her stories of school and college.

"I can't believe you're not dead!" she exclaimed more than once. "I was so sure you were dead."

"No," he assured her. "I'm very much alive. Here," he offered his arm. "Pinch me and see. I'll yell."

"But, when you didn't come back…"

"And what of boyfriends? Anyone special?" Tom's eyes were twinkling with mischief.

"And why should I tell you that?" Kate's response was guarded.

"Ah, then there is someone. The friend who was with you after the funeral perhaps?" He grinned with satisfaction as her blush deepened. "Who is he, then?"

"I don't think I want to tell you."

"Come on," Tom cajoled. "What's his name? What does he do? How long have you known him?"

"Grief! It's like a third degree, father. What is this? The inquisition?"

"Just want to check out my daughter's boyfriend."

"Well, without wanting to seem disrespectful, what business is it of yours?" Kate snapped.

"Sorry!" Tom raised his hands in surrender. "Sensitive area is it?"

"Not particularly. I just don't happen to think it's your business to cross-examine me about that, or anything else really."

"Touché," he said quietly. "I don't suppose it is. It's just, you are my daughter. It may seem as though I haven't cared, but I have… and I do."

"Funny way you had of showing it," Kate muttered.

"Sorry," Tom sighed. "Look. Can we just start again? We were doing great, till I overstepped. I'll try to behave in future," he said with a grin.

Disarmed by his ready charm, Katie returned his smile.

"Pax?" he asked, holding up his hand.

"Pax," she laughed, striking it with her own, the old, familiar ritual calming her irritation with him.

"Anyway, what about you?" she asked after a while. "Anyone special?"

"Only your mother," he replied. "But I don't suppose you'll believe that any more than she would."

"Well, like I say, funny way of showing it! Eleven years is a long time for any torch to burn without fuel."

"Yes," he sighed. "I know."

They walked in silence then for so long that they became awkward with one another, as they hadn't been in their first delight at meeting. Several times one or other of them would prepare to speak but then would not. It seemed difficult to find anything to say, among the many things that clamoured to be said.

"Did you..." Katie's voice was nervous. "Did David contact you before he... before..."

Tom looked surprised. "No, pal. He didn't. That would have been nice. To have seen him," he added sadly. "But why do you ask? Did you think he tried to?"

"He had your address. That's how we knew where to write."

"I wondered about that." Tom nodded in understanding. "But how did he get my address?"

Katie shrugged. "We've no idea. We only found it after he... after... In his things. In his room."

"That's just a mailing address you had. He had. That's not where I live. Even if he had called there, he wouldn't have found me." Tom scratched his ear, a puzzled gesture that Katie remembered well. "How on earth could he have traced me? "

"Would it have been so hard?"

"Well..." He looked sheepish. "I don't go under my own name, you see, for, well, for reasons we don't need to go into just now. Honest reasons, I hasten to add," he hastened to add, by way of reassurance and in reply to the cynical look on Katie's face.

"That would make things a little more difficult for anyone who wanted to find you. For any reason, any 'honest' reason, I hasten to add."

"Yes, well. But you say David had my address. I wonder how on earth he came by that."

"Don't look so worried," Katie laughed. "I doubt if he'd have passed it about or anything. He won't have 'blown your cover'."

"Oh, now, it isn't like that at all, Katie."

"No, Dad? I'm sure lots of people have good, honest reasons to change their name from time to time. And use a mailing address."

Tom stopped walking and turned to look at her face. "Look. This is not going so well, is it? Do we call it a day, walk away and each get on with our lives. Or shall we change the subject and have a nice time together?"

Kate thought for a while. Could she just walk away again when, at last, she could get to know her father? Even if 'getting to know him' wasn't going to be the bright, sunny experience she had imagined in her girlish dreams. She had wanted to see him, had never stopped wanting to see him, for eleven years. Could she just walk away now, because things were a bit strained? What did she really expect of their first meeting after so long a time?

"Let's change the subject," she decided.

"Great! Pax?"

"Pax," she nodded.

And so the afternoon continued, with carefully chosen words on carefully selected topics, a measured degree of personal revelation amid immeasurable taboos.

As they strolled through the gardens, Tom made a valiant effort to lighten the mood again, joking and teasing, gradually charming her and helping her forget their differences. As they chatted and walked, they engineered 'natural breaks' to ease the inevitable tensions, pausing here and there to admire the displays of flowers or to watch the squirrels at play.

"Did you know that squirrels don't really store their food for the winter?" Tom asked as they watched one disappear into the branches above them.

"Don't they?" replied Katie. "I always thought they did."

"No. They gather the nuts like you would gather snowballs in the winter, to have a ready supply for pelting the opposition," he laughed as they were showered from above.

Katie laughed as they dodged and walked on down the hill, Tom tentatively offering his arm and Katie tentatively taking it, awkwardly at first, but then warming to the old familiarity a little.

"Dad, I have to go now," she said some time later, gently pulling her arm from his. She smoothed the grass in front of her with the toe of her shoe. "Can I see you again?"

"I'd like that, pal. I'd like that. Thank you."

He didn't try to make her stay. The few hours they'd spent together had been precious to them both, a start, albeit not a totally smooth one, to their renewed relationship. For now, it was enough.

He walked her to the gate and watched her climb into the car that drove up a moment or two before she reached it. He smiled as he recognised the driver as the boyfriend of the blushes.

* * *

"Well. How did it go," Mike asked as she climbed into the car beside him.

"Not yet, Mike. I don't want to talk about it yet. I'm too confused."

"That's okay, pal."

"Please don't call me 'pal'," she said a bit sharply.

"Sorry, pa... Sorry. I didn't realise you didn't like it. I've always called you 'pal'." He sounded puzzled and a little hurt so Katie leant against his arm as he drove.

"I'm sorry, Mike. It's just that, well... that's what Dad called me today. I'd forgotten, he always called me 'pal'." She started to cry quietly.

"Okay, love." He looked at her for a reaction to the endearment. She gave him a watery smile, so he continued. "I'll take you home."

"No," she sat up quickly. "Not yet. Could we just drive for a bit till I've sorted out my feelings?"

"Sure. Anything you want, love," he grinned.

"Don't push it," she grinned back.

Mike headed for the seafront at Portobello, where they could get out of the car and walk on the prom if she wanted, which she did and they did, in a companionable silence.

"You looked very flushed when I picked you up," Mike remarked while they sat on a bench staring out to sea. "Pleasure or pain?"

"Pleasure, I think." She tried to analyse the warm feeling that was growing inside her. "Yes. Overall, I think, pleasure." She was, as she had said, confused, but she had enjoyed many aspects of the afternoon. The awkwardness and mutual wariness had been there, but so had the fun and familiarity. Unlike her mother, she was not bitter about Tom, possibly as a result of the fantasies she and David had concocted around his disappearance. They had never doubted that he had a good reason for going until the later years. The fantasies had protected them from the harshness of the realities for long enough to cushion the impact a little when they fell into place. She had missed her Dad and found that she was able to forgive a lot. Enough? She didn't know, but she was willing to try if it meant having him back in her life.

* * *

A week later, it was Tom who stood waiting for Katie. This time they had chosen Princes Street Gardens, and he was there at the gate when she arrived.

"Sorry I'm late," she said as she approached.

"No bother. I'm just glad you came," he said, with obvious relief. "Thought perhaps you wouldn't."

"Why wouldn't I come?"

"Oh, a million reasons. Second thoughts. Bitterness. Your mum." Tom laughed nervously.

"Mum wasn't difficult... just indifferent," Kate said with a shrug.

It was true. Sarah had not been difficult. She had just not wanted to talk about it. As far as she was concerned, Katie could meet Tom again if she chose, but Sarah herself chose otherwise. And chose too, to tolerate rather than bless the arrangement.

"Never mind," Kate linked her arm with his. "I'm here. Let's walk." She looked back at the gate. "Do you remember how David always used to run straight in this gate, onto the grass and roll down that hill?"

Tom laughed, remembering. "Until the time he rolled right over that woman's sandwiches!"

"And her cream cookie!" Katie added. "I thought I'd die laughing."

"I thought your mum would kill David. His trousers were covered in cream and sardine paste."

"But Mum couldn't be angry for laughing. David's face was so funny. He didn't know whether to laugh or cry."

"Didn't he cry in the end?" Tom tried to remember.

"Well yes, but only because the woman hit him with her umbrella before he could get out of the way!" Katie reminded him. "And that's when Mum did get angry. Do you remember? You had to pull her away before she clouted the woman back with our umbrella!"

"Oh yes. Yes. Woe to the body who dared to touch her kids!"

"She's still like that. Protective. Especially of David. Whenever anyone... oh... she used to... we... we miss David, Dad," Katie faltered. She hadn't wanted to talk about David. Not yet. But somehow he was almost there with them. This had been another of his favourite places. They used to come here so often on a Saturday afternoon.

"Do you want to tell me about David?" Tom asked gently. "You know, what happened, how he died. I'd like to know."

"Sorry, Dad. No. I can't. Not yet." Kate remembered Sarah's firm determination that Tom was not to know the details of David's death. "Not yet, Dad," she repeated quietly, though she wondered how long Sarah really thought she could hide the truth. "It was an accident, very upsetting. I can't talk about it," she mumbled, unable and unwilling to concoct a lie. "Let's just remember how he used to be."

"Aye, he was a canny wee lad. A real bright spark. Full of fun, wasn't he?" Tom said with a proud grin. "And full of energy. He could run up and down that hill three times before we could walk to that bench over there."

"But he couldn't catch the squirrels, no matter how hard he tried," Katie added, laughing. "It's funny," she said softly. "I'd forgotten how full of life he used to be. He had quietened down a lot before he... before he died," she added resolutely. She had to be able to say it. David died. She had said it, she could almost believe it. But oh, the pain. "I'm sorry, Dad," she sniffed. "I still find it hard. Only a few weeks. I still can't believe it. I keep expecting him to come walking towards us, with his silly smile and floppy hair." The tears were very close now.

Tom took her hand and they walked on, each wrapped in their own thoughts, each wanting to reach out to the other but afraid to reveal the wounds beneath the bindings.

It was Katie who spoke again after the long silence. "I wish David had found you before he died."

"I do too, Katie. I can only remember him as a wee boy, but he must have been a young man."

She smiled. "Oh, there was still a lot of the wee boy about him. He was very sensitive, vulnerable." She took a deep breath, determined not to give way to the tears that stung behind her eyes. "We used to come here a lot, David and I," she said in a resolutely bright voice. "We used to sit and talk and pretend that you'd be there when we went home for tea."

It was Tom's turn now to take a deep breath. "I… erm, I…" he cleared his throat. "I'm sorry, Katie."

"Where were you, Dad? Why did you go?" Kate dropped his hand and turned to look straight at him.

"Katie, I…" Tom raised his hands, placed them on her arms. "I'm sorry, Katie. I can't talk about that just now."

"Can't?" She shrugged his hands off. "Or won't? Don't you think you owe us that?"

"I can't, Katie."

"Don't you realise how much we needed you? How much David needed you? Perhaps he'd be alive…"

"Don't, Katie! Don't even think like that. I can't take that on just now."

"*You* can't? *You* can't? What about Mum? Have you stopped to think about what she's had to 'take on'?"

"Katie, don't do this."

"She blames herself. Thinks, if she hadn't had to work, if she had been able to give him more time, if she hadn't nagged you."

"Is that why she thinks I left?"

"One of the reasons," Kate shrugged. "She doesn't know why you left. Somewhere along the line decided it must have been her fault. Like she's decided now with David's…" She stopped short, realising she had gone too far, said too much, "with David's accident," she finished lamely.

But Tom was not a fool. "What happened to David?" he demanded. "How could the accident be your mother's fault?"

"It wasn't. She just blames herself because she... because she can't... Oh, I don't know why. She just does."

"What kind of accident was it?"

"Look, Dad, I said I didn't want to talk about it yet. And anyway you've changed the subject. *I* asked *you* why you went away."

"And *I* told *you* that I didn't want to talk about it."

They stood glaring at one another, father and daughter, two of a kind, both stubborn, both determined, both seeking the high ground.

Without speaking, they turned and resumed walking through the gardens, oblivious now to the fragrant flower-beds, the playful squirrels and the happy picnickers, secrets unspoken simmering between them. But, like any simmering pot, with time to cool the contents settle so the tension between them subsided slowly as they walked.

"Do you still like to play 'make-believe'," Tom asked as they came to the bandstand.

"All the time," she replied sullenly.

Before she knew what was happening, Tom had pulled her to one of the seats then had jumped onto the platform.

"Ladies and Gentlemen," he bellowed. "By royal command, I'd like to introduce to you... fanfare... tum-te-tum-tiddy-tum-tum... the Thomas Reed Orchestra."

Katie laughed and clapped her hands, her sullenness gone in a moment, captured by her father's exuberance. She watched in delight as her father proceeded to dash about the stage, pretending to be first one instrument then another. The years had flown, or been blown away by his trumpet blast. She was a little girl again, playing 'make-believe' with her father as they had played so often. No wonder they had loved him, this endearing clown of a man.

"And now, a guest appearance by the world famous, beautiful, exciting, fabulous musician... fanfare again... she comes onto the stage," he said, holding out his hands until she could no longer resist the invitation and joined him on the bandstand, whereupon he immediately twirled her around and with another loud fanfare, introduced her, "Ladies and gentlemen, Miss Katie Reed. Loud applause, rapturous applause. She takes her bow." He led her, by the hand, to the front of the stage and bowed to her, making her bow back, turn to the 'audience', bow again.

With serious face, he proceeded to have an elaborate conversation with the imaginary orchestra members as to which of the many instruments she was accomplished at she should play, deciding at length on the clarinet.

Joining in the game, Katie did her best to make sounds as close to clarinet sounds as she could muster, accompanied by Tom running from 'instrument' to 'instrument'.

With eyes closed, she let herself float with the tune they had somehow drifted into, a mixture of 'Stranger on the Shore' and something she couldn't name, both well remembered favourites from the days when she was a little girl and he had sung her to sleep.

The last notes hung in the air as she lowered her 'clarinet' and opened her eyes, flushed with the warmth of bedtime memories, held in the magic of the present game.

It was only as she bowed to Tom's applause that she became aware of the small crowd they had gathered, tourists attracted by the noise of their fun and curious to know what it was about. She blushed deeply, not knowing how to escape, but Tom bowed elegantly to their audience and swept her off the stage.

They ran, laughing, until they had no more breath and had to rest on an empty bench, still laughing, then subsiding into a happy warm silence, their laughter echoing back through the years.

Kate remembered a time when they had 'staged' a 'play' on that very bandstand. One summer, aeons ago. She and David had played 'Babes in the Wood' to Tom's 'Wicked Witch'. He had tickled them mercilessly as they pretended exhausted sleep.

'You're not supposed to do that, Dad,' David had reprimanded him with great seriousness.

'The witch is supposed to be nasty.'

'How's this then?' Dad had growled, lifting David high in the air, pretending to eat him.

'Help me, Kate! Help me!' David had chortled.

But it was Mum who had come to his rescue, luring the 'wicked witch' away with the promise of chocolate biscuits for tea.

'Choccy biccies!' Dad crowed, putting David down and snatching the packet from Mum. 'And they're all for me!'

The ensuing scuffle to share out the biscuits had brought the 'play' to an end amid the tumultuous applause of the imagined audience.

Warm, funny memories of childhood, summer days with the family together the way it should be, the way it never could be again.

They were almost asleep in the heat of the sun, Katie's head resting on her father's shoulder, when a man approached, obviously trying to attract Tom's attention.

"Harry. Could I see you just for a minute, Harry? Please Harry, it's urgent."

"I'm sorry, you've got the wrong guy," Tom smiled. "Must have mistaken me for someone else, right?" he smiled again.

"But Harry...."

"My name's not Harry. Now would you clear off and stop pestering us or...." Tom turned to Katie, pulling her to her feet as he rose. "Oh let's give the stupid drunk the bench."

"Please Harry, I'm desperate."

"Besides," Tom added, roughly brushing the man's hand from his sleeve and pulling Katie away from the bench. "I'm starving! What's it to be? A pizza or a hamburger?"

"Yuck! Neither!" replied the twenty-one year old Kate. "But I could murder a baked potato."

"Harry…"

"Race you to the gate, then," challenged Tom, without another glance in the man's direction, and the incident seemed no more than the starter's call for their sprint.

Chapter 5

"After a while you learn the subtle difference
between holding a hand and chaining a soul..."
1971 Veronica A. Shoffstall

The weeks passed and Kate saw her father several times more, each time coming home feeling happy and carefree, each time feeling a stab of guilt when she saw her mother's anxious face watching for her return.

Sarah was not recovering well from the shock of David's death and she refused to meet Tom, not ready yet to receive the comfort she was afraid he could give. When she thought of him, it was still with bitterness and anger. The mellowing she had felt at the crematorium had been temporary, brought about by the special circumstances. Whenever she knew Kate was meeting him, her stomach tightened into a knot, the pain holding her fiercely in its grip. He was a stranger now, an unknown quantity, someone to be feared. What if he disappeared again, only taking her precious Katie with him next time?

Reason told her that Kate was old enough to resist, to know better than to go with a stranger. But what if he became something other than a stranger? Each hour they spent together would be building familiarity; each word spoken, cementing their relationship, bonding them together, pulling her from her mother.

Sarah knew he was a charismatic man. Hadn't he charmed her away from her own mother?

He had entered her life like bright, lively music; when he was with her, she wanted to dance; when he wasn't, she couldn't get him out of her head.

Older than her by several years, thirty-one to her twenty-three, he had danced into her sheltered world and shocked her parents like 'Rock'n'Roll' never did.

Hers had been a tight... tight, rather than close... family: her father a sullen, taciturn man with firm ideas on things like 'propriety' and 'decorum'; her mother, subdued by her husband's overbearing manner; her older brother eager to break out of what he considered their stifling upbringing, and Sarah herself reluctantly submitting to her father's rule and enjoying her mother's affection.

Tom blew them apart.

She was personal secretary to Mr Finlay of 'Finlay & Baxter', a small, local printing firm, in the little, central-belt town where they lived. She had been sitting in her usual position at Mr Finlay's desk, dealing with the morning's mail, able to ignore the interruptions of telephone and receptionist, not even lifting her head when the door was knocked and opened in response to her boss' 'Come in!'

'Ah, it's Tom Reed, is it not?' Mr Finlay was saying as Sarah continued to sort through the mail and the notes she had already accrued that morning. 'Come away in. It's good to see you, lad.'

'Good to see you too, Mr Finlay,' was all he said, but something in the timbre of his voice made her look up.

He was talking to Mr Finlay, didn't even notice that she was there, but Sarah held her breath. It wasn't that he was strikingly handsome, because he wasn't. It wasn't that he flirted with her, because at that point, he didn't. The attraction she felt came from nowhere.

Blushing, embarrassed by the unexpected warmth of her feelings, she headed for the door.

Before she made her escape, Mr Finlay spoke her name.

He was introducing her.

She felt about fifteen years old, awkward and shy, unable to make the required responses, feeling angry with her own ineptitude.

Tom smiled.

Mr Finlay went on speaking, something about Mr Reed being a salesman, selling office supplies, she would be able to help him.

Irritatingly, he demanded some kind of response from her.

Absently, she muttered something vague about checking their supplies.

Infuriatingly, Tom watched the exchange and grinned.

He knew! He *knew* he had thrown her off-balance! And all he could do was grin!

She continued her retreat to the door, at some point resuming breathing, though she wasn't aware of it. Her world was spinning. She had never believed in love at first sight, didn't believe in it now, being a firm believer that love grew slowly, with good roots... something she was in no rush to cultivate, preferring to have a career than a romance, convinced that she had more sense than to subject herself to the whims of a man the way her mother had. But here she was, all of a flutter over someone she hadn't even spoken to!

She didn't know this man, had never seen him before, how could he have this affect on her? It wasn't 'love', she knew that. Just some animal attraction. Some very strong animal attraction.

Fumbling with the door handle, desperately clutching her notes and files, she excused herself and tumbled out of the room and into the cool sanctuary of her own office.

Her room was filled with the perfume of daffodils and hyacinths, the spring flowers she loved to have around her, but their perfume didn't soothe her, only heightened her excitement. She needed air.

Flinging her burden on the desk she lunged at the window, opening it with a desperate urgency. The breeze from the open window cooled her and brought with it the sounds of traffic and bustle, the normality and warmth of life from the street below. She breathed it in greedily.

She intended to get control of these silly, girly feelings, laughing at herself for being so unsettled by them. She'd had boyfriends, some casual, some more serious, but she'd always been totally in control. There was too much at stake. Happiness was something you worked for and planned... not something you risked on impulse or emotion.

What a strange thing attraction is. Inexplicable. Unaccountable.

She shook her head and sighed. Back in control. She would not be taken by surprise again.

Suddenly, he was there in the room with her.

'May I come in?'

'You seem to be in, Mr Reed.' She tried to put ice in her voice. 'What can I do for you?'

Stupid, banal question.

'You can have dinner with me tonight, Miss Thompson.'

Quick worker. Smoothie. Not her type at all.

'I meant, could I assist you?' She vaguely indicated the papers on her desk.

'And I meant, can you have dinner with me tonight... please?' he repeated. 'Or dancing, if you prefer? We could go dancing?'

He surely cannot be serious!

Uncertain how to reply, she chose to ignore his request. She opened a filing cabinet, pretending to look for something, then froze as she sensed him move closer. Too close.

'What are you afraid of? I'm not going to hurt you.' His breath was toothpaste fresh.

'Excuse me please,' she said as she tried to push past him.

He blocked her path. 'But you might run away. I want you to promise that you'll have dinner with me tonight before I let you go.'

'No, thank you.' She tried for cold, managed cool.

He lifted her left hand. 'No rings. No attachments? Too busy?'

'No! Just don't fancy you,' she lied.

'Moving too fast for you?' he asked, still holding her hand.

'Wrong direction,' she retorted, pulling her hand away. 'Now, was it an order you were hoping for? Can we deal with that before I report you for sexual harassment?'

He held his hands in the air. 'Can't blame a boy for trying!'

'Wolf, more like!'

'Me? No! I just don't believe in wasting time. I like you, you like me...'

'I don't know you.'

'We could soon change that.'

'But I don't want to know you.'

He raised an eyebrow. 'Yes you do. You know you'll like me. I'm clean, I'm not too loud and I won't embarrass you in public.'

'You're very sure of yourself.' She rearranged the papers on her desk, scanning them, sorting through them for something to attend to. 'Sorry!' She looked up, pretending surprise that he was still there. 'The answer is still no.'

He pulled a face. 'Pity! Could have been nice. You, me, candle-lit dinner, romantic music....' He swayed in an imagined waltz.

She shook her head. 'Mmmm, no. Doesn't appeal. Sorry!' And went back to the papers.

But Tom was not easily put off. He kept appearing at the office on one pretext or another 'chatting her up', making her laugh, making her blush, until, eventually, she gave in and agreed to go dancing with him.

Within a month, he had won Sarah's heart and lost her father's approval. He was brash and breezy, called her father 'Pops' and waltzed her mother round the kitchen whenever he called for Sarah. With his encouragement, brother Robert 'grabbed hold of his life' and emigrated to Canada. Tom was never forgiven by her parents.

But, like any piece of music, once you're familiar with the melody, you begin to hum along. Tom's easy, lilting life became hers too. Until he suddenly left, leaving jangled emotions and crashing hopes. It had taken a long time to learn to move to her own music again. A long time to hear any music at all, in fact.

So, while trying to understand Kate's need to see him, her own need *not to* was drumming out the beat. She didn't want to dance to his tune again.

"Why won't you see him?" Kate asked one day.

"Because I don't want him back in my life."

"But he's great. He's fun and..."

"He's dangerous!"

Kate shook her head. "I'm sure he's not."

"Tom runs through life. I'm too old to be running all the time. Too old and too tired."

"But you loved him once."

And that was true. She had loved him once. Loved him enough to go against her father, to walk out of his house, unwelcome ever to return. She thought it wouldn't matter, that Tom's love would be more than enough to make up for the estrangement from her family. And it was. Until he'd gone, too late for reconciliation with her parents, her mother already dead, her father bitter and reclusive. Loving Tom had cost too much.

"Come on, Mum."

"Leave it, Kate. You don't understand."

"But Dad loved David too."

"I said, leave it!"

"But perhaps it would help."

"How? Working on the principle that stubbing your toe makes you forget your headache? Can I just tell you, it doesn't work. I've tried it. All that happens is that hopping about holding your toe makes the headache worse."

"But…"

"Drop it!"

"But…"

"Kate. Your father abandoned us eleven years ago. What could he possibly say now that would make me feel better about that?"

Kate grimaced. "I don't know, but…"

"That's right. You don't. I'm not going to see him and that's the end of it!" Sarah threw the words over her shoulder as she walked away.

Kate shrugged her disappointment, following her mother into the living room. "Will you at least see a counsellor, then? Talk to someone? Maggie from your work phoned yesterday. She says you've still not called her back. She's worried about you. *I'm* worried about you."

It was a familiar theme. Kate felt that Sarah needed help: Sarah wanted to be left alone with her grief.

Sarah sighed. She knew she would have to give in, for Kate's peace of mind. It wasn't what she wanted. She doubted if it was what she needed. But there seemed no other way to keep Kate happy except seeing Tom. And that was by far the worse alternative.

So, eventually, she allowed herself to be persuaded to see a counsellor from Omega House, a support and advice centre.

"Great Mum. Mike's very good. He'll help you come to terms with everything. He's helped me a lot."

"I didn't know you'd gone to Omega House? How long have you been going?"

"Oh, a while," Kate mumbled. "But I knew Mike before David died. He's a good friend."

"Was it Mike who looked after you at the funeral," Sarah's eyes narrowed.

"That's right. I forgot you met him then. He's nice isn't he?"

"Yes, I'm sure he is, Katie dear. But how did you meet him? Through Omega House?"

"Well... sort of."

"What does 'sort of' mean? Did you or did you not meet Mike through Omega House?"

"Well, yes. But..."

Sarah looked long and hard at her daughter. "Kate, did you *know* that David was doing drugs?"

Chapter 6

"Oh, Katie, Katie! Why didn't you tell me? Oh, why didn't you tell me?" Sarah cried out painfully. Once more, guilt flooded through her.

'Oh, dear God,' she pleaded. 'How could I not have known?'

"Mum, I'm so sorry," Katie sobbed. "I wanted to tell you, really I did. But David made me swear that I would never tell."

"How did you find out? Did he tell you?"

Kate shook her head. "I just knew," she shrugged. "I recognised the signs, knew others who did drugs when we were at school."

"Did you confront him, or what?"

She nodded. "Oh, he denied it at first."

"You should have told me right away."

"I wanted to, but when David realised I was going to tell, he promised he'd stop if I didn't. I kept on at him, till, eventually, he let me get help from the agency."

"How did you know about the agency?"

"I looked it up in the phone book and I made David come along with me."

It should have been me. I should have been with him.

"That's when we met Mike. He was great. He really reached David," she smiled through her tears. "Honestly, Mum, he was doing so well for a while. Mike had even got him to go to Doctor Mitchell."

"Doctor Mitchell?" Sarah gasped. "Are you telling me now that *Doctor Mitchell* knew David was on drugs?"

Realising too late that she was making things worse for her mother, Kate could only nod sadly, fresh tears running down her cheeks.

"Doctor Mitchell knew?" Sarah repeated incredulously. "Doctor Mitchell knew as well? Who else knew? Did *everybody* know but me? Was it only his own mother who was blind?"

She was too shocked for tears, but sat motionless, pain coursing through her veins, throbbing in her temples, betrayal sharper than a knife in her heart.

He was my son. Someone should have told me.

Kate did her best to comfort her mother but was brushed away, so went through to the kitchen to put the kettle on. Making a cup of tea was the only thing she could think to do right now.

Mike was a kindly, gentle young man in his early thirties, who had worked as a volunteer in Omega House for six years and was competent and helpful with his counselling. He came to see Sarah at the house as soon as she gave Kate her permission to arrange a meeting.

After the initial, awkward introductions, Kate left them in the living room and tactfully withdrew, leaving them space to explore the possibility that Mike could help Sarah with the myriad feelings that swirled her off-balance since David's death.

"Please, sit down, Mr...er.."

"Mike, please."

Sarah waved him to a chair. "Kate wanted me to see you."

"Yes. I hope I can…"

"It was her idea."

"Yes."

Sarah walked across the room, straightening already straight cushions. "I'm not at all sure it was a good one."

"Perhaps if I…"

"You know it wasn't what I wanted?"

"Yes."

"She's worrying about me, of course." She repositioned the clock, dusted non-existent specks from the mantelpiece. "There's no need for her to worry. I'm fine," she said with what was supposed to be a reassuring smile. "Just fine."

"I'm sure you are, Mrs Reed."

"Sarah. Please, call me Sarah. 'Mrs Reed' makes me feel so old. David's friends always call me... oh!" she faltered, her hand to her mouth. Sitting down, she lifted the cat onto her lap, letting herself relax a little as she stroked its warm back. "Well, perhaps I'm not *just* fine."

Mike smiled kindly. "No. Perhaps not."

"You seem very young."

He shrugged. "Sorry. Would you have preferred to see someone else?"

"No, of course not. I didn't mean that. Forgive me. That was rude. It's just that, it seems sad that you have seen so much. Kate tells me you've been working at Omega House for a few years already."

"That's right."

"So you'll have dealt with, well, with people like me. Mothers. Mothers who've lost their sons."

"Yes."

She closed her eyes and breathed deeply, her head pressed against the back of the seat. "How could I not have known, Mike?" she asked. "My son was on drugs and I didn't even know. How can that be?"

"D'you know, that's the question I'm most often asked." He leaned forward in his chair. "You see, drug users can become very crafty, secretive. It isn't unusual for the parents of an addict not to know for a while. In fact, you'd have to be quite shrewd to detect the changes, it's such a creeping, gradual thing!"

Sarah got up, pushing the cat from her lap as she rose. "I should have known he was having problems."

Mike raised his shoulders. "He..."

She was pacing now, "I tried to be a good mother," looking at Mike, appealing for understanding. "I tried to be there if he needed me. It wasn't easy. I had to work."

"I don't know that David turned to drugs to sort out problems, Sarah. I think it was more of a social thing." Mike sat forward on the chair. "He was inquisitive, experimented a bit, wanted to fit in with the crowd for a while, that's all. The problems came later. Not that he saw drugs as a problem. Users seldom do. But his dependency began to give him other problems. Then he would have seen drugs as the solution to *those* problems, or, at least, a help."

"What kind of problems?"

"He was restless, agitated, became unreliable. He could no longer hold down a job. He'd started to drift from one thing to another."

"What do you mean?" Sarah sank into the chair. "He was working in the bookshop. He liked books. He was happy there. He told me."

"Not latterly."

"But I don't understand."

Mike sighed. "It seems he left there some time ago and had several jobs since."

"Left the bookshop? Why would he leave?" Sarah shook her head.

"I'm sorry Sarah." His face grimaced in recognition of her pain. "I'm afraid he was dismissed from the bookshop, and the other jobs after that. As I said, the drugs were making him restless, unreliable."

Sarah leaned back, her eyes closed. "So, the bookshop, going to the bookshop each day, not really going to the bookshop each day, letting me think… All that was part of… of the drugs thing?"

"'Fraid so," Mike confirmed with a rueful look. "Another of his symptoms was that he became a very convincing liar and that, of course, is the real reason why you didn't know what was going on."

A liar? My David, a liar?

Wearily, she rose from the chair, wandering about the room, seeking an anchor somewhere for the shipwreck of her heart.

David had *never* been a liar. If anything, he had been too honest for his own good, had always been quick to own up to any mischief he was found out in, sometimes taking the blame for things that were as much Kate's fault as his. As a little boy, the story of 'Pinocchio' had affected him deeply, possibly aided by Tom's vivid story-telling, so much so, that he'd tearfully confessed to various trivial lies he had already told, begging forgiveness and assurance that his nose wouldn't grow.

Kate said he was 'soft', but he was a good boy.

"He was such a good boy, you know. Always ready to help in the house, always loving. He'd become a bit of a loner, but I thought that was just the way he was. He'd always liked quiet things, reading, music. He was never any trouble." Sarah walked over to the sideboard. "This was his last school photo." She held it carefully, her fingers tracing the lines of his face, her eyes searching it for understanding. "Like his father. He looks like his father. So dark. Funny, isn't it? That Katie should take after me, and David, his Dad." She put the photograph down. "Always good school reports. Quiet though. Teacher thought, too quiet. Just his way, I thought."

A small tin on the sideboard caught her eye next. She laughed as she picked it up. "We used to tease David, Katie and I. He never put any money in the telephone tin, didn't really use it much. Funny, nothing in it now," she remarked with surprise, shaking it to make sure. "We usually have enough to cover the calls we've made. Oh well, no matter," she sighed, fighting off the significance of the empty tin. The bill nearly due, there should have been twenty pounds in it, maybe more.

Mike allowed the silence to stretch out, letting her have her thoughts.

"Like I said, he was a good boy. Thoughtful, always seeing what he could do to help, always regular with his keep... His keep!" She turned to Mike. "How did he pay his keep? If he had no job, how did he pay his keep?"

"I don't know, Sarah."

"Money for drugs?"

Mike gave an embarrassed shrug. "Pawn shop maybe?"

'I can't find David's ring, Mum. And the watch we bought him. I thought he'd like to wear them''

"Or..." he broke off uneasily.

"Or stealing." She held up the empty tin. "You were about to say 'stealing', weren't you?"

"Oh, I..."

"It's alright. You don't have to spare my feelings. I'm getting the picture. He'd have to support the habit somehow, wouldn't he?"

53

Mike nodded uncomfortably.

Putting the tin back on the sideboard, she slumped into the nearest chair, covering her face with her trembling hands.

Stealing? Like his father?

"We can't know for sure."

"But we can imagine," Sarah sniffed, her voice small and tired. She leant back in the chair and closed her eyes.

"That's enough, I think, for today. What do you say, Sarah? Enough just now?"

She nodded.

There was nothing Mike could say just now that would make it any easier to accept the facts as they were. David, her gentle, sweet boy, had become a liar and a thief. He hadn't been born that way, he hadn't been brought up that way. He had turned himself into these things. To feed the habit that was taking over his body, he must have starved his conscience.

"One thing your daughter is very good at," Mike was saying, "is making a nice hot cup of tea. I'll give her a call, shall I?" and he rose to do so when Sarah held him back.

"Do you know... did he... did he have AIDS or anything?"

"As far as I know, he hadn't started injecting, not part of a crowd who were sharing needles. Unlikely that he had HIV or anything of that nature, certainly not that way. I don't know if he was involved with anyone?"

She shook her head, "No." pain sharp in her chest, "Oh!" her hand covered her mouth. "How would I know?" she asked, knowing the answer already in her heart. "So much I didn't know. He didn't talk about girls. Not like that." She closed her eyes. "It was just, I just wondered, thought, perhaps, maybe that was the reason he took an overdose. If he'd got AIDS or something," She shuddered. "Couldn't face…"

Mike put his hand on her shoulder. "I doubt it," he said. "Kate didn't seem to think he had been with anyone and, as I say, he wasn't sharing needles. Anyway," Mike added kindly, "we don't know for sure that David intended to overdose. It could have been an accident. In fact, it probably was. The inquiry returned a verdict of accidental death, remember?"

An accident? Please God, let it have been an accident. Let him not have meant to take his own life.

"And Kate's sure they were right," he reassured her. "Don't forget, he was still comparatively new to the drugs scene, especially hard drugs. He could just have made a mistake, or he might have been sold a 'bummer'. Lots of these drugs are cut with other substances."

"Cut?"

"Mixed. Adulterated. If he'd been sold adulterated drugs, he wouldn't have known." He put his arm round Sarah's shoulders. "The inquiry found traces of several different substances in his body."

"An accident then?"

"Seems like it."

Sarah closed her eyes.

They sat for a while in silence, their discussion weighting the air like the eerie calm between thunder-claps.

"That cup of tea now?" Mike suggested.

"There is one thing more I'd like to know," she sniffed, drying her tears. "Who was the animal, the *pig*, the *scum* who gave my son drugs?" Her face contorted with the disgust and hatred that seared through her.

"I wish I knew."

"I'd like to get my hands on him!"

"David would never reveal his source, afraid, of course, that it would be stopped," Mike shrugged. "No-one wants to finger them," he continued, "afraid of the repercussions, or of losing their supply if they can't stay clean. So," he spread his hands, "the dealers are enmeshed in a web of protection and deceit."

"They must be the dregs of humanity!" Sarah spat out, hatred sparking an ugly fire in her eyes, a fire that would burn long and hard, its flames licking hungrily at her peace of mind.

Mike sighed.

Sarah knew the fire was not to be put out until it had scorched the man who lit it.

Chapter 7

Mike tried to coax her along to the family support group run by Omega House but she was very reluctant.

"Don't you think it's a bit late for that? David's gone. There's nothing I can do," she argued.

"But it might help *you*," Kate reasoned. "It might help you understand."

"Oh, I understand all right," she retorted. "I understand that my son became a drug addict under my very nose, when I was too busy to help him!"

"Mum! Don't do this to yourself," Kate pleaded. "If you won't go for your own sake, please will you go for mine?"

"What d'you mean?"

Kate reached out to her mother, touched her arm. "Oh, Mum. I know how much it hurts. I'm hurting too," she said gently. "But we have to find a way to keep going. I'm worried about you. You don't go anywhere, you don't see anyone."

"I see Mike. You asked me to see Mike and I do… for you."

"Now I'm asking you to go a step further. Come along to the group. It really helps. Talking to others, understanding the problems."

"But…"

"I need you to, Mum," Kate begged her. "I can't bear seeing you like this any more."

"Like what?"

"Brooding, hating yourself, bitter. It tears me up just looking at you." She pulled her mother's arm, leading her to the mirror on the living room wall. "Look at yourself," she commanded. "Look at the bags under your eyes, the lack of colour about you. Look at your hair. It hasn't been cut for months, doesn't that often see a brush or a hairdryer. You've let yourself go. You've lost your pride, your self-respect. You won't see any of your friends, won't let anyone near you. How much longer can I watch you shrivel up like this?" She started to cry. "It hurts so much to see you like this. I need you, Mum. Not David. *I* need you. I need you now."

So, with a great deal of reluctance and trepidation, she allowed Kate to take her to the hairdresser, tidy her up a bit and introduce her to the family support group: a group made up of those needing help and those giving it, the 'helpers' mostly volunteers, the 'helped' not necessarily. She noted some less than willing participants among the weary, group. Some angry ones too. And many, like her, sad and confused.

Panic threatened to overwhelm her at first and she checked her bag repeatedly, making sure she had her purse, her bus fare, her house keys. Just in case...

She looked around the ill-assorted gathering, wondering why she had allowed herself to be persuaded to join them. She could never relate to these people. They were each locked in their own circumstances, feeling their own pain, their own guilt. What did they care for hers? Or she for theirs?

But, as she listened to their discussion, she found herself wondering about them. What brought them here? What did they really hope to find? Comfort? Forgiveness? Absolution?

Is that what Kate sought for her?

Until now, her grieving had been such a private thing: unimaginable that she should ever display it publicly. To talk openly about it would be to let it loose to do what harm it dared. And who was to restrain it?

Sarah was mute: too soon to let the beast roam free.

But she watched and listened.

There was Rena. Her husband held her hand as she spoke of her long struggle with prescription drugs: anti-depressants, tranquillisers and painkillers. Her fight was far from won, but she was 'in the ring' at last. The doctors who had so readily pushed her onto the ropes, serving now in her corner as she tried to scrap her way out of the bout.

And Jake, who had been clean for seven years and wanted to help others achieve the same victory.

Elsie, the wife of a recurrent addict, giving the group a last-ditch chance before leaving him to his latest decline into incoherence. Sarah couldn't relate to her, with her foul-mouthed denunciation of her husband. His failure to stay drug-free after the last spell in rehab had been one too many for Elsie. She was giving notice that she quit. The group could write this one off, she said, or words to that effect.

One of the people Sarah met, and felt she *could* relate to, was Joan, the mother of a young lad in hospital after an accidental overdose. Joan was trying to understand her son's drugs habit and how she could help him break it. She needed to know what support would be available for them when he came home. Like Sarah, she had talked to Mike and had been persuaded to come along to the family group session where there were others in a similar position. They discussed how they cope, what they had tried, what had helped, what life was like living with the daily fear and despair.

Sarah could see what the group was about now. Too late for her. She hadn't had the chance to cope.

Joan and Sarah often had a coffee together after the session.

"Well," Joan declared, sitting down with a weary sigh, the first evening they met. "That was better than I thought it'd be. I was dreading coming here."

"Me too," Sarah concurred.

"Wasn't sure what to expect."

"Yes."

"Afraid people would look at me, thinking, 'How could she let her son get in a state like that.'"

"I know just what you mean."

"But it was okay."

"Better than I thought too."

"I suppose everyone's in the same boat, or similar."

"Your son, Gary, isn't it? How's he doing?" Sarah asked tentatively.

"It looks like it's going to be a long haul," Joan sighed. "They're trying to get him off the heroin. He's going through hell… and so am I," she confided.

"At least you're finding out how to help him," Sarah sighed. "I wish I'd had that chance. I feel such a failure," she added almost inaudibly.

Joan touched her hand. "I know, love. So do I. For ages after I found out about our Gary, I thought I was going out of my mind. They keep telling me it's not my fault, but I still blame myself."

"Mike reckons David started off just taking pep pills and stuff. For kicks, to be one of the boys. Who really knows?"

"Gary, too. At school." Joan's fist clenched. "I wish I could get my hands on the scum who take drugs into school playgrounds!"

Sarah supplied a few alternative names for what Joan politely called 'scum', her hatred for them sparking in her eyes. "I intend to find him, whoever sold my David drugs at the end. I'll find him. Somehow, I'll find him."

"Meantime, *we* have to come to terms with the results of their greed. They're the ones who should be put through the hell my Gary's going through!"

"Too good for them," Sarah fulminated.

"Yeah!" Joan agreed. "But they don't get caught. Too damn clever! So what can you do?" She was pacing round the table, smoking cigarette after cigarette. She looked in disgust at the one in her hand. "Huh! Same goes for this damn weed! If I could get hold of Jenny Wilson now, I'd wring her neck. Got me started on fags in primary school. Ten, I was. And her a monitor too!" She stubbed it out viciously. "I'd stopped, you know. Gave it up three years ago, but with all this…" Her voice trailed off and she looked helplessly at Sarah.

"I know," Sarah reassured her. "But at least you can still help Gary. You can do it together." Her voice was not steady either. "I only wish I'd had the chance. It was so sudden. The end came before I knew it had begun. Like finding the last page of a book torn out, only you're left holding the page. It's the story that's missing."

They found comfort in their common pain; talking coming easier to another mother, a mother looking into the same well of despair and failure.

"Why don't you come with me to see our Gary?" Joan asked one evening. "He's in a rehab. unit. I've told him about you... and David. I'm sure he'd like to meet you."

Sarah smiled. "Thanks, Joan. Perhaps I will sometime." She shook her head. "But not yet. I don't think I'm ready."

* * *

"You should go," Kate said, when Sarah reported the conversation. "It might help... find out what makes a young lad..."

Sarah shook her head. "Couldn't cope with that," she said, raising her hands as though warding off a painful blow. "Too soon."

"But it's been weeks, Mum, months, in fact."

"Five months," Sarah stated.

Only five months! Dear God, I carried him for nine!

"Perhaps it's time to..."

"No, Kate. It's not time for anything yet. I've hardly had time to believe it's true, never mind anything else."

"But..."

"I've done as you asked. I go to Omega House. I talk to Mike. Don't ask for more. Not yet, Kate. Not yet."

Kate held her close. "Okay, Mum," she sighed. "It's okay."

Okay? No. It's not okay. It's far from okay. It's living hell. The pain doesn't go away. The emptiness can't be filled. I want my boy back. I just want him back. I want another chance.

"All right, love," Sarah whispered into Kate's hair. "I'll be fine in a bit. Just give me a wee while longer." She took a deep breath. "I just miss him so much."

Summer had long since fallen into autumn: leaves, green for David, blazed then died, falling withered to the damp earth suffocating his ashes. She had barely noticed, registering only vaguely the changes in temperature and humidity, adapting her wardrobe mechanically, her heart also withered, her will extinguished.

To please Kate, she continued going along to Omega House... it was almost the only place she did go, leaving Kate to do the shopping on her way back from her work, refusing invitations to visit friends, going to the doctor's surgery only when she needed to extend her sick line for work.

She had refused to see Doctor Mitchell after she discovered that he had known about David's addiction, refusing to forgive him for withholding the information from her.

"But what about patient confidentiality?" Kate demanded.

"What about it? As far as I'm concerned, 'patient confidentiality' should have been a non-runner here!"

"But doctors can't..."

"Doctor's!" Sarah spat out. "Doctors can't give me back my son! Doctor Mitchell didn't save my son's life. Perhaps if he hadn't been so precious about his 'patient confidentiality' David would have been alive today."

"And me, Mum? What about me? I knew," Katie breathed. "Does that mean you can never forgive me either?"

Sarah stared at her daughter, afraid to answer, knowing there was a fragment of truth in the accusation.

Kate turned away. They were standing in the kitchen, clearing away the dinner dishes. Kate had been trying to persuade her mother to talk to Doctor Mitchell instead of just picking up the sick line from whichever of the other doctors was available.

"Of course I can forgive you," Sarah replied at last. "You're my daughter. You're all I've got."

"But you can't really forgive me?"

"Yes, I can. I have. I said so."

Kate shook her head. "You had to think too long before you answered," she said, turning to look at her mother. "But it's all right," she smiled sadly, "I can wait. Perhaps you will... in time."

"But I do!"

"No. It's okay." She put her hands on Sarah's shoulders. "I can't forgive myself, Mum, so why should you? We both just need time." And she drew her mother to her, both knowing there was no more to be said for now. The emotion that gripped them permitted no pretence.

61

Sarah knew that sooner or later, she would have to go back to work, face the knowing looks, the wagging tongues. Or look for a new job. Six months was a long time to hold her job open.

The doctors had been understanding, seeing her obvious pallor and nervous distress: her hands still shook as they picked at her coat, her collar, her neck; she was still losing weight, still not sleeping, the dark rings under her eyes verifying the fact. They had no hesitation signing her off. But then, none of them knew her well, none of them understood that her self-inflicted isolation was no longer helpful. She was drowning in an ocean of empty hours. Instinctively, she knew Doctor Mitchell would be different: he would send her back to work, get her fighting for life again.

But not yet. She couldn't face anybody yet, couldn't make those kinds of decisions yet. It was too soon. *Too soon.*

* * *

Not everyone in Omega House brought a positive contribution. There was a man, Alan Hoddle, about thirty, Sarah thought, who made it plain that he didn't feel he had a problem. He was morose and rude to those who attempted kindness. His clothes and hair were dirty and unkempt, adding to his sinister air of hostility and he was usually what Sarah thought of as 'spaced out'. She watched him closely, wondering where he got his supply, how she could find out. But he was not someone she could ever strike up casual conversation with, never mind trick him into telling her his most closely guarded secret. She watched nevertheless. He came because his partner made the continuation of their relationship conditional on his seeking help for his drugs habit. His resentment and minimal co-operation soured the sessions.

"Why do you let him come?" Sarah asked bitterly as Mike gave them a lift home one evening.

"You know why, Sarah."

"But shouldn't you see him separately or something?"

"We've tried. The nearest we can get to him is what you saw. Him sitting in for the last ten minutes or so when he comes to pick up his partner."

"Well, he certainly manages to spoil the whole session in that ten minutes. Leaves everyone else with a bad taste in their mouths."

"But we don't want to close the door to him. We're hoping that we can reach him somehow through his partner."

"*She* certainly seems to be hoping that, banking on it, even," Kate said.

"But if he doesn't want help…"

"It certainly makes it difficult, if not impossible to give it," Mike agreed. "But we have to try."

"He doesn't want to stop."

Mike shrugged.

"He must have a supplier. Do you know who it is?"

Mike shrugged again as he negotiated through the traffic. "Could make a few educated guesses."

"Yes?"

"No better than guesses though."

"Have you ever followed him?"

"What? Twenty-four, seven?" Mike glanced across at her. "That's what it'd need. Who knows where or when he meets up with his supplier, never mind how the stuff's passed," he said as he rounded a corner. "They tend not to walk up to one another with hands outstretched, you know."

"I suppose not."

"Anyway, that's not my job. Or Omega House's. Our role is to support family and friends, leave the villains to the Drugs Squad. These people are dangerous to be around, especially if you seem to be taking too much interest," he warned her.

"I know. It's just… oh… It doesn't matter."

"Be careful, Sarah."

"Mum." Kate leant forward, putting her hand on Sarah's shoulder.

"I will, I will."

Mike slowed as he approached the lights. "I see you watching him. I can read your face. You hope he could lead you to David's supplier."

"But..."

Mike turned to look at her, his earnestness settling as a frown. "He can't, Sarah. He won't. His supplier is *not* necessarily David's."

"But..."

"Leave it, Sarah. Don't let him see you watching him. Like I said, these people don't like it. They can be dangerous."

"Okay!" she sighed. "Anyway, the lights have changed."

Mike turned his attention back to the road, checking his mirror, waving his apology to the driver behind as his delay had caused them both to miss the lights.

"You're right, Mike," Sarah conceded. "I'll be more careful."

"Good."

"Was David like that?"

"Like what?"

"Uncooperative."

Mike put his hand over hers. "No. Not at all like that. He wanted help. He already wanted to kick the habit when Kate got him along to us, but it was hard going."

From the back seat, Kate murmured her agreement.

"But he was trying?"

"Yes, he was trying." He put his hand back on the wheel and waited till the lights ahead changed to green. "You know, Sarah," he said carefully as he changed up the gears. "I know how you feel about Doctor Mitchell."

She stiffened in her seat. "I don't want to ..."

"I know you're still angry with him."

"Yes."

"But he really was very supportive. He was doing his best for David."

"But it wasn't enough, was it?" Sarah cried. "He should have..."

"If only... a little longer. If only we'd had a little longer. I'm sure David would have made it."

"So what went wrong?" She held up her hands. "What happened?" She had turned to face Mike. "If Doctor Mitchell was doing so damn well, what the hell went wrong?"

"I wish we knew," Mike sighed. "I only wish we knew," he slowed the car, his hands sliding down the wheel, his shoulders drooping. "Why don't you go along? See Doctor Mitchell? Talk to him?" he pleaded. "He was your family doctor for a long time." He looked in the rear-view mirror, accepting Kate's encouraging nod. "I know from Kate that you used to think well of him."

"Used to," Sarah sulked.

"I'm sure he'll want to help you."

"Like he helped David?"

"Not fair, Sarah. He tried to help David."

"He did his best," Kate chimed in from the back seat.

"Well it damn well wasn't good enough!"

"Not fair," Mike repeated. "David was getting all the help he could be given."

"Except his mother's," Sarah said bitterly.

Mike sighed. "Go to see Doctor Mitchell, Sarah. Please."

"He should have told me!"

Chapter 8

"You should have told me," Sarah accused him.

"I couldn't, Sarah. Not against his wishes. He was not a child."

"He was my child."

"But he was old enough to know his own mind, old enough to marry, to vote, to drive a car, whatever. Old enough to be treated as an adult, to have his right to confidentiality respected. He trusted me, Sarah. I could not, would not destroy his trust by betraying his confidences."

"Even to his mother?"

"Even to his mother," Doctor Mitchell reaffirmed. "What do you think would have happened if I had broken his trust?" he asked. "Do you think he'd have been back here for help? Instead of picking up his prescription from me, where do you suppose he'd have sought his solace? No, Sarah, I could not have told you."

"No," she sighed, her anger ebbing away in the flow of his reason. "But I wish I had known."

Doctor Mitchell nodded. "I do too, believe me. I asked him to tell you, but even the thought of that distressed him. He didn't want to disappoint you." Doctor Mitchell looked steadily into her eyes. "He thought he was going to beat it, you know. He really wanted to."

"So everyone tells me," she cried. "So what happened? Why the overdose? Why the hard drugs? If you were giving him prescriptions, then shouldn't that have kept him off them?"

The doctor shook his head. "I don't know the answers, Sarah. All I know is that the last time I saw him he hadn't had anything except what I had prescribed for more than a month. Where he got anything else, I have no idea. Why he got it," he shrugged, "who can say?"

"Or who sold it to him." she added bitterly.

"Anyway, Sarah. What can I do for *you*? Are you sleeping yet? Is it time to get back to work, do you think? What about if I sign you off till after Christmas?"

Christmas! Oh, God, not Christmas! Not Christmas without David.

"Get that over then start picking up some of the pieces? What d'you say? It might help. There's a certain amount of truth in the old sayings about keeping yourself busy at times like these."

It was just as she'd thought: Doctor Mitchell encouraging her to get her life 'up and running' again. Instead of getting through the days, he wanted her to live them again... but not till after Christmas.

With his help, she slept through Christmas.

Work had given a steady rhythm to her life over the years and it felt good to 'get back into the old routine' at the start of the new year, after she braved the curiosity and sympathy of the first day.

Crisp winter mornings, dark but looking forward towards spring: she had always liked the turn of the year, the feeling of being at the start of something. 'The Start of the Rest of Our Life,' Tom used to say, raising his glass to hers as the bells struck midnight. Hollow empty words ringing with insincerity, she had often thought since he had gone, but, this year, she needed their optimism.

Life goes on. The old truism.

To outward appearances, Sarah's life was 'up and running' again, life 'going on'. She got up at seven every morning, made her bed, tidied her room, showered and dressed, cleaned the bathroom, made breakfast. She and Kate had never talked much at breakfast, both needing time to find their sociability in the morning, but now the silence seemed to worry Kate and she tended to babble while the kettle boiled, fussing over her mother while she buttered toast.

..."Will you be all right?"

..."Don't forget to call me at work if you need me."

..."Shall I get Mike to pick you up when you finish?"

Sarah tried to smile and reassure her.

…"Yes. I'll be fine."

…"Yes, I'll phone if I need you."

…"No, I'll be fine getting the bus."

It was all a sham, a charade.

The alternative was unthinkable.

To leave Kate with double grief would be an act of selfishness that the mother in Sarah recoiled from.

So life did 'go on'.

Snow fell and deteriorated into slush, wetting her feet as she trudged home. Cold rain fell on her uncovered head, chilling her though she hardly noticed and didn't care. Winter reached out to touch spring.

The routine clicked back into place.

She went to work, picked at her lunch, talked about the weather, the telly, the news, whatever was being discussed around her. She began to reaffirm old friendships: her boss; one or two of the other secretaries, and Maggie, the typist she shared an office with.

Maggie was enjoying relating stories of the 'temps' she had had to put up with while Sarah was on sick leave.

"Some of them could hardly type," Maggie complained. "There was one girl who only used one finger. Goodness knows how she got on the agency's books. Mr Tasker gave her a try, but it was hopeless. I had to retype practically every letter! She only lasted two weeks. And she was lucky to last that long."

"Well, Mr Tasker's very patient," Sarah remarked. "After all, he put up with me going AWOL for months."

"Hardly AWOL," Maggie defended her. "You had a sick line. And a good reason. He was legally bound to hold your job for you."

"Still, he was kind about it. Sent flowers and everything."

Maggie chuckled. "Yeah, I think he still fancies you!"

Sarah blushed. "Don't even go there, Maggie!"

Maggie leaned over the desk and lowered her voice a little. "Rumour has it that he was quite cut up when you turned him down, y'know!"

"He was fine, as you well know. He hadn't been serious about wanting to date me anyway."

"Not what I heard!"

"Well, you heard wrong!" Sarah told her firmly. "And now, can we get back to work, remembering that this is not the school playground."

"Ooo, sorry, Miss!"

Sarah shook her head, but she was smiling too. She liked sharing an office with Maggie. They had always got on well, from the day Maggie had joined the firm and was shown into the room. When they chatted, they found they had a lot in common, and they worked well together. But their friendship rarely blossomed into their personal life outside office hours. Maggie was younger by a number of years and had no children. She and her husband had a busy social calendar and Sarah was often invited to dinner parties and cocktail evenings at their home but she rarely went, at first because she was a single parent, bringing up her two children on a limited budget: she had no funds for fancy clothing and babysitters, and little free time, having the cooking, cleaning and housework to do after leaving the office. When Kate and David were older, she had grown accustomed to her own company and rarely sought to socialise in the evenings or at weekends, being tired: happy to get her feet up if she had the chance.

As for James Tasker: he was a nice man, a widower for the past five years, lonely, seeking companionship. He had asked her out once or twice, just for 'drinks' after work. At first, she had gone and had enjoyed his company but, really, she didn't want more than friendship and didn't want to lead him to believe otherwise, so she stopped accepting his invitations. Her timing had been good: the relationship had not gone beyond friendship: they could still work together without embarrassment. He had expressed his pleasure that she was back, having enjoyed the various 'temps' no more than Maggie, it seems.

All in all, it was good to be back at work, back among familiar friends, who understood and didn't ask too much of her.

Sometimes she did a little shopping on her way home, just the essentials, wanting nothing new, nothing different. When it was her turn, she made the evening meal for herself and Kate, even began to eat a little better, her weight steadying, a little flesh returning to her face, the dark rings fading as sleep returned to bless her for a little longer each lonely night.

And the nights themselves began to feel shorter as spring drew closer.

She wrote long letters to her brother, Robert, telling him about her work, the news, the weather, the growing romance between Kate and Mike, trying to sound 'back to normal', not wanting to worry him, praying he could not read her pain between the lines.

He wanted her to go to Canada.

'A holiday would do you good,' he wrote. *'Besides, I need to see you, see for myself how you are. Your letters tell me so little of what's really going on. I mean really going on. I need to sit up all night with you, eating toast and talking, the way we used to. You have to come over. I just can't get away yet. If I could, you know I would.'*

She knew he would. If he could, he would. But Douglas, their youngest, had been so ill. He'd just had yet another heart operation, and he was only a kid, barely ten years old. So she wrote back telling him how well she was doing, that she was getting counselling, that she was coping well with her grief. There was no need for him to fret. She'd come over one of these days. Just not yet.

She needed to get 'back to normal'.

She stopped folding and refolding David's clothes, caressing them, holding them to her face, searching for a whiff of his scent, the way she had done before, with Tom's things but, this time, without hope. She knew he was never coming back.

She started putting clothes into bags to take to the charity shop. Then she'd unpack them all again, put them back in the drawers for another day. But the time came, as time relentlessly does, when she was able to part with bits and pieces. Not everything at once, just a few things here and there, now and then.

She started carefully emptying drawers and cupboards, each one staring vacantly back at her reproachfully, as though she had vandalised it. Reason told her she had to do it, probably should have done it months ago. But it was so final.

His clothes and shoes were hard enough, his books and music impossible. As for his personal belongings... she hadn't even been able to open those drawers, afraid of the secret life they would reveal.

Gradually, she started listening to his CDs as she worked in the room, hauling her own CD player in when she failed to find his, trying to get hold of the *essence* of him. They say music can reveal a soul and that's what she sought.

Often she would cease the sorting, the folding, the packing up and just sit and listen. He had loved a wide variety of music, but the ones she dimly recalled hearing him play were classical, orchestral pieces, Mozart, Beethoven, Vivaldi, the usual favourites, but beautiful nonetheless.

He even had a taste for opera. That surprised her. She had always thought of Kate as the dramatic one. But there were a number of Opera CDs, some of them compilations of well-known arias that were vaguely familiar to her.

Listening to his music let her feel close to him.

Gardening had the same effect.

As winter turned to spring, she became aware of the need to care for the garden. If it was not to become a wilderness, she was going to have to do something with it.

At first, she merely pulled up weeds and generally tidied around a bit, but gradually the different bulbs he'd long ago planted began to push through the soil. New life. Life he'd touched. Fresh and green, filled with eager energy. She found a little of his soul here too.

So she cared for his garden. She would always think of it as his garden because he was the one who had planned it and cared for it for so long: he was the one who had loved it, she and Kate only admiring its beauty and enjoying its produce.

She could breathe in his garden.

They say time heals. Time doesn't heal. It only lets you get used to the pain. Learn to tolerate it. Learn to live with it.

And she thought she could... until she found his diary.

Chapter 9

"...and you learn that love doesn't mean leaning
and company doesn't always mean security
And you begin to learn that kisses aren't contracts
and presents aren't promises..."
1971 Veronica A. Shoffstall

It was rain beating against her bedroom window that woke her. The luminous hands of the alarm clock told her it was 03:17. She lay listening to the rain and the wind for a while; sleep being blown further from her with each noisy gust.

03:34... Wide awake, with no hope of sleep returning, she sighed wearily as she pulled herself out of bed, reluctant to leave its warmth, anxious to leave its solitude. She padded downstairs without putting any lights on, not wanting to risk disturbing Kate. The house was cold and she shivered, hugging her housecoat closer round her body. Still in the dark, with only the glimmer from the distant street lamp, she made herself a warm, milky drink. 'Just what the doctor ordered'. She had become adept at this nocturnal routine.

Carrying the drink upstairs, she tiptoed into David's room and, having closed the door quietly, she switched on the little bedside light and put her mug on the table beside it.

She smoothed his bedcover, her hand lingering on his pillow, covered with a fresh, clean pillowcase every week, sadly unwrinkled by his beloved head.

With a deep sigh, she sat down in *his* chair by *his* table to sip her soothing drink as she had so many nights before, waiting patiently for the feeling of peace to creep over her. But the wait was long tonight. She had noticed it was taking longer each time now, the feeling of being near him, the essence of him. She used to feel it here. It used to bring her comfort.

Having never been particularly religious, her knowledge of doctrine was hazy, but that didn't trouble her, knowing how much ambiguity there was in Church dogma and doctrine. Yet she felt there had to be something...

Not knowing where else to look, she had studied David's Bible as she had sat here through long, searching nights. He had been proud of that Bible: had won it at school for 'Scripture Knowledge'. She was surprised to find it well-thumbed, with certain texts underlined, passages highlighted, comments written carefully in tiny writing down the sides of pages marked by scraps of paper. She let herself be led by his hand to read the same words he must have read, trying desperately to read the mind that wrote the thoughts. She had yet to find the answers that would bring her comfort. Instinctively, she felt that this was where she would find them, but she wearied of the search.

She came into this room during the darkest hours, wanting to be close to him, knowing he was gone. There was no ghost, no 'soul' or 'spirit' to haunt this room. But she used to be able to feel something left of the life he'd lived here.

However, it was getting harder to imagine him lying there, reluctant to be woken for school or work, warm from his sleep, his hair tousled and his face hiding from the morning light: getting harder all the time to see his smile, hear his voice. How she wished she could draw back the duvet to see again that precious face, to rumple his hair, to stroke his cheek. Even here, in his room, he was moving further from her every lonely night. The memory of him was fading but the ache for him was just as intense as when she'd let them carry his lifeless body away.

Seeking to aid her traitorous memory to bring him back into focus, she started rooting around the room, searching for some object, some treasured possession, something he had touched, something he had loved...

They had already noted his camera was missing, and his binoculars. Even his precious CD player must have been pawned or sold at the last.

Most of his clothes were gone now, only the few things she had been unable to part with remained: the jumper she had knitted him years ago. It had never really fitted, but he wore it to please her, said he liked to huddle in it to watch TV or listen to his music. It was comfortable, he said, made him feel loved.

But even that no longer smelled of him. She fingered it longingly as she folded it back into his cupboard, regretting the empty shelves, the empty drawers, but knowing too that their contents had become mere cloth and stitches, with the capability to hurt but not to heal.

Her fingers trailed along the neat row of CDs. She would not have played them just now even if his CD player were there, even without the risk of waking Kate. They could only tear at her heart, the pain unbearable though the music beautiful. She could never play them in the lonliness of night. Catholic taste: jazz and rock neatly slotted in beside opera and orchestra. So much glorious sound, so much pain and longing.

The titles of his books were equally varied, their spectrum wide. Sometimes she would read the books he had read, Tolstoy, Grisham, Garfield, the Bible: trying to see them through his eyes. He loved true stories, stories of adventure and courage, stories of men like Scott and Shackleton. He'd never been anywhere very exciting, foreign travel being well beyond their budget, but he loved to read about adventures in the Himalayas, in the African bush, the Amazonian rain forest, the North Pole, Antarctica. He used his books as working books, jotting his comments in their margins, underlining passages that stirred him, revealing his admiration for the men and women who walked their pages. Much of the information he gleaned would have been used to authenticate the 'letters' from his adventurous father. Sadly, the books and the annotations helped her get to know him better in death than she had in life, and while this had, at first, drawn him closer to her, the more she read his mind, the more she realised him to have been a stranger.

She recognised him a little better in his choice of poetry. Kate had once declared it 'brought out his feminine side' and perhaps that's why she related more to that than some of his other literature. She had loved his gentle, meditative nature, had feared the more restless, venturesome moods, but had a need to know him in all his guises.

So, sometimes she would sit here and read his books.

But concentration eluded her tonight; there were none to divert her mind from its restless longing, the longing for something more tangible.

In the nine months or so since David had died, Sarah had never opened the drawers beside his bed: Kate had searched them for his watch and ring before the funeral; the police had searched them for whatever they thought they might find there. Drugs perhaps? Needles? A syringe? Something to lead them to the explanation of the unexplained. But Sarah herself had not opened them.

These were his most private possessions. The violation of their sanctity had troubled her at the time; it troubled her still, but she knew, eventually, she must empty them. Reason told her it was not healthy to create a shrine to David, not healthy to preserve his belongings as holy relics. Sooner or later, she must move on. She had done it before. She must do it again.

Sitting on the bed, and with a resolve born of reason rather than desire, she steeled herself to open the top drawer.

All the usual treasures were there. The things everyone keeps. Photographs and memorabilia, things no longer useful or decorative but precious none the less. His old teddy bear, bought one Christmas by Tom, given with love, accepted with joy, treasured after all these years. A baseball cap, reminder of summer play in the park, too small to be worn latterly, too big in the memory to be jettisoned. Old toy cars that must have had meaning for David but were unremarkable to her. A pencil case with a broken zip, well used in days past, empty and idle now. Sunglasses, football cards, and assorted bits of paper, receipts and the like, things that may have had memories for David or may have been kept by default.

Pawn tickets, one for his camera and one for his binoculars, dated last April, ten months ago and still redeemable. Dizzy with the pain of this discovery, she rested her head against the headboard. So, Mike was right, David had resorted to pawning his precious belongings to get money for drugs. How desperate he must have been. He had loved his camera, photography being one of his favourite hobbies for many years. Wherever they went, whatever they saw, David had a record of the views, the buildings, the flowers, the fauna. No outing was considered complete without the click of his camera. Some of his work was displayed around the walls, mostly close-ups of flowers or birds and some spectacular sunsets.

With a sigh, she put the tickets in her housecoat pocket. She would find the place tomorrow and buy back his things. She searched further, but, disappointingly, there was no ticket for his watch or his ring and no sign of them in the drawer. He must have sold them. She decided to check the other receipts after looking through the rest of the drawer's contents.

She didn't realise, at first, that it was a diary she held in her hand. It had no year emblazoned on its cover, no dates printed in its pages. Just a notebook, a medium sized, ordinary, ruled notebook, the kind you might buy for a student or a schoolboy. And that's what she thought it was, a book of notes from his English class at school, one he'd kept for some sentimental reason or just because he'd not bothered to discard it.

She flicked through it idly, expecting nothing, wondering only how it came to be among his special things and was about to put it aside when something caught her attention.

Here and there, dates appeared in the margins: not dates that went far back in his schooldays, though, on closer inspection, that was, in fact, when they started, but dates drawing inexorably closer to the date of the end of his life.

'Oh, God, help me,' she prayed out loud. 'It's his diary!'

She hadn't known, hadn't guessed he'd kept a diary.

She closed the book with shaking hands; she could not, would not commit this final violation of his privacy. And yet…

Without wanting to, she opened it again. Did the rules, *her* rules, stretch beyond the grave? He had left her. He had not warned her he might go. He had left as a stranger. Did he now have the right to deny her this last, desperate clutching at this last, desperate straw? This chance to know, to understand her own son?

Her hands were shaking; she dared not look down at the pages before her. Sweat was breaking out on her forehead, she could feel it trickle down her face, on her neck, her chest, down her back. She could hardly breathe, the fear of what she might read was almost overwhelming, suffocating, making her light headed.

This was *his* diary, *his* personal belonging. She had no right...

But he had gone away, he had left her. She needed to know why. Needed it so much that there were no longer any rules.

Her heart was beating so fast that she thought it must burst, her breathing becoming laboured.

Why is this so hard? What do I fear? What could he have written that could possibly hurt more than his leaving?

Trying desperately to steady her breathing, she turned to the last entry in the notebook, the one she dreaded most, the one she needed to read, the one she should never have read.

The date was the day before she found his lifeless body. The entry was short and stark :

'I just want to die!'

Chapter 10

Her heart was beating in her throat, choking her. The pain in her chest made breathing difficult. Clutching her shoulder, she lowered herself to the floor, gasping for air.

He wanted to die! He wanted to die!

It was what she feared. Much, much worse than the fact that he *had* died. He *wanted* to die. He had *meant* to die. To leave her.

She lay on the floor, her lungs gripped in the vice of her chest, her heart squeezed beyond endurance.

She knew she must lose consciousness soon and she prepared herself to welcome it.

She clutched the diary tighter, *David, oh David!* reaching out to his memory, going towards his resting place, waiting to join him in his sleep.

Her chest was so tight, breathing difficult, sweat on her neck, tears on her face.

Oh, God. If I'm to die tonight, take care of Katie. My Katie!

Katie!

The world swung round, changed direction.

My Katie! How can I leave my Katie?

"NO!" she gasped.

The pain was crushing. She could hardly bear it, but she knew she must fight to stay conscious. She must get help. She *must not* die.

Katie needed her. She said so.

"Katie!" she called. But it wasn't a shout. Her voice was too weak. "Katie," she tried again, her fingers clawing at the carpet, her knees trying to push her towards the door. The pain was unendurable, the effort too much.

Chapter 11

Katie's alarm rang out into the cool, spring morning, last night's storm having freshened the air and chased away the clouds. She sang as she showered, enjoying the brightness of the day, looking forward to what it would bring. Dad had asked her to come see his shop, hoping that she would report back favourably to her mother, no doubt. Kate was happy to be going there, excited to see where he worked, a little bit more of his life.

He was such fun, so much as she remembered him, so ready to laugh, getting more out of life than everybody else. Surely this bright, easy-going man could not have left without good reason? David always said, 'It takes two to make, *or break* a marriage.' He always reckoned Mum held back the truth, knowing why he went, unwilling to face any fault of hers. Kate wasn't so sure. She had seen more of Mum's pain, knew more of her loneliness and longing. But still, his reasons must have been good. He wouldn't have gone on a selfish whim... would he?

She turned the thermostat down and let the cooler water cascade over her body, scattering doubts, refreshing hopes. Yes, the day stretched ahead invitingly and she was ready to run with it.

Cosy in her bathrobe and slippers, she dried her hair and creamed her face and body, still humming, still feeling good. She would wear something bright and cheerful, something to match her mood, the mood of the day. Red, perhaps? Or the russet and gold top Mike likes so much? Laughing at the memory of his obvious appreciation of her looks, she decided that, even though she'd not be seeing Mike till later, she'd wear the russet and gold. She laid it on the bed beside the trousers she had chosen and went to make some breakfast.

"Mum?" she said softly as she tapped on her door. "Ready for a cup of tea?" she asked, opening it, surprised at the empty bed, knowing that, if Mum woke when she heard the alarm, she would usually look into her room before she went downstairs, blow her a kiss as she dried her hair. Frowning, Kate headed for the stairs.

Funny! David's bedroom door was tight closed. Mum liked to keep it slightly ajar. 'It doesn't seem so empty, then,' she would say.

"Oh, Mum," Kate muttered as she pushed it open. "I hope you've not been moping in here again." her voice tailed off and she dropped to her knees beside the still body of her mother.

"No! Oh no!" she cried out, bending down to feel for a heartbeat, praying there would be a soft breath on her cheek as she put it close to her mother's face. "Mum! Mum!" she cried again.

She was so cold, her lips blue, her face still and colourless. Any breath there was, imperceptible.

"Don't leave me, Mum. Please don't leave me," Kate begged, rubbing her cold hands, shaking her, pulling her up onto her lap, willing life into her motionless body. "Wake up, Mum. Wake up!"

"Oh, Kate," the whispered reply, the longed for reply, the welcomed reply.

"Mum, Mum! Are you all right? What's wrong? Oh, God, I thought you were dead!" Kate was crying, with fear, with concern, with relief, with love.

Sarah's hand stole into hers. "I'm so tired, so very tired," she whispered.

Kate pulled the duvet from David's bed and covered Sarah. She was very cold, very pale. "Here, let me put this under your head," she said as she gently eased David's pillow under her mother's head. "I don't think I should try to move you. I'm going to call for an ambulance." She got up from her knees, then bent again to kiss the beloved face. "Are you all right? Oh, you know what I mean. Oh, I love you. You're going to be all right. I'll get the ambulance. Now, don't you move, Mum," she added quite unnecessarily. "I'll just be right here in the hall. Look, if I leave the door open, I can see you all the time. You're going to be all right. Look, I'm dialling now. They won't be long. You're going to be fine, Mum," she kept assuring her, aware that she was prattling but aware too that she needed to reassure herself as much as her mother. Her hands were shaking so much it was difficult to dial, difficult too to speak calmly into the phone, to answer the inevitable questions, to summon assistance.

With tears in her voice, she called for an ambulance and she phoned Doctor Mitchell, her panic soothed a little by his calm, reassuring voice. Then she quickly pulled on the clothes she had laid out earlier, feeling them too bright, too brash now that the day had taken on a different hue, but not wishing to be far from her mother's side for a moment longer than necessary.

"I'm all right," Sarah assured her. "Just tired now. No pain any more. Just tired." She closed her eyes for a while, resting, gathering strength for the things she needed to say before they took her from this room: before the moment had passed, the right time to say the things that needed to be said. "Kate," she said, a little louder this time, a little stronger.

"It's okay, Mum. Don't try to talk."

Sarah shook her head almost imperceptibly. "Listen, Kate," she demanded. "I need to tell you…"

"Yes, Mum."

"Kate?"

"Yes?"

"I didn't want to die. I want you to know, I didn't want to die."

"I'm glad."

Sarah raised her hand to silence her daughter. "I didn't want to die… for *you*. I didn't want to leave *you*. I love you, Katie. Love you so much."

"Oh, Mum," Katie wept, as she tenderly wiped her mother's tears. "I know you do. I never doubted it."

* * *

Angina pectoris, a pretty name for an insidious condition. Angina pectoris, 'pain in the chest due to insufficient oxygen being carried, in the blood, to the heart muscle.' 'Usually occurs when the demand for oxygen is increased during exercise or at times of stress.'

"In your case," the doctor was explaining. "The ECG and the coronary angiograph show no permanent damage," he consulted the file, "blood tests, okay." He looked up at her, his expression kindly, his demeanour reassuring. "The pain would have been caused by coronary artery spasm: the blood vessels narrowing suddenly, for a short period of time, returning to normal with no permanent obstruction. Undoubtedly due to stress. Your GP has explained your recent loss, not been eating, sleeping badly." He put her notes away. "A warning, Mrs Reed. You must take it as a warning. I think we'll keep you one more night... just till we see you well on the way to recovery. Then just the medication I've given you, when you need it. The nurse will explain. She'll also arrange a return appointment. We'll do a treadmill test in a week or two. Keep an eye on you. Okay?" He smiled kindly, shook her hand and moved on to the next bed. Another patient reassured, his evening round almost completed.

The hospital routine clicked on. Nurses bustled here and there, administrating medication, answering the phone, taking temperatures and blood pressures: never a restful place, a hospital ward. Gone were the days of soft-soled shoes and whispered conversations in the corridor: modern nursing was carried out in a brisk, businesslike fashion with no time for the luxuries of peace and quiet.

Trolleys rumbled along, lights blazed down, people came and went. Life: the noise and movement of life. It was so good to be alive!

Sarah lay back and closed her eyes, reflecting on the events of the day: a day filled with tests and examinations, anxieties and reassurances. Kate had stayed with her most of the day, had finally been persuaded to go home to get something to eat when they were certain that Sarah was going to be all right, showing signs of recovery.

'Mike and Dad both send their love,' she had told Sarah, returning from a trip to the public phones in the hospital foyer, before she'd finally gone.

So Tom had sent his love, had he? She smiled. Kate had often conveyed his love to her after being with him. Sarah had always been disdainful, not believing or accepting the sentiment. Love: a word can become meaningless when uttered lightly. 'Actions speak louder than words,' they say. She had seen no reason to believe his words, no actions to support them, but she was more charitably disposed towards the world today so she was more inclined to receive the gift, though not setting too much store by it.

She had expected Kate and Mike to pop in at evening visiting time so it was no surprise when they interrupted the short nap she was enjoying.

"Oh, you're looking so much better," Kate declared delightedly, bending to kiss her mother's cheek. "Still a bit pale and tired around the eyes, but so much better than earlier."

"Good."

"Mind you, that wouldn't have been hard. You looked dreadful!"

"Thank you."

"Your lips were blue. I thought... I thought I'd lost you."

"But you haven't," Sarah said, taking her hand. "So let's not even think about it."

Kate smiled. "Agreed!" She handed over some parcels. "We've brought you some things," she said, her excitement bubbling up like a child's. "A new nightdress." She shook it out of its wrappings with a flourish.

"Oh, that's beautiful," Sarah laughed.

"And a housecoat." This too was released from its layers of tissue and pretty paper.

"But Kate. There's no need for this."

"And a new toothbrush and soap bag and things."

"I'm only going to be in till the morning."

"And Mike brought you some flowers." She pulled him forward.

"Thank you, Mike," Sarah smiled, putting them to her face, taking a deep breath of the delicious scent of life. "They're lovely. But really couldn't you have stopped her buying all these things?"

"Don't you like them?" he asked.

"Of course I like them."

"Then why should I have stopped her?"

"Everything's perfect," she said, examining the silky soft nightdress and housecoat, far too glamorous for a hospital stay. "But it's ridiculous. I'm only going to be here overnight."

"Oh, let us spoil you," he said with a smile. "You deserve a bit of spoiling."

"But…"

"I'll go and see if I can rustle up a vase," Kate offered, picking up the flowers and rushing off with them.

Sarah shook her head. "What is she like? She's so…"

"She's so pleased you are alive," Mike supplied. "I think she got a terrible fright, finding you on the bedroom floor like that."

"Me too," Sarah said quietly. "I thought I was going to die, and, instead of the relief I thought I'd feel, I suddenly realised how much I wanted to live."

"Good."

"I know now that everyone is right. Life does go on. Oh, I'll not stop missing David. That'll always be there, it'll always hurt, sometimes unbearably. But I want to live… for Kate."

"And for you, Sarah. There's still a lot of living for you to do."

She nodded. "And for me, I suppose, though, right now I find it hard to imagine anything I want to do other than just *be* here. With Katie."

"Give yourself time."

"That's what I've been saying, what everyone's been saying for months now. Nearly ten months!"

Mike shrugged. "Ten months! What's that in the scheme of things?"

"True. True."

I carried him for nine. Nursed him for fourteen. Loved him for… her mind baulked at the work involved in the calculation… *eighteen times twelve…*

"Anyway, the main thing now is that…"

"Look who I found in the corridor!" Kate announced triumphantly as she entered the room, pulling Tom behind her.

"Tom!"

"Hello Sarah," he said shyly, offering her another bunch of flowers, shuffling a little uneasily on his feet, not sure whether a handshake or a kiss was more appropriate... or acceptable.

She took the flowers, not quite looking at him. "Thank you, Tom. That was kind."

"Carnations," he said. "I know you like carnations."

"Yes, I do. They always last so well."

"Mum! Why do you always have to be so practical? Dad's brought you your favourite flowers, not because 'they last so well', but because he remembered they're your favourite flowers!"

"Sorry," Sarah blushed, accepting the reprimand.

"Come on," said Mike, leading Kate by the elbow. "I think you and I need to search for another vase."

"How are you?" Tom asked.

"Not so bad. 'A warning,' the doctor says. I think I got off light."

Tom nodded. "Need to look after yourself."

"Yes."

There seemed nothing more to say.

"It was good of you..."

"I'm glad you seem..."

They broke into the long pause together.

"Sorry!"

"Sorry!"

Tom indicated that she should speak first.

"It was kind of you to come."

He shrugged. Katie's shrug, she realised. "I wanted to see for myself you were all right. Katie was very worried."

"She got a fright, poor thing. Thought she'd lost me, I think."

He nodded.

A few more minutes of awkward silence.

"I'll let you rest, then," he said, moving to the door.

Sarah's turn to nod. "Right. Yes. Thank you for coming, Tom."

The shrug again.

"No, I mean it," she said. "Thank you."

Tom smiled. "Good to see you." And was gone.

85

Kate was furious when she came back with the vase. "Why did you let him go so soon," she scolded. "He barely had time to say 'Hello'!"

"We had nothing more to say to each other."

"Mum!"

"It was kind of him to make the effort. But I'm sure he stayed as long as he wanted," she said wearily. "It's nearly twelve years since we had a conversation. We've nothing to talk about."

"I don't suppose you gave him any encouragement," Kate sulked.

"Why should I? It was his choice to come. His choice to go."

"I had hoped…"

"Kate. I don't mind you seeing your father. That's up to you. If you hold out hopes that he'll remain a part of your life, then you're deluding yourself. A man who is capable of running off once, is capable of doing it again. I want nothing to do with him."

"Suit yourself," Katie continued to sulk.

"Thanks. I will."

"But it was kind of him to come all this way, from wherever it is he lives?"

"Yes," Sarah sighed, smiling. "It was kind and I told him I thought so."

"Good!" Kate was a little mollified.

* * *

When they got home the next day, Sarah went upstairs while Kate made their lunch. After unpacking the few bits and pieces she had with her in hospital, she quietly went through to David's room. Bending down, she felt under the bed, her fingers searching for the notebook she had pushed under while she lay there, semi-conscious, two nights before. With a sigh of relief, she retrieved it, glad that Kate had not found it when she had remade the bed. Clutching it close to her chest, she looked round the room.

Nothing had been moved, nothing altered. Yet everything had changed. "Goodbye David," she said softly, knowing that she would never feel the same in this room, the place where she had faced her personal demon and survived, the place where she had realised how much she wanted to live... even without him. "I'm sorry, son. But life must go on."

It hurt so much, knowing that her love had not been enough to make him want to live. But if that was so, then she must accept it and let him go. It must have been what he wanted.

Katie called up the stairs. "Lunch, Mum!"

She put the diary back in the drawer for another day. Not to read. Certainly not to read. Her hand hovered over the open drawer. She looked at the diary. No, it wouldn't be right. A diary is a private thing, personal, not for other's eyes. And yet...

Didn't he owe her an explanation? She had carried him in her body for nine months... he had fed from her breast. She had cared for him, worked for him, worried for him, fought for him, loved him for eighteen years. Didn't she deserve *something* back? Didn't she deserve an explanation?

Another shout from Katie: "It's getting cold, Mum."

"Coming," she called back.

Not today, not just yet. She would need to be stronger, couldn't afford another angina attack. Not so soon. She closed the drawer. She would pack it away with anything else they decided to keep. She looked around in the doorway.

They must change the use of this room, perhaps making it a little sitting room where she could come in the evenings when Katie and Mike were watching television or just needed a little privacy to talk, to cuddle, whatever. She caught herself blushing. Well, she was young once... and in love.

Yes, they would change the use of this room. David had no further use for it. She would let go. In a few weeks, when she was fully recovered, when she felt stronger physically, she would sort everything out, keep a few bits and pieces, let the rest go. It would be better that way.

Chapter 12

"Good grief, Mother, what in the name are you doing? You do know it's only ten past five in the morning?"

"Sorry Katie. I couldn't sleep..." Sarah hastily wiped the sleeve of her dressing gown across her tear-stained face. "Needed to be doing something, getting on with things." She cleared her throat. "Thought I'd sort through some of David's things. I really can't keep this room like some kind of shrine or something."

"Fine. Great. I'm glad you see it that way..." Kate stood in the doorway of David's room, rumpled and warm from sleep. "But did you have to start moving furniture at such an unholy hour?"

"Sorry dear, did I wake you?"

"Wake me! Did she wake me?" Kate asked no one in particular as she wandered back to bed. "No, of course you didn't wake me, Mother. I always wander about the house at ten past five in the morning!"

"Oh look Katie, David must have kept that old cricket set Dad bought him years ago!"

"I'm trying to sleep, Mum," Kate called back from her own room.

"Sorry dear. Do you think your Dad would like to have it?"

"Why don't you ask him?... in the morning!" she added with emphasis.

"Yes, perhaps I will. It'll maybe mean more to him than us. It was the two of them, the cricket, wasn't it?" she asked rhetorically, remembering the two of them, David and Tom, playing cricket in the park, on the beach, anywhere there was a bit of space, enough to bowl and hit a ball without doing too much harm.

"Good night Mum!"

"Yes dear." She turned the cricket set over in her hands, feeling its weight, remembering the pleasure it gave, the pride David took in it. "D'you think you could give it to him when you see him next?" Then louder, "When do you see him next? Katie," she called when there was no reply. "I said... when will you be seeing your Dad again?"

"I'm sleeping!"

"This Saturday, isn't it? I'll put it in a bag and you could give it to him."

"Why don't you come too... give it to him yourself?"

"I thought you were sleeping?"

* * *

When the post dropped through the letterbox a few weeks later, Sarah was having a good day. There were more of them now. Her winter was passing; there was new growth in her heart. Little buds of something resembling happiness occasionally popped open in the wasteland of her emotions. Some days she felt almost normal, happy to see the sunshine or the spring flowers, to smell the freshness of the newly dried washing as she brought it in from the garden. This was one of those days, so she read Tom's letter with an unaccustomed lightness.

'Dear Sarah,' she read, *'Thank you for sending the cricket set with Katie. It doesn't half bring back memories! David could only have been five or six that year when we went to Middlesex. Didn't he love the games of cricket we played in the park that holiday? Fancy him still having this old bat and things! I'm really pleased you sent it to me, and I shall treasure it.'*

Sarah smiled as she read on, *'Katie is a real credit to you, Sarah. She is a lovely girl, with a fine sunny nature. I remember she always was a smiler. I'm grateful for the chance to get to know her again. I wish you'd give me the chance to get to know you again too, Sarah. Wouldn't you meet me, just you and me, so that we could talk?'*

Sarah put the letter down on her lap. Perhaps it would be nice to get to know Tom again. Perhaps not.

Certainly not just now. Not when she was getting her life back, when she had stopped looking into the precipice of despair. She was not far enough back from the edge to risk involvement with

Tom, for she knew it would unbalance her. She was afraid she would fall.

So she put the letter away in her own private drawer, to review another day. Beside the diary.

She had brought it through to her own room, feeling it less likely that Kate would come across it there, not ready to share it with her.

Knowing it existed tormented her.

Her hand hovered over it after dropping in Tom's letter.

She had never been the kind of mother to read her children's letters, had never even realised David kept a diary, let alone presumed to read it. She respected their privacy and expected the same respect from them.

Dual standards. She knew she had dual standards. Here, on the one hand, she believes in the right of her children to protect their privacy, while, on the other, she was furious with Kate and Doctor Mitchell for withholding information from her, information that David obviously considered private. Like his diary?

But she wanted so much to read it, knowing that, of all that was left, this would be what could give her back a bit of David… possibly the most precious bit. His thoughts, his emotions, his hopes, his fears: remind her of all the reasons she loved him. Not just because he was her son, but because he was the person he was, the kind, gentle boy she had known.

To read the diary now would be like letting him explain himself, helping her understand the 'why' of it.

So, while Kate was at work that day, Sarah tentatively opened the notebook and began the journey that would take her to hell and back again.

Chapter 13

Tom was surprised to get Sarah's phone call: she could hear the surprise in his voice and she smiled to herself when she detected there was pleasure there too.

"It's good to hear you, Sarah."

"You asked if we could meet. In your letter?"

"Yes."

"I think … Yes. I'd be grateful if we could. I need to see you about something in particular."

"Intriguing!"

"Please?"

"Of course. How could I resist?"

"Perhaps I could come to the shop? Kate has been desperate for me to see it anyway, so…"

"Kill two birds with one stone, so to say?"

"Something like that."

"Okay. When shall we say, then? Saturday?"

"No, not Saturday. Kate is home Saturday. Through the week would be better. Friday. I don't really want her to… well, to be around, while we talk."

"It gets more intriguing by the minute!"

After she put the phone down, she sat quietly for a few minutes, waiting for her heartbeat to steady from its crazy thumping. She must keep calm. *Nothing served by getting ill again. Perhaps another of the little tablets?* But there was no pain, a certain amount of tightness, but no pain. *Relax, deep breath. Getting better, getting better…*

Still in the hall beside the telephone, she rested her head against the wall behind her. The telephone seat was hard and unyielding, with no support for her back. Really, she needed to sink into the cushions of her sofa but she was waiting till her heart rate returned to normal before she moved.

It would have been more comfortable to use the extension in her bedroom, more comfortable... but more intimate.

Intimacy was far from what she wanted with Tom. Nor could she imagine he really hoped for it either. Enough if they could talk civilly to one another, satisfy Kate that they, that *she*, Sarah, had tried. An exchange of information, pretence at cordial relations, that was all, that was enough.

Was this really such a good idea, to go to Tom's shop on Friday? To meet him anywhere, anytime? Was she ready for the emotions that would inevitably arise, being with him, talking with him? She had already gone through every conceivable emotion since he had left her : agony, thinking he'd been in an accident ; disbelief that it could be anything else ; anger, hot, red, seething anger ; loneliness, cold, blue empty loneliness; frustration; grief... the list went on, throwing her this way and that. Was it wise to start the roller-coaster again?

Wise or not, good idea or not, she decided she had to see Tom.

* * *

The temptation had been to start at the end of the diary, to find out what happened just before David died. What had led to that last awful declaration. But she was afraid of the revelation, unsure of her strength to face it. Better to build towards it, find out what was driving him to that bitter end.

So, she started at the beginning, four years ago, when David was fifteen.

The first few pages were the random musings of a hormonal teenager, not in any discernible pattern and with no dates to place them in time. She was relieved to read that he had a normal, healthy interest in girls. Homosexuality was something abhorrent to her, unnatural, though she knew she would be considered 'out of date' in her views, and not 'politically correct' in expressing them. But what was fashionable morally was not her concern, only what she knew to be the 'old-fashioned' morality of the Bible. She had been brought up, by and large, with those standards and she had in turn taught them to her children.

And there was one of her problems! Dual standards again!

She had not always practised what she preached and she was afraid that David may have suspected as much, *must* have suspected as much, and yet he'd never said, never confronted her with his discoveries.

As far as she could discern, he just accepted her impropriety without censure. Gone was the little boy who raged at the hypocrisy of the school chaplain who preached about the sanctity of life and joined the territorial army: gone the teenager who railed at the teacher who punished the smokers but smoked in the staff room. At some point he had accepted the 'do as I say, not as I do' of the adult world: the transition from idealist to cynic. She hadn't seen it happen and grieved that it had.

"I feel like I never knew him," she had said to Joan one evening.

"I know what you mean. My Gary's a complete stranger to me. I thought he was still a boy, still into bikes and skateboards and suddenly there's a girl on the scene and motorbikes and drugs."

"What happened to the in-between stage? The awkward, fumbling stage where they blush and stutter when a girl talks to them?"

"Must've blinked and missed it with my Gary. He's always been one for the girls. Never slow at coming forward."

Sarah frowned. "I had no idea what David was like with girls, never saw him with one. He certainly never talked about them." Her frown deepened. "There were one or two turned up to his funeral, come to think of it now. Didn't register at the time."

"Not what you'd've been thinking of, love," Joan sympathised.

"No…" Sarah agreed thoughtfully. "Tough to realise your children have grown up and become strangers, isn't it?"

But before she realised that, she had the joy of reading about the fun and fantasies of a normal, though fairly innocent, teenage boy. The boy she *had* known, the boy she recognised, the boy she thought he'd stayed.

The first dozen or so pages of his diary were easy reading. Once she had cracked his code. He always used the initials of his friends, and always in reverse. She discovered this when she came across a story she remembered, something that happened here at home, and she knew the friend who featured. After that, it was okay as long as he wrote of people she had heard. Unfortunately, there were many she hadn't.

Then, the first date he had entered in the margin was the date of his sixteenth birthday. A day he obviously considered to have special significance because he was now old enough to marry without parental permission, to ride a motorbike and to leave school, if he chose... which he soon did. It was also a date of some note because, as far as she could decipher, it was the date he lost his virginity... and the date he first tried drugs.

If Sarah was shocked to read of his dalliance with the young lady who seduced him into the bushes after dark, she was horrified to read of his first taste of the poison that would kill him.

S.M. gave me a drag! This was no ordinary fag! Wow!
High! High! High! --- I like!

Sarah felt anger rise like a tide, washing over her, throwing up debris, exposing the shipwreck of David's life.

S.M.? M.S.? Martin? Mike? Did he have a friend who was Mike? or Martin? Or Matthew? Or Marlon? Or... Martin! There was a Martin! But it was Martin Brice. M.B/B.M. not S.M. She couldn't think of anyone else. But maybe it wasn't a boy at all: maybe it was the girl he'd been with. If she was loose enough for sex... She checked again. No, different initials.

Who were these people, this crowd he'd taken up with? Young folks she had never met, he had never brought home?

Frustrated, she rummaged through the rest of his drawers looking for an old class photograph, something to jog her memory, help her identify M.S. She found all his class photographs together, neatly stacked, in order, in the second drawer down. The individual photos of both her children she kept among her own things, displaying a selection as it pleased her. The class photos were theirs and David's were here, filed in chronological order.

She scanned the faces. So many of them she never knew, faces or names. A useless exercise!

With tears of anger and frustration stinging her eyes, she gathered the photographs together, seeing in every one of them the beloved face smiling out at her, changed from one year to the next, yet always the same laughing eyes, the same cheeky grin. He'd loved getting his photograph taken, saw it as an opportunity to charm.

'Poser!' Katie's accusation.

'Jealous!' His riposte.

Smiling back at him, she put the photographs away again.

With a sigh of resignation, she realised it didn't matter now. What use was her anger after all this time? What could she do if she got hold of S.M.?

If it hadn't been him, it would probably have been someone else. David seemed keen to have new experiences to mark what he saw as a 'coming of age'.

After that, there were other entries seeming to suggest occasional 'drags', but it was a while before it was regular, more than a few 'drags' or 'pills'. His code became more elaborate as his involvement increased, making it difficult to follow the course of his habit or trace its source.

She was still going occasionally to Omega House, and her reading was reinforcing the assumptions Mike had helped her make. It seemed to be that David started taking drugs for fun, had underestimated the danger until it was too late. In the early part of his diary, he wrote so lightly of 'smokes' and 'pills', showing no fear of addiction, no understanding of its nature.

Weren't they supposed to show schoolkids films and things about the danger of drugs? Had David failed to appreciate the information? Or was it bravado rather than ignorance?

Sarah shook her head as she read. It certainly seemed that way. *Oh David, David, David!*

If only she had known. If only he had talked to her, asked her about it. But she knew that was unrealistic. What teenager would ever ask his mother's advice about the wisdom of taking drugs? No matter how much she wished it, he was no different from any other boy his age, no closer to his mother, no more likely to see her as a 'pal', a confidante. Any chance she might have had to influence his inclination to experiment with drugs was lost long before. It was something she should have discussed, a lesson she should have taught before the temptation arose. To her great regret, it had never occurred to her to do so.

Drugs had just not been an issue in her own schooldays and she had not taken enough notice of the changing times, had made the dangerous assumption that her children would automatically hold the same values as she did, as though these were inherited rather than taught.

The questions came to her unbidden: Would it have been different if Tom had been around? Would he have been more in tune? More observant of the passing scene?

The answers chilled her in their probability.

David started to write about finding his Dad and, strangely enough, that upset Sarah more than reading about his sexual exploits or the illicit smoking and non-prescription pills.

It frightened her because the tone of his writing changed, became more intense, more desperate, the elaborate codes sometimes forgotten in his earnestness. He obviously felt a deep lack in his life, perhaps sensed that Tom would have understood, advised, helped where she failed.

He wanted his father, needed him with a profound longing that stung Sarah and made her heart contract.

She had need of her own 'pep pills' several times during the days it took her to read the first quarter of the diary.

......Had a chat with J.F. today. He's just found out he's adopted. How hard can that be? To find that out now! He's pretty devastated. Didn't get on much with his old man before... don't suppose its gonna get much better now! At least he's had an old man of sorts around till now.

Hell, I miss Dad. Man, I keep getting the feelin he's somewhere around... nearby, I mean. You know, I bet he's wishing he could call or something. Probably scared of what

Mum would have to say about it if he did. She'd go ballistic! Gets her knickers in a twist if we even mention him! Which isn't helpful when you're trying to find out the gen. Wish he'd phone though. Could ask him what to do about A.L. Even just to hear him would be cool.

* * *

.....Looked up Ed direc today. 47 Reeds ~ only one T.Reed ~ no Tom or Thomas. Tried it, but not him ~ neither were any of the 47. Had to phone from phone box. Itemised bills are a curse! Besides I never use phone. She'd wonder what I was up to. Don't know where to try next. Maybe Newcastle area? Have to start somewhere. 'Missing ~ Last heard of driving to Newcastle'!

* * *

....Told Mum football prac. Went to Telephone House. Looked up all Reeds in Newcastle area. Tried them all. All 54!! Incl 8 T.Reeds. One sounded hopeful. Wifey said hubby called Tom. Phoned back. Wasn't him! He was only 37 ~ Dad must be about 50 ~ 52 by now. So, no go! Shattered! Must've got hopes up. Need to chill next time. London next. Know he had business or stuff down there sometimes. Worth a try. Anything worth a try! Getting desperate. Want to talk to him.

Wonder if he's ever had a beard? Think I'd suit one. Think I look like him. Don't look much like Mum ~ so, reckon must look like him. Hope so. Got her eyes unfortunately. Bit of a bummer. Kate has his ~ brown. Bet he's worn well. Bet he's cool.

Always felt a bit weird Dad not being here ~ him not being dead or anything and them not being divorced. I mean, what d'you tell folks? Still ~ not his fault. Told A.L. they were separated ~ felt lousy. London direc next. Capital, old man, capital!

He tried the London directory, then the Liverpool, then Manchester, Glasgow, Blackpool... everywhere. He'd systematically gone through every telephone directory in the United Kingdom! It had taken him months and had cost him a small fortune to make the calls. What he earned from his paper round and his Saturday job must have been sorely stretched between one thing and another.

He would not have been much better off once he started work. The bookshop hadn't paid much, he had 'keep' to pay, his drug habit was growing and that's when he really got in the swing with his telephone search. Sarah understood better why he didn't go out much to clubs, pubs or cinemas. The poor soul couldn't afford to. She had just thought he preferred to sit upstairs with his music for company. Apart from the occasional CD, he rarely had money for casual spending.

As for the telephoning, he seemed to have got it down to a fine art, honing and perfecting his spiel until he found out as economically as possible what he needed to know. She had to admire his perseverance though she pitied his passion.

...Tried the last of the phone books at the library. Thought I was on to him. Phoned this T.Reed ~ guy said his father was Tommy, said he'd get him. Sweating while I waited. Tommy turned out to be ok, but never been to Scotland. Married, kids, never travelled. Another dead end.

Either he's ex-directory, or not got a phone, or living abroad, or changed his name. Most likely ex-direc.

Face it: Everyone's got a phone.

2. can't imagine he's ex-pat

3. why would he want to change his name?

So ~ what next?

* * *

…..Woke up with brill idea! Birth Cert! Must get from Mum in morn. How? What reason could I need it? Don't know what hope to find. Haven't clue what's on birth cert! Father's old address? Grandparents? Worth a try!

* * *

*…..Mum doesn't have birth cert ~ at least hasn't clue where to find it! Not helpful! Told her **must** have it for work ~ s'thing to do with tax. Says look for it, pop it into old Brennan! Told her not to bother ~ too late. Hard time explaining why 'must have it' doesn't really mean 'must'. She seemed relieved not to have to look for it.*

Wonder if could get copy? Where?

* * *

.....Asked at library. Wifey suggested Register House in Edinburgh. Seems can pay to get copy. Phoned. Going in tomorrow.

Sarah moaned softly. She hardly dared to turn the page.

She remembered him asking for his birth certificate. It was the only time he had. Whenever it was needed, she'd managed to handle matters without him having to see it.

Same with Kate. Even when Kate wanted to learn to drive. She'd told her she'd search out the certificate and pop it in the envelope with the form, post it for her, get it away quickly. Then, she'd watched for the envelope returning it, fortunately, separate from the provisional licence. Kate seemed oblivious to the subterfuge, excitement at having the licence crowding out any questions she might have had.

Her heart quickened.

She should have known one of them would eventually find out. She should have told them.

The moan became a sob. The sob became a wail.

And he never said a word.

But perhaps he didn't understand the significance of what he found out.

When she read on, she discovered that he did go to Register House.

.....Cost me a tenner for the afternoon! Was only there an hour! Scarey place, like a tomb. Big domed centre with rows of files in corridors round it. Weird, man. Computers everywhere ~ cool! You do a search on the computer then get the right microfiche from the files. If had longer, could've traced family tree but had to get home before Mum suspicious.

He paid for a copy of his birth certificate, not an abbreviated one, as he was offered, but a full copy, seeking as much information as possible. But, whether due to his excitement at possessing it, his disappointment at its scant information or his innocent ignorance, he didn't seem to understand the significance of his purchase.

.....Birth cert not much cop!

Think know where T.G. is though. Might call on him. See if he's good for any info.

T.G.? G.T. Who on earth could G.T. be? How could he possibly know anything of Tom? Who would know anything of Tom? G.T.? Damn his schoolboy codes! Why could the child not just write in plain English?

.....Visited T.G. Very cagey with me. Didn't let him know who I am yet ~ told him from the council, on job experience, come to do garden. Man, it needs doing! Poor sod's too old for it. Didn't try getting info yet. Better get to know him first. Seems miserable old sod!

After that, there were a number of entries mentioning T.G. Or G.T. as it would be, whoever he was. It seems David really did 'do' his garden, even wrote with pleasure of the order he was bringing back to it, but had little encouragement from its owner as far as she could make out. 'Miserable old sod' was what he remained in David's estimation. However, he persevered with the work without receiving any thanks, or any 'info.' G.T. seemed to have little conversation and no inclination towards it.

Sarah puzzled over the identity of the mysterious G.T. and David's conviction that he might have knowledge of Tom.

Chapter 14

Friday was not a good day for Sarah. The early summer sunshine seemed too thin to warm her, clouds seemed to have gathered around her since her telephone conversation with Tom and she couldn't emerge from the gloom. Failure and guilt floated like spectres in a mist of despair. She was sliding back into winter though summer tried to cheer her forward.

She tried to postpone her visit to his second hand furniture shop, but left it too late and there was no reply when she phoned. Perhaps Tom was already on his way to their meeting place. There was nothing else for it but to go through with the day's plan.

She hugged her coat round her as she waited for the bus, cold with apprehension. She hugged it closer as she walked from the bus to the shop with Tom beside her.

This part of Leith was not well known to her and her apprehension only deepened as she surveyed the clutter of small shops, selling everything from clothes to electrical goods, from vegetables to second-hand books, many of them displaying tattered sale signs and handwritten price tickets, all of them seeming to be pushing their wares at her, none of them looking inviting. The street here was narrow, with too many cars parking too close together, their tyres mounting the pavement in some places. There were too many people: mothers pulling grizzling toddlers along in their wake or pushing overloaded buggies before them; delivery men with boxes on their shoulders shouting as they pushed into the interiors of the shops; youths with transistors blaring; old men with dogs, and everywhere puddles and dirt.

She picked her way along the pavement, her collar turned up, her mouth turned down.

Perhaps it was only her dark mood, perhaps it was the dinginess of the shop but Sarah shivered as she surveyed the outside of it. Warning bells were sounding somewhere deep in her memory. Something didn't feel right.

"Why have you called it 'Fame's Furniture'?" she asked, nodding towards the painted sign above the shop. "Why not Reed's?"

"Oh, that," he laughed, "was my feeble attempt at a joke. Fame, as in famous. It's supposed to give the illusion that the furniture might not be just anybody's old junk. It might have belonged to someone famous, been their old junk?"

"Oh," said Sarah, unimpressed.

Inside, the shop was cold and dirty. Tom had made a good attempt to clean it up but it needed more than a quick flick of a duster or sweep of a broom. He'd tried to brighten it up but it needed more than a few vases of flowers. The windows were filthy, any light filtering through them, dappled and murky.

Some of the furniture looked as though it had been here a long time, dust lying thickly in the corners where his token duster had failed to reach.

A dusty, musty, un-cared-for smell permeated the place, making her want to hold her breath, cover her mouth, protect herself from the plague of doubts assailing her.

He drew her attention to one or two of his 'special' pieces: an ancient gramophone, its long brass horn polished recently, a stack of old '78's' beside it. "Fabulous, isn't it? Antique," he said proudly; a tall vase patterned with elaborate flowers and leaves, garishly coloured but sparklingly clean. "Worth a mint," he whispered conspiratorially; a willow-patterned plate; a carved cigar box. All ostentatiously displayed on a table in the middle of the shop, all obviously assembled for her benefit, all carefully cleaned for her inspection... and all contrasting sharply with their room-mates.

"Do you do much trade, Tom?"

"Enough," he said cheerfully. "I'll never be rich on it, but it keeps me well enough in the manner to which I have become accustomed," he joked as they threaded their way through the stacks of dusty merchandise.

"And what is the manner to which you've become accustomed, Tom?"

Proudly, Tom threw open the door to his office. "Welcome to the inner sanctum," he announced. "Please, take a pew!"

Sarah gazed around her as she accepted the well-upholstered chair Tom pushed towards her. The office was better. It didn't have such a musty smell and it was cleaner and brighter. Not for Tom the second hand furniture of his trade. The captain's chair Sarah sat in, like the others, was fairly new and expensive, though somewhat gaudy.

"You always had expensive taste, Tom," she said, indicating the thick carpet, the teak desk. "Yes, it's very nice. You must be doing all right for yourself. So, how was it you got started in this business, Tom?"

"Right time, right place, I suppose," he answered with a casual shrug. "I met this guy...."

She raised an eyebrow.

"He was wanting to retire, and I'd done him a good turn."

Higher.

"So he helped me get set up."

Sarah looked straight at him.

He met her look briefly, then turned away. "You don't believe me?" he sighed.

"No."

Tom scratched his head and stretched elaborately. "Yes, well, you always could see through me," he said with a roguish grin. "Okay, I'll come clean! I had a win on the horses." He looked hopeful. "Better?"

"Better," she said doubtfully.

"But you don't buy it?"

Sarah shook her head.

"I bought the business with my 'ill-gotten gains'," drawing apostrophes in the air, "from a job I wasn't done for." He turned away.

"Yes," she nodded. "That's sounds more likely."

Tom swung round and leant over her, grasping the arms of the chair. "But that was a year ago Sarah, more, eighteen months.

That's past history. I've gone straight since. I swear I have." He turned to lean on his desk. "You can examine my books if you like. They're straight. I'm straight. I swear it Sarah."

He strode over to the filing cabinet and pulled out account books, receipts, files. "You can look at them, Sarah. All of them. I have nothing to hide. I'm clean."

"Can we go for lunch now, Tom?" she sighed. "I don't like the smell in here. I think it's the chrysanthemums."

* * *

"You wanted to talk," Tom prompted when they were settled in a pretentiously chic little restaurant in the 'new' part of Leith.

"What was this place before?" she asked, looking round the ultra modern, 'minimalist' interior, all metal and stone, grey and cold.

"I'm not sure," he shrugged. "Possibly some kind of warehouse? A loading store for one of the shipping companies? We're so near the docks, I suppose."

"Probably," she shivered, no longer interested.

"You're cold. Would you like us to go somewhere cosier?"

She shook her head.

Tom, in turn, looked around. "This place is supposed to be very fashionable, but the décor's a bit sparse."

"It doesn't matter."

He started to get up, reaching for his jacket on the back of the chair. "We could…"

"No. It really doesn't matter, Tom."

So he sat back down, rearranging his jacket, accepting the menu from the waiter, fiddling with it, not looking at it, watching her face, waiting for the inevitable questions.

"When did you come back to Edinburgh?"

Tom stroked his brow, smoothing the furrows. "About eighteen, twenty months ago."

"Any reason for coming back after all this time?"

He shrugged. "Homesick?" he grinned.

She looked up from the fancy menu she was pretending to study, her eyebrows raised.

"Well, that was part of the reason."

She didn't look away.

The familiar shrug again. "Business, I suppose. I had good contacts here before."

"Yes," she said, remembering.

"......*Saw Dad today!!! This time, for sure!*

Me on bus ~ him walking along Princes Street. By time got down stairs & off bus, he'd disappeared. Walked all way back to where saw him, checking everyone out, but no sign. Must've gone into shop. Went into every shop that block. Impossible. Needle in haystack job. Too many people, too long a time.

Sure it was him this time, though. I <u>knew</u> he was in town, I just <u>knew</u> it!

Man ~ imagine if I'd found him ~ bumped into him ~ just like that!?! Freaky!..."

"Were you never afraid we'd bump into you?" she asked

He leaned back, the metal chair scraping on the slate flagstones of the floor, his indrawn breath hissing a little in his throat. "Always hoped you would," he breathed out softly. "It would have been such a relief. To have met you by accident, saved all the hours of wrestling with the dilemma of how I could get in touch."

"You thought of getting in touch?" Sarah asked, her face augmenting the scepticism and contempt in her voice.

"You obviously find that hard to believe."

"Very!"

"But I wanted to."

"So?"

"It got harder all the time. The longer I'd been away, the harder it was going to be to explain. Whenever I decided I would, there were a million reasons why I wouldn't. But I did want to." He looked at her for understanding. Tossing down the paper napkin he had balled in his fist, "Ach! What's the use? You don't believe me. Next question?" he demanded, his elbows on the table, his face thrust forward, the challenge offered.

He waved away the approaching waiter. "You want some answers? Okay. That's fair. But the answers you get are the answers you get. Okay? Take it or leave it."

Not in the slightest intimidated by his manner, Sarah continued with her unwritten agenda. There were things she needed to know, things she was curious about and things she would rather not hear. Any claimed desire to return to the bosom of his family belonged to the last category.

So, she let it pass. Let pass too the invitation to ask, 'Why? Why had he gone?' She no longer cared to hear the answer. Strange, that after eleven years of wondering, she had absolutely no curiosity about it any more. Time enough for excuses and lies.

It mattered not his reason for going, only that he had gone.

"Are you ex-directory?" was the question she asked instead.

He looked puzzled, was taken by surprise by the change of direction. "Why?"

"Are you?"

"Well, yes. But what does that have to do with anything?"

"David tried to find you by phoning up every 'Reed' in every phone book in the country."

"Phew!"

"Exactly. It took him months. It cost him money he could ill afford and it brought him nothing but disappointment."

Tom rubbed his forehead, the furrows not so easily erased this time. "Hell! That's... that's..."

"Sad? Pathetic?"

"Poor kid."

"Poor kid indeed. He desperately wanted to find you."

"I wish he had."

"Do you?" She pushed her face close to his, causing him to draw back, flinching. "Do you, Tom? You could have seen him any time you wished. *He* would not have been hard to find."

"I didn't know..."

"No. You wouldn't, would you, Tom? How could you know?" she gave a very elaborate shrug, a parody of his own. "You knew where we lived, Tom," she continued, hard tones flattening her voice, anger lighting her face. "Eleven years, Tom! Eleven years

106

before you turn up. Too late and even then, only when *we* find *you* under a stone!"

"I didn't leave..."

Her laugh was harsh and loud, causing the waiter to step in their direction, but seeing or sensing that his interruption would be unwelcome, he put his order pad back in his pocket and attended elsewhere.

"I didn't mean to leave."

"Come again? You didn't *mean* to leave? Took you by surprise did it?"

"I mean, it was not my *intention* to leave."

"Oh?" Raising her shoulders, spreading her hands, the gesture open, inviting explanation, the tone of her voice daring it.

"Something happened."

"Yes?"

"I was detained..."

"Go on."

He looked around, checking the waiter was out of earshot. "At Her Majesty's pleasure," he confessed.

She shook her head. "Won't do!"

"I'm telling you!"

"I checked the papers, court reports, even phoned a few prisons. Here, Newcastle, London, a few others."

"I'm telling you, I served time," he hissed.

"Where?"

"London."

"Why could the police find no trace of you then?"

Once again, he looked round furtively, uncomfortable with the venue for such disclosures. "Look, Sarah, if you want all the details, can we maybe go back to the shop, the back office, privacy?"

"Even if it were true..."

"I swear, Sarah."

"What stopped you getting word out? Alcatraz, was it?"

He pushed his chair right back, pulled his jacket from the back of it, stood up to go. "Not here, Sarah. Come on, let's go."

She didn't move. "What have you told Katie?"

"What?"

"What have you told Katie?"

"About what?" He sat down again.

"About us?"

Hand to forehead, perspiration there to grease the gesture this time. "You've lost me, Sarah. I don't know where this line of questioning is leading."

"It's not difficult. You've been seeing Kate. I presume you talk? She must ask questions?"

"Yes."

"So. Has Kate asked you anything about us?"

"Like what?" he said with exasperation.

"Like why we weren't married?"

Chapter 15

He'd talked to Katie. After getting the copy of his birth certificate, David had asked her if she'd ever seen hers.

.....she hasn't, so that's not much cop. Still ~ don't suppose hers much different to mine. What next?

Back to the drawing board!

But it was back to Register House he went, this time looking for his parents' marriage certificate.

And, of course, he found no entry.

Because there was no entry.

They had never married.

And what Sarah needed to know: Had he told Kate of his non-finding? He hadn't recorded in his diary any conversation he might have had with his sister. In fact, there was no entry for many months after his discovery. It was as though he'd taken time out, from searching, from thinking, certainly from writing, while he assimilated the information, or lack of it. But that didn't mean he hadn't talked.

Hence her question to Tom, "Has Kate asked you why we were not married?"

He shook his head. "No. She hasn't said anything. Why? What have you told her?"

"Nothing."

"What d'you mean? "

"I mean, I've told her nothing. She doesn't know we weren't. Unless David told her."

"David?"

"He found out."

"Had you not told them?"

"Don't sound so shocked. Why should I? You were dead. It wasn't discussed."

"But…"

"No 'Buts', Tom. You were dead as far as we were concerned. And never mind the injured look. What did you expect? Did you think I set the table for you every night for eleven years?"

"But…"

"Why should I tell them? You were their father, now you were gone. What would it matter to them if we were married or not? I just wondered whether Kate knew."

"Well, she hasn't said anything to me," Tom said. "Why don't you ask her?"

"What?"

"Why don't you ask Kate if she knows we were never married?"

It was Sarah who looked round the restaurant this time, almost as though she expected Kate to be there, at the next table, watching the drama unfold, hearing the secrets revealed, the years of pretence peeled away.

"But she might not know."

"Aren't you going to tell her anyway?"

"Why should I?"

"Because I'm not dead. I'm back. I'm here in Edinburgh, Sarah. She wants to see me. She's my daughter."

"Huh!"

He ignored her derision and leant forward, his arms on the table. "Don't you think this is something she might find out anyway?"

"Not if you don't tell her!"

The aluminium frame of the chair objected noisily when he lurched back, his hands thrown up in frustration. "Whatever," he acceded. "What does it matter?"

"It matters to me! It always mattered to me, Tom." Sarah, in turn, leant forward, refusing to let him distance himself from this issue. "Let's see now, why was it we never married?"

"You know why."

"I know what you told me," she snapped back.

"Well?"

"What was it again?" She leant back, pretending puzzlement, scratching her head, closing her eyes. "Oh yes, I remember! You

110

were already married, weren't you?" Her eyes opened wide, the mocking question in them, the incredulity too.

"I told you..."

"Yes, so you did, Tom. You told me. So it must be true, mustn't it?"

"You know it's true."

"Do I, Tom?" she asked. "And how would I know that?"

"I told you. I told you right at the start. You knew I wasn't free to marry before you ever agreed to live with me."

"True. But why, Tom? Oh yes, I remember! Because *you* told me."

"Yes."

"You told me you were married. She was a Catholic, that was it, wasn't it? She was a Catholic, so she wouldn't give you a divorce, isn't that what you told me?"

"Exactly!"

"So it must be true, of course!"

Tom sighed elaborately and shook his head, tired of the game, weary of the interrogation.

"What was her name, Tom?"

"Her name?" Again, the hand to the brow. Again, the perspiration.

"Yes. What was your wife called? Let me think," she bit her lip, pretended concentration. "Oh, I forget. But *you* must remember, Tom! She was your wife after all. What was her name again?"

Tom stood up, his chair falling noisily to the slate floor. "I'm going back to my office, Sarah. I've business to attend to. If you want to continue your interrogation, that's where you'll find me."

"Forgotten, have you? Surely not! Surely you can't have forgotten your own wife's name?" she hissed, standing now too, the suppressed rage of eleven tormented years oozing from her every pore. "You're a liar, Tom. A liar and a cheat. You always were. It just took me a long time to figure it out."

"You're wrong, Sarah. Come with me, somewhere private," he gestured around him, taking in with a sweep of his hand the waiters and the silent diners pretending indifference to the scene. "Come over to the office."

She shook her head.

"Where then?"

She buttoned the coat she had never removed, picked up her bag and walked towards the door. "Not today, Tom." She looked around at the cold, grey restaurant, its metal chairs and lack of comfort. "I've had a bellyful of contrivance today."

* * *

Kate helped to clean up the shop. She polished the furniture, scrubbed the floor, washed the windows.

"And just where do you think you're going with my hoover, young lady?" Sarah asked as Kate prepared to load it into Mike's car.

"I'm borrowing it. Just for an hour or two."

"I can see that, and I see you've borrowed Mike's car. I hope he had more say in the matter than I had."

"Oh Mum, you don't mind, do you?" She planted a kiss on Sarah's cheek.

"Depends where you're taking it."

"Mum..."

"Don't think I haven't guessed. I know fine that you've been down at Tom's shop every spare minute the last few weekends. Is it any cleaner?"

"Drat! I thought I was going to surprise you. Don't laugh! When you didn't say anything, I thought you hadn't noticed. I wanted to make it nice so you'd go there again. Dad's really upset you didn't like his shop you know," she said as she lifted the hoover into the open boot.

"It wasn't the shop I didn't like, " Sarah muttered.

Kate was leaning over the boot, so didn't hear the muted comment. "What did you say?" she asked as she closed the lid.

"Nothing Katie, nothing. So, he's upset is he?"

"Dad hopes you'll come down again. He says he wants to talk to you. Owes you some explanations."

"True!"

"He says you guys didn't hit it off too well last time."

"You could say that!"

Kate leant on the back of the car, the keys dangling in her hand. "He'd really like to try again, Mum." She swung the keys casually, pretending nonchalance to the conversation they were having. "You will try again, Mum, won't you?"

Sarah shrugged her non-committal. "Perhaps."

"Please, Mum. Say you'll try again," she pleaded, all pretence gone, her eager expression catching at Sarah's heart.

"Does it really matter that much to you?"

"You're my Mum, he's my Dad. It's not amazing that I'd want you to get on!"

"No. But..."

Katie put her arms round her mother's waist. They stood more or less eye-to-eye. There was pleading in her look, but understanding too. "Mum, I know how hard it's been for you. I'm not asking you to fall in love with him again though that would be nice," she grinned. "Just make friends with him," she continued. "I love you both. I want you both in my life."

Sarah stroked her hair, held her face between both hands, gazed into the deep pools of her eyes. "I love you too, darling, and I will try if that's what you want," she said softly, kissing her on the forehead.

"Oh, it is Mum. It really is."

Sarah drew her daughter into her, holding her gently against her chest. "Then I'll try," she said, giving her a hug then letting her go. "So, what do you want me to do?" she asked.

Kate walked round to the driver's door of the car and leant against it. "Dad says, if only you'd come to the shop again maybe he could explain. Will you?"

"Will I what?"

"Go to the shop again."

"Oh! I don't know."

"Please?"

"We'll see."

"Good! I'll tell him." She opened the door and prepared to sit in the car.

"That doesn't mean 'yes', Katie," Sarah laughed. "It means we'll see!"

But Katie would tell her Dad anyway.

She told her Mum that she had been in the shop three times now when customers had bought things. "Quite expensive things, for second hand, I mean," she added, fitting the key in the ignition but not turning it yet. "His business really does seem to be above board, Mum."

"Let's hope so," Sarah sighed.

"I'm sure it is Mum. It just feels, well... okay. It feels okay somehow."

"Maybe you're too trusting, Katie," Sarah leaned into the car to stroke her beloved's head. Katie caught the hand and held it.

"And maybe you are not trusting enough," she said softly.

"Maybe... maybe..."

* * *

Trust! She had trusted Tom. She had believed him when he told her he loved her. She had believed him when he told her he couldn't marry her, he was married already.

'I want to be with you but Mary's a Catholic. We've been separated for two years but she can't divorce me,' he'd told her.

'It doesn't matter,' she'd said. 'We can pretend we're married. No one need ever know.'

But people did know. Her mother and father knew... and it did matter.

'He'll leave you, like he left her,' her father prophesied. 'But it'll be easier next time. He'll just walk out without a backward glance, you mark my words!'

'But he loves me. He never loved Mary. They were too young.'

114

'Pshaw!' her father's old-fashioned retort. 'Not solid enough, too fly-by-night. You mark my words, my girl. You'll see I'm right. When it's too late.'

'He's not 'fly-by-night', whatever that's supposed to mean, is he, Mum? You don't think that, do you, Mum?'

'Of course she does,' supplied her father.

'Do you, Mum?' Sarah persisted.

'You're not really going to live with him, are you dear? I mean, people will know you're not married. You'll not be accepted.'

'Accepted! Don't be ridiculous, Mum. People don't get 'accepted' or not because they're married or not. You're living in the past. Nobody cares any more.'

'Oh, but they do, dear. I know I do. It would bring disgrace on our family.'

'Mum! You're talking like a Jane Austen novel! I don't believe this.'

'It'll all end in tears, my girl, you mark my words!'

'Dad!'

'And we'll not pick up the pieces when it does,' he intoned. 'If you walk out that door to go to that waster, you can stay out. You're no daughter of mine!'

She thought he was bluffing. Expected him to soften through time. Was certain her mother would.

She overestimated their capacity for forgiveness.

When Tom left her, he left her alone, with two young children and no family to help her support them. She could only suppose her father felt some kind of satisfaction in being proved right. His door stayed closed to her.

Letters from her brother, Robert, became her source of family information. Ridiculous that she should hear of her mother's illness from Robert, living halfway round the world, when she lived only an hour's journey from her. Worse to learn of her mother's death from him.

Robert had somehow retained his father's favour, despite his unblessed departure as a young man, so it was he who was informed of all the news, never Sarah. Robert tried hard, over the years, to mediate between their father and Sarah, but he too was surprised by the unrelenting opposition he met. Even at their mother's funeral, Dad would not speak to Sarah, giving her and Tom the 'silent treatment', caring nothing what friends or neighbours thought, letting Robert's pleas on her behalf fall on deaf ears.

When Tom disappeared, Robert came over again for a few weeks and Sarah had been grateful for his loving support and help as she tried every conceivable avenue of approach to her search.

Robert had liked Tom, had declared him 'sound' and 'cool', the brother-in-law he wanted, so he found it hard to believe Tom's disappearance could have been intentional, having always disagreed with his father's prophecy that Tom would inevitably leave Sarah the way he had his wife.

'Tom loves you, Sarah. I just know he does. He wouldn't up and leave you without any warning like that. He's not a coward. He'd tell you if he wanted out. There has to be another explanation. Something out of his control. '

By the time he rejoined his family in Canada, Robert was convinced Tom must have died.

But, when Tom had been gone for a while, when she had checked everything she could check, searched everywhere she could search, Sarah began to wonder if her father *had* been right… that it *had* been easier this time. Had Tom given 'a backward glance'? Or, was that the problem? Had he glanced even further back? Gone back to Mary? Had he picked up a life he'd discarded before, finding it fitted again?

Or had he moved on to yet another model?

She found herself imagining a trail of discarded 'wives' left in his wake as he tried on relationships, shimmying into their lives for a while then wriggling out when the fit was too tight.

You can imagine a lot of things in eleven years.

Chapter 16

She had stopped reading David's diary for the time being... just as he had stopped writing for a while. Having come up against a bit of a brick wall as regards tracing his father, David didn't seem inclined to write about anything for a few months. When he started again, his code became more complex and Sarah hadn't sussed it out yet, so she gave herself a break from trying to decipher the workings of his mind, discouraged by the realisation that she hadn't known her son at all.

She had proudly told Mike that David was a good boy, he never lied. But he had. Even then, as a young lad, before the real lying and double-life began in earnest, he had forgotten his 'Pinocchion' fear. Little lies, like where he'd been when he came home late for tea. Bigger lies, like what he was doing when he was tracing his father. Sometimes lies of omission rather than commission, but lies none the less. Lies, subterfuge, call it what you will, she felt deceived. She had thought she knew him so well.

Reading the diary no longer made her feel close to him, only disappointed and sad, and she had had enough of sadness for a while. David had left her long before he died. She was coming to terms with that.

Kate would be next. She and Mike were seeing a lot of each other, he almost lived in their front room. Sarah liked him and was happy for them, but she knew the time would soon come when they'd want to be on their own, in their own home, married, she hoped, though she knew she had no freedom of speech to suggest it. She just wanted them to be happy. That was the priority now. Ensuring Katie's happiness. Kate could not be happy if Sarah was miserable, so, Sarah put aside the diary for a while, turning her attention to the clearing and decorating of David's room.

At first, it was a traumatic exercise. More often than not, she would start with good intentions and finish without achieving very much. But, gradually, the room began to be less David's Room and more The Spare Room. Then, by the time she had redecorated it and disposed of the bedroom furniture, it had become a little sittingroom, Her Room. Somewhere for her to sit quietly with the cat and her thoughts or watch television or read, whatever she was in the mood for. Perhaps even to entertain a friend, like Maggie from work, leaving the downstairs livingroom for Katie and Mike.

They protested, of course, that they enjoyed her company and there was no need for such an arrangement, but the truth was, she preferred it this way. It had been the right thing to do. They needed space to be together, to talk in private, to plan their future together, and she needed somewhere fresh to block out the past and learn to live in the present.

She had taken care over the choosing of colours and fabrics. Wanting this to be a sunny room, a room for pleasant reflection rather than gloomy thoughts, she had taken time and trouble over it and was happy with the results. The walls and ceiling were shades of pale golden yellow, light, bright but not cold, the colour of early summer sunshine. A soft carpet of deeper gold covered the floor. Creamy curtains, layers of cottons and voile, dressed the window and matched the little bed-settee and chair she had searched out in a second-hand furniture shop and re-covered herself. At last, she had let the season warm her, allowed its glow to colour this room, a room where she hoped it could always be summer.

She could even imagine enjoying 'entertaining' here. Sitting with Maggie some evening that her husband was playing bowls or cards: chatting over a cup of coffee or a glass of wine: something they had occasionally done before. She knew that would please Maggie. She had been trying to visit for months, but Sarah had always had an excuse ready, a reason why it was never convenient. She hadn't been ready for company then. But now? Well… perhaps. Perhaps in this lovely summery room she could pick up some more of the threads of her life.

A selection of books lined up neatly in David's old bookcase, one of the few things she had kept, repainted and repositioned. Mike gifted her the telly from his flat, assuring her he rarely turned it on and was even less likely to now that he spent most of his time here with Kate. She accepted it graciously and retrieved and renovated David's little bedside cabinet to set it on, beating the bucket-man by a whisker!

Mike helped her to do away with the old centre light fitting and Kate treated her to some delightful crystal lamp bases and together they made soft shades for them from the same fabric as the curtains.

Sarah dug out her mother's crystal vase, the one she had loved as a child and had begged from her father as a keepsake after her mother died. It had been handed over grudgingly, negating much of the pleasure of having it, but now she washed it lovingly and filled it with the roses Kate brought her each week.

"You don't have to do that," she protested.

"I want to," Kate said firmly.

"Let her," Mike nodded.

So, she allowed herself to be spoiled, loving the luxury of fresh roses filling her little room with their perfume, watching their enchanting journey from bud to blossom as the week wore on.

With patience and hard work, they had transformed a bedroom of regrets into a living room of promises.

The arrangement worked so well, that Kate wondered if she and Mike could stay in the house when they married.

"It would only be the kitchen and bathroom we'd have to share," she pleaded.

"*Only* the kitchen and bathroom," Mike spluttered. "What d'you mean *only*? The kitchen and the bathroom are the most difficult to share."

"The bedroom?"

"...even for a married couple," he continued, ignoring her interjection.

"But I already share them with Mum."

"But *I* don't! I've got used to living on my own. It's going to be hard enough to share with you, never mind your Mum!"

"But she's easy to share with. She likes to go to bed early and get up early."

"Probably just when I need to get into the bathroom to shave."

"She pops down for a cuppa and takes it back to bed."

"Just when I need to grab some breakfast, preferably without conversation."

"She's never chatty in the morning."

"Only because you're incapable of conversation till half past eleven."

"Rubbish!"

"She'd probably feel obliged to talk to me in the morning. I'd end up being thoroughly rude to her and there goes a beautiful relationship," he said, flinging his hands in the air.

"You wouldn't be rude," she wheedled. "You're not capable of being rude."

"In the morning, yes, I am more than capable of being very, very rude. I am not a 'good-morning' sort of person!"

"Perhaps that depends on who you spend the night with," Katie purred in his ear, curling her body onto his lap.

The discussion arose from time to time over the next few weeks, but Mike was unwavering in his refusal to countenance the idea.

"It won't work," he kept saying.

"But it *is* working," Kate reasoned. "You practically live here already and we don't get in one another's way."

"But I *don't* live here. The times we might are the times I'm not here."

"But you're flat's too small."

"We'll find somewhere."

"We can't afford a bigger place."

"We'll find somewhere."

"I like it here."

"Yes, I do too, but *not* sharing a house with your mother."

"She's not so bad."

"I'm not saying she is. I'm not saying anything about your mother. Just that I don't want to share a house with her, or anybody else for that matter."

"Except me?"

"Except you," he agreed, pulling her into his arms. "Though you'll really have to remind me why!"

Then, one evening, their peace was shattered by a loud crash from the kitchen. While changing the water for her roses, Sarah had dropped the vase in the sink. It had hit the taps as it left her hand and lay in jagged pieces, the tap water coursing over it, mingled with the dark red of the blood oozing from Sarah's hand.

"Mum!"

"T.G/G.T I've got it! Gordon Thompson. My Dad!"

"What are you talking about, Mum? Look at your hand. You've cut it."

But Sarah just stood, shaking her head, an expression of horror on her face, but not horror for her wound. "G.T., Gordon Thompson. David was seeing Gordon Thompson! He was doing his garden!"

"But your hand! The vase, you've..."

"The vase? It was their wedding present from my granny. Granny Thompson ."

"Mum," Kate was holding her mother's hand under the running water. "Mum," she repeated loudly. "Your hand! You've cut your hand!"

"G.T., Granny Thompson. Only it's not *Granny* Thompson."

"We'll need to get her to the hospital," Mike decided. "She needs stitches in that cut. It's very deep."

"It's *Gordon* Thompson!"

"Get a towel or something, and some ice from the fridge. Wrap it in the towel. Give me something to bind it to her hand with."

"Mum, Mum? Can you hear Mike? We're taking you to the hospital."

"The 'old sod'! That was my Dad!"

"She's in shock. Just grab the keys. I'll get her to the car."

"He was doing his garden."

"Put her in the back seat. You get in beside her. Here, put this blanket round her, she's shivering."

"I've not got her bag, her heart pills..."

"Hell! I'll run in for them. Where's the bag?"

"Hall table, I saw it on the hall table."

"It was Granny Thompson's vase."

"Okay, Mum. It's okay." Kate hugged her mother closer, buckling the seat belt round her. She sat in the middle seat, beside her, so that she could hold her mother tightly, fearing for her, willing her to be all right, for the shock to pass, for the muttering to stop.

Sarah looked at her, smiling briefly, not really seeing her at all. "He called him a 'miserable old sod' and that's what he is. I doubt if he'd have got much out of him."

"Who, Mum?"

"Here's her bag," Mike threw it onto the seat beside them.

"'Miserable old sod,'" Sarah mused, getting weaker now, shivering uncontrollably, but her mind far from the pain of her wound. The wounds she was feeling now were from a different time, a different injury. "Wouldn't even part with the time of day."

They got her to the hospital, where her wound was stitched and dressed and the doctor set up a saline drip to replace some of the fluid lost. "She'll be fine," he reassured them. "We'll keep her in overnight, keep her warm. We've given her something for the pain and to help her sleep. She just needs rest now. It was a nasty cut and she was losing a lot of blood. I think we've managed to save her fingers. You did well."

"She didn't seem to know she'd cut herself."

"Shock. She'll be okay now. As I say, you did well getting her here so quickly. It's a good job you were with her."

Kate looked at Mike and knew that there would be no further debate. They would be moving in with Sarah when they married.

Chapter 17

Kate wrote to her uncle Robert, telling him of Sarah's accident and of her concerns for Sarah's future. He wrote back that he too was worried and was preparing a 'sister-flat' attached to his own house, so that Sarah could spend at least part of each year with him and his family.

"The kids would love to get to know their Scottish auntie better," he wrote. *"And you would love it over here, Sarah. Everything is bigger somehow. So much open space, so many places to see, things to do, people to love you. You wouldn't be leaving Katie, just letting me share you with her for some of the time."*

"You should go," Kate assured her. "It would be good for you."

"I hate other people telling me what's good for me all the time."

"Well, it would be. Something fresh, something new. Uncle Robert is great. You get on so well with him and Angela. You'd have a ball. Just think, you could sit up all night playing Baccarat like you used to, or talking! You and Robert never seem to run out of things to talk about."

Sarah nursed her bandaged hand moodily. "Where on earth would I get the money to go jetting off to Canada?"

"Uncle Robert says he'll send you the ticket, you only have to tell him when you'll go."

"I couldn't let him do that."

"Why ever not? He wants to. He's your brother, he…"

"He's not rich."

"He seems to be 'comfortable'!"

"He has his own family to care for."

"You *are* his family."

And she had no answer to that. Robert had told her the same thing.

"You are family. And family matters ~no matter what Dad seems to think."

"Oh, I don't know, Katie. Your Uncle Robert is very kind, but I'd feel in the way." She held up her helplessness.

"You wouldn't be. Your hand will soon heal. Besides, he misses you. He says the kids miss you too."

"I know, but he would say that, wouldn't he?"

"Only if he meant it. If he didn't hope you'd go over there, he wouldn't be building on a 'sister-flat' for you."

"I worry about that. It costs a lot to extend a house."

"Obviously he can afford it or he wouldn't do it."

"I suppose so."

"Mum. You're just putting obstacles in your own way."

Sarah sighed. "But…"

"Why don't you think about it some more? Uncle Robert says the flat won't be ready for a few months anyway, so there's no rush. It's just so kind of him, I don't think you should dismiss the idea out of hand."

"No, you're right. It is kind. Very kind. But your Uncle Robert always was kind, so it's no surprise."

"And you'll think about it?"

Sarah smiled at her lovely, caring daughter. "I'll think about it."

* * *

Meanwhile, Tom was becoming part of Katie's life. Like it or not, if Sarah wanted to stay close to Kate, she was going to have to get used to Tom being around. She wouldn't trust him, *couldn't* trust him. She would be careful, not get involved, not let him into her own life but she would watch him, she would guard her Katie.

Tom was Kate's father, but he was not Sarah's husband. She owed him nothing.

He owed her a lot… starting with the promised explanations. Sarah wasn't bothered to hear them but Kate championed Tom and won him the right to be heard.

So, here she was, back in his shop, trying to keep an open mind, trying to 'be fair' as Kate had asked.

She looked around at the shiny, polished furniture and it didn't look so shabby. Late summer sunlight shone through the clean windows. The flowers here and there didn't look so out of place any more. As she wandered between the rows of sideboards and cabinets, coffee tables and hat stands, she could see that there were even some reasonable bits and pieces, one or two things that could probably sell for a fair price. Perhaps it was all right after all. Perhaps it was 'above board'. Perhaps.

Suddenly, the bell sounded. *Ah, a customer. How nice.*

She looked round expectantly, catching a look of surprise on the man's face before he backed out, muttering something about it being "A mistake."

"Oh! I thought I had a customer," Tom said as he came through from the back shop.

Sarah laughed. "I think you nearly had, but my face frightened him off."

Tom raised his eyebrows.

"I think the chap had made a mistake or something. He was looking for someone called Harry. At least I think that's what he called as he came through the door. Then he said something about it being the wrong shop, a mistake. I thought I recognised him, actually," she continued, a little puzzled by the look of alarm that passed momentarily across Tom's face. "But perhaps not," she shrugged. "I don't know. He seemed rather confused anyway."

She watched Tom carefully, feeling she must have been mistaken about his earlier expression. Perhaps it hadn't been alarm, just a flash of disappointment at losing a prospective customer. He seemed perfectly at ease, unconcerned.

"Oh, what a pity," he said, confirming her thought. "I'd have liked you to see things at work."

"You mean you'd have liked me to have seen *you* at work, Tom Reed," she laughed. "You'd've enjoyed showing off to me.

Using that smooth talk to convince someone they desperately needed something they have no use whatsoever for."

Tom's hands were in the air. "Touché," he acceded. "But, you're too hard on me. No-one ever comes back to complain."

"They're probably too scared they'd end up buying something else they don't need, " Sarah said as she walked into the office with him. "A bit like... you know? Did you ever watch 'Last of the Summer Wine'? What was the old lady called? The one with the second hand shop? Auntie something?"

"Auntie Wainwright."

"Yes! You do know it," Sarah laughed. "Well, I bet you're just like her!"

"Are you calling me an old bat?"

"Would I ever?" she asked innocently. "Now, where's the cup of tea you were supposed to be making? Or were you selling the teapot while I was browsing?"

"Do you..?"

"How's the..?" they began in unison when the cup of tea was poured and they were sitting awkwardly in Tom's office.

"Sorry…" Sarah said.

"Please..." Tom leant back in his chair with a gesture that she should be the one to speak.

"I was only going to say, I was going to ask, how's the second-hand furniture business?" Sarah shrugged.

"Oh not bad, not bad. I'm able to get about a bit, looking for good buys and bargains. I like to travel."

"I remember."

"Yes, I suppose you will." He paused before asking, "Was that hard for you, Sarah?"

"I didn't mind. I didn't grudge you the travel. I never wanted you to feel hemmed in."

"You were better than I deserved, Sari."

"Sarah."

"Sarah," he smiled. "You never liked being called 'Sari', did you?"

"No, it always makes me think of the Indian dress, or a cat, or something. 'Here, Sari, Sari,'" she leant down, her fingers beckoning the imagined animal.

"I don't suppose you've still got the cat?"

"Not the same one," Sarah laughed. "She'd be about a hundred and five if we had!"

"That's what I thought. But she might have lasted. She was such a lazy cat. She might have been conserving her energy for old age."

"Very old age!" Sarah laughed.

Tom looked up from the biscuit he was crumbling between his fingers. "Sarah," he began, "Sarah..."

"Is it just furniture you deal in?" she asked in a sudden flash of insight.

He was taken by surprise by the unexpected question. He scratched his head, leaving a dandruff of biscuit crumbs. "What d'you mean?"

"Well, jewellery, watches, things like that?"

"Yes, these too. Why? Looking for something?" he asked, putting down the biscuit, rubbing his hands together.

"Could be. Could be. Depends what kind of discount you give me," she teased.

"Seriously?" He walked over to a cabinet. "I've got one or two nice pieces just now."

She followed him over.

"Ladies' rings, brooches..."

"Any men's rings, or watches?"

He looked up at her, his surprise showing.

"Mike. I thought I'd like to give him a gift. He's been good."

"Yes, of course. Well," he said, opening the cabinet, pulling out a drawer. "I've a few watches, not many just now. Some of them not up to much," he shrugged.

She looked over them carefully, a frown of concentration on her face. "That one," she pointed. "May I see that one out?"

"Course."

She turned it over in her hand, noting the engraving on the back, the scratches on its face.

"They're second hand, of course. You can't expect them to be perfect," Tom said defensively, mistaking her hesitation for criticism, and holding his hand out to take the watch back.

"No! No, I know that." Sarah's grip tightened.

"This one here's in better condition." He offered her another watch.

"No, it's all right," she said quietly. "I like this one. It's got character. Reminds me of… of someone," she faltered.

"Then, it's yours," he said, pressing it into her hands.

"How much do you want for it?"

"No. It's yours. As a gift."

Sarah shook her head. "No. I couldn't do that. I want to buy it. I want to give it as a gift myself, so I must pay for it," she reasoned.

"A fiver, then."

"Okay," she agreed.

"Done!" He offered his hand.

"I hope not," she said quietly, looking up at him. "And I want a receipt."

"A receipt?" Tom spluttered. "Don't you trust me?"

"No."

"Okay. A receipt it is," he conceded, searching on the desk for an invoice pad.

"Got to keep the books right," she teased.

"There's a pad here somewhere."

"If you could just fill in the details," she suggested, once he'd located a pad of invoices.

"Details? What d'you mean?"

"You know, the serial number on the watch, the engraving, things like that. Just so I can prove it's not stolen, if asked."

"It's not stolen!" Tom exploded.

"Good. Then you'll not mind filling in the details."

"You just don't trust me, do you, Sarah?"

"No," she agreed with a smile.

"Here then, you fill in the details, I'll sign the bloody thing!"

"Tom!" she remonstrated.

He grunted by way of apology and pushed the pad of forms towards her.

The business concluded, they sat down again. Sarah put the watch carefully in her handbag, taking her time about it, her hand still lightly bandaged, making her awkward, giving her heart a chance to steady, wanting to be calm, wanting to be in control.

"Aye, you always were hard," Tom joked.

"Was I?"

He shook his head. "No, Sarah. You were never hard. Anything but."

And so they sat for a while, quietly drinking lukewarm tea and nibbling biscuits, ostensibly a companionable scene.

"Sarah, I… " He shifted in his seat. "I was wondering, Sarah. I, em… "

"Yes Tom?" Sarah's eyes met his.

"You're a very attractive woman."

"Don't, Tom."

"Always were. You've hardly aged at all. What are you now? Forty-five? Forty-six?"

She nodded.

He looked at her ring finger. "Never married?"

"Tom." She put her cup down on his desk.

"Did you ever meet someone else?"

"This is really *so* not your business."

"But did you?"

"Tom Reed, if you are going to pry into my love life, I'll just go home right now!" Sarah said, not ready to admit to Tom that, in the eleven years of his absence, she had kept other men well at bay. Oh yes, there had been opportunities, there had been interest shown and she had enjoyed the attention, but no one had been allowed to get too close. Like a fool, she had waited for him until loneliness became a habit, she supposed.

"I always wondered."

Sarah gathered her bag, started to rise. "Tom, let it drop!" she warned.

But Tom persisted with his serious study of her face. "I didn't leave you for another woman, Sarah," he said at last.

"Didn't you, Tom?" She tried to sound casual, as though it didn't really matter, feeling that it shouldn't really matter after all this time, but knowing somehow that it did. It mattered more than she wanted Tom to know. She sat down again and waited.

"No Sarah, there was no other woman."

"Not even Mary?"

"Mary?"

"Your wife. Remember? I thought you might have gone back to your wife."

"Oh. Mary!" He shook his head, cursing. "What on earth made you think that?"

She shrugged. She had to believe him, the look of bafflement on his face was too swift to be pretence.

"I left you because the law had caught up with me, as you always said it would. I had to get out of the country fast, lie low for a while. But they got me in the end. I served three years down in London."

Watching Sarah's silent face, he continued, "I served another three after that before I learned my lesson."

She nodded.

He raised his hands. "Truth, Sarah. That's the honest truth." He added a few oaths to authenticate it.

She sat silently, watching his face, his body language.

"You never liked my jaunts to London, did you, Sarah?"

Sarah shook her head, remembering too well the fear she used to feel each time he announced that he had to go to London 'on business'.

"I should have listened to you. Shouldn't have made that last trip."

"But you told me it was a short haul, Newcastle, you said."

"I didn't want you to worry. I knew how you felt about me going to London," Tom continued, "You were right too. I was up to no good. Only not with another woman. I had another identity, another name and address, but not another woman."

"No. I don't believe you Tom."

"It's the truth, Sarah. I swear it is."

"But why couldn't I find you? The police had no trace of you."

"I'm telling you, I had to leave the country. Spent a few years incognito on the continent."

"Why didn't you contact us?"

"I was in hiding. I didn't dare make contact with anybody over here. They were looking for me, might have been watching the house, intercepting the post, tapping the phones. I didn't know. I couldn't risk it."

"No, I can't believe you mattered that much to them. What, in God's name had you done?"

"That's not important! It was nothing wicked, like murder or rape. That's all you need to know. It was just the usual stuff."

"Your petty thieving? No. I can't believe Interpol would have cared about that, unless it was something bigger?"

"It was big enough, Sarah. That's all you need to know. For your own sake!"

"For my own sake?" she spluttered. "Since when did you care about 'my sake'?"

"I didn't want you involved. If I'd tried to get word to you, you might have got drawn into the mess I'd made."

"You could have found some way, Tom. There must have been some way."

"Believe me, there wasn't. There just wasn't!"

"And after they caught you?"

"It was under a different name. I had been using an assumed name," he repeated, "and a London address for my, ahem, my 'business'. I didn't give our address so that you could be spared the shame and humiliation of having a jailbird for a husband."

"Pardon?"

"I said... "

She was out of her seat, pacing the office. "You wanted to spare me shame and humiliation?"

"Yes."

"*Spare* me? *Spare* me shame and humiliation? You have to be joking, Tom!"

"No."

"You stupid, silly, foolish moron!" Sarah exclaimed, seeking words to express her incredulity, unused to using strong language, having to settle for meaningless euphemisms. She punched the desk with her good hand. "You idiot! All these years! All these years! Did you really think that it would hurt less to believe that you were dead? Or, that there was less shame, less humiliation in losing you to another woman, than to know you were in jail?"

Tom hung his head.

"*Save* me shame! *Save* me humiliation! You cannot be serious! How do you think I explained your sudden disappearance to everybody? To the kids? The neighbours? The busybodies? What conclusions did you think they might jump to?"

He shook his head, studied his shoes.

"'Oh we really don't know where Tom is, Mrs Jones,'" she mimicked. "'He's left us. No, no, I'm sure he's not gone off with another woman. I mean, how could he possibly do that? No, no, something must have happened to him. He'll turn up soon, you'll see.'" Her voice hardened with bitterness. "Unless, of course he's dead! Disappeared without trace! But don't worry, there's no shame in that. It happens all the time!"

"I didn't think…"

"I couldn't grieve, couldn't mourn properly. You might not be dead. They never found your van. No word of an accident. It didn't turn up in a ditch anywhere, abandoned. You could turn up any time. Then again, maybe you were with *her.* Maybe you'd gone back to your wife."

"Oh Sarah, I'm so…"

"Sorry? You're sorry, Tom? Yes. You should be sorry. It was eleven years of pure hell!" She paced the office, throwing words at him like stones. "Not knowing! Not knowing what to think! How to feel! Loving you one day, hating you the next. If you were dead, then it was okay to love you because you couldn't help that. If you'd gone back to Mary, then I could hate you, but what if you hadn't?"

"I'm so sorry, Sarah."

"I did think you might have been in prison, but it didn't occur to me that you could use another name! I assumed that, if you'd been caught, I'd hear, they'd tell me. *You'd* tell me!"

"I was ashamed."

"You were a fool!" She stopped pacing and stood in front of him. "Why didn't you trust me, Tom?"

He looked up as she continued to speak. "Why didn't you trust my love for you? I knew you were a fool with all your shady deals. Sooner or later you were bound to get caught. But I had been preparing myself for that. I would have stood by you, waited for you. I wouldn't've cared about prison bars. I loved you!" She was almost weeping. The wasted years strangled her.

"I was ashamed."

"Oh Tom, I thought you'd never truly loved me. That all the good times had been a sham, as dishonest as your damn business dealings. I thought you had cheated! I thought you had cheated." She sat down wearily, defeated by his stupidity.

"I never cheated on you, Sarah."

They gazed silently at one another, trying to understand the enormity of the mistake Tom had made so long ago.

"Why are you telling me this now, Tom?" she demanded.

"Because I want to come back, Sarah." Tom stated simply. He reached across the desk to place his hand over hers. "I love you, Sarah. I never stopped loving you. I'll not pretend that I've been celibate for twelve years, but no one else has ever mattered. I want to try again to make you happy."

"You ask too much, Tom," she gasped, snatching her hand away. "Too much too soon."

"I know, but, if we…"

"Too soon for me to know you, to trust you."

"I'll not let you down again, Sarah."

She shook her head. "I can't take that chance, Tom. I can't let you hurt me like that again."

"I won't, Sarah."

"I can't risk it. It's too soon, much too soon."

"But…"

"And too soon after David's death. It's not much over a year since I lost David. It still hangs like a cloud over me. My mind isn't clear. I live in a fog. I don't know what I feel about anything."

133

He reached for her hand once more. "I love you, Sarah. Never stopped."

She looked at him, shaking her head. "I don't know if I believe that, and, even if I did, I doubt I could ever love you again. Oh, I know my heart leaps at sight of you, that your touch is still like an electric shock," she said, indicating his hand on hers. "But I don't think I could ever trust you again." And she pulled her hand from under his and moved further from him.

"I know it's too soon, Sarah," Tom replied. "All I ask just now is the chance to show you that I've changed. I'm straight. You *can* trust me, honestly, Sarah. Let me show you."

Sarah scrutinized his face. "Have you changed, Tom?" she asked. "I want to believe you. For Kate's sake, I want to believe you. She wants so much for us to be friends but I don't know. I don't know if I can. As you say, you'd have to *show* me you've changed."

Hope rose hesitantly in his face like the sun on a cloudy day. "I will, Sarah. Just give me the chance and I'll make it all up to you."

"That won't be easy," she murmured.

"I like a challenge," he grinned, the hope dawning more surely now. "And I'll take it real slow."

"*Real* slow," she emphasized. "Friendship only, nothing more."

He held his hands up innocently. "Nothing more."

"No promises!"

"No promises."

They sat staring into one another's eyes, not as lovers might, but as animals do, sizing one another up, feeling for the ground rules before making any move.

Chapter 18

The house had hardly changed at all, only become older and shabbier: the door hardly recognisable as the proud, deep red it had been painted many years ago, the paint faded and peeling, the letterbox hanging askew; the window frames and guttering in need of repair and repainting; the front step littered with the detritus of autumn storms and birds' droppings: but otherwise the same. The same grey stucco effect walls, the same useless, little half-porch, the same flagstone path, some of the flagstones cracked and crumbling.

The grass was tall with the growth of several seasons, the flowerbeds lost in its envelopment. Even the windows stared bleakly back at her, the old net curtains greyed and torn.

Where was the self-respect her father used to flaunt so proudly? Where the pride? These were all jobs he used to do himself, climbing the ladder nimbly. Okay, he was no longer the young man he used to be, but surely he would want the jobs done nonetheless, would hire someone to do them? Was that not what people normally did? Was that not the responsibility of a home-owner? This looked the home of a no-hoper, a down-and-outer. She shuddered as she negotiated what was left of the path.

He didn't respond at first to her insistent knock and she had almost given up before the door creaked open and he stood before her.

"What d'you want?" he demanded querulously.

"Dad, it's me, Sarah."

"I know who you are. I'm not blind. I asked what you want."

She looked around at the gawping strangers who had been her neighbours, older now, but still nosy, their sudden need to be in the front garden signalled first by the twitching of the curtains. "Can I come in for a moment?"

"Why?"

"Please, Dad."

He looked at her without affection. "Why?"

"Why are you making this so difficult, Dad?"

"What do you want?" he repeated, but, after a moment, he shuffled down the hall assuming that she would follow him.

Suddenly, she was overwhelmed with longing for the security of her childhood: for her mother, always there when she came home from school. She would call through from the kitchen, 'That you, love? How was school today?' and Sarah would sit at the kitchen table watching her mother prepare the vegetables, peel the potatoes, cook the meat, while she recounted her day, enjoying the quiet attention her mother gave her in those few precious minutes before Robert came bursting in the door to claim his share.

For her father as he'd been when she was little, always taciturn and strict, but ready to fight her case at school. No-one bullied the Thompson kids. Strong, dependable, steady. There was always food on their table, coal in their grate. Before the years of disillusionment had soured him and loss had embittered him.

She walked slowly down the hall behind him, noting his halting step, his need to hold on to the wall at his side, the rasping of his breath. How much he had aged.

This was the living room of her teenage years. Nothing had changed as far as she could see. Even the wallpaper was the same. But his neglect had stopped at the front door. The room was clean and tidy, the furniture old and worn, but cared for. Relief flooded through her. She doubted if she could have borne the same lack of pride in here, the home that had been scrubbed and polished so assiduously by her mother.

His chair had changed. Instead of the old leather armchair that used to have pride of place by the fireside, there was an orthopaedic chair, one of those with a firm, high seat, making it easier for a less fit person to hoist themselves up. How much that must have hurt his pride, to admit his strength was failing, that he needed help in any way. There was a walking stick too, resting against the chair, forgotten when he went to open the door? Or spurned?

"Dad..."

Ignoring her presence, he sat in his chair, picking up the paper that lay on the table beside it.

"Dad... I wondered..."

He opened the paper with somewhat of a flourish, maximizing the noise a newspaper can make.

"Please Dad. I wanted to..."

He turned the page with an even greater flourish, making even more noise.

"You're not going to make this easy, are you?"

Another page, another flourish, more noise. But no acknowledgement.

Sarah sat back in the armchair across from him, her mother's chair. She closed her eyes. What would her mother have done with this stubborn, non-communicative man? How did she deal with this mood? She waited quietly for inspiration. The old clock on the mantel ticked off the minutes.

Cabbage? Or sprouts? Yesterday's dinner no doubt, the smell lingering after the food departed. Boiled potatoes and cabbage, remembered odours, though her mother would have opened the window in the morning, clearing out the reminder of yesterday's fare by now. Polish, a faint hint of polish too, though, this time, not familiar, a different brand perhaps. Her mother always used beeswax with lavender, a distinctive smell, not as stringent, as manufactured, as this: the old-fashioned tin of polish replaced by a spray can.

There was a photograph of her mother on the mantel, where it had always sat. One of the very few there was of her. She smiled out of it uncertainly, her discomfort showing in her eyes. Whenever Robert's old Brownie came out, Mum would hide herself away somewhere, in the kitchen if they were at home or behind the nearest tree if they were outside. She'd been caught in the garden; caught by the cunning of her son; caught as she smiled up at his approach, unaware of the camera until it was too late. Robert had been jubilant, dancing round the garden whooping his triumph. It was a beautiful photograph and Sarah found herself smiling back at her mother, such a gentle woman, such a shy soul.

Martha Thompson had lived quietly, unobtrusively, her demeanour one of constant apology. She bowed to her husband's every opinion, any argument dying before it was uttered, as though she had no right to any of her own. It used to annoy Robert and Sarah when they were young, but no amount of reasoning or coaxing would persuade her to stand against him. 'Your father knows best,' was her constant reply, even when they strongly felt that he did not.

'What hold did he have over you?' Sarah silently asked the faded image on the mantelpiece. 'What made you feel you owed him such total, all-encompassing loyalty. Even when he was wrong?'

She looked across at him, sitting there, stiff with resentment, pretending to be absorbed in yesterday's paper. How did he command such devotion? Had Martha been so grateful to be rescued from spinsterhood that even a man capable of so little affection was to be adored? Sarah shuddered.

Many years ago, sitting in this room, silently observing the scene, she had decided that was not to be for her. She would choose carefully. She would only marry someone who was her equal in every way, someone who would deserve her loyalty without needing to demand it, who would earn her respect without needing to command it. She sighed wistfully for the innocence of that youthful decision.

Had her mother had such dreams as a girl? Was this the husband she envisioned when she sat on the rug, observing her own parents at rest? How did he win her heart? *Had* he won her heart? Or just some kind of gratitude and loyalty? Sarah thought she would never know, but she would always wonder.

The hearth needed sweeping, coal dust and ashes covering it like a grey snowfall. Her mother would not have let it lie there for more than a moment, yet this had obviously lain since the fire was lit this morning. She checked the 'tut' on her lips, aware of an impulse to kneel before the fireplace and tidy it up with the old brush and shovel that hung on its brass stand in the corner, knowing instinctively that the gesture would not be appreciated by the old man. He had never accepted help or criticism well, and that would imply both. His unspoken adage through life had been, 'What I can't do myself is not worth doing!'... though, in truth, it was not how he had ever lived. The hard work her mother did in his behalf was taken for granted, didn't count as outside help, was his by right, without recognition or thanks.

Sarah closed her eyes again, letting the smells and sounds of the room draw her back to her childhood.

He hadn't always been so morose, so severe. She remembered a time when he would tell them stories at bedtime, always Bible stories, always with a moral. 'Jonah and the Big Fish' was their favourite. They would lie, holding their breath in suspense as the story unfolded, marvelling at its clever twists and turns, amazed at his skill as a raconteur, a skill used rarely and reluctantly, as a reward for exceptionally good behaviour.

The minutes ticked peacefully by. It's strange the companionship sitting either side of a fire can engender. The coal in the grate shifted and settled, the flames stilling to a warm glow. Silence stretched its limbs like a lazy cat.

She let her breathing deepen, her body relax into the chair. She was in no hurry, had nowhere to rush away to.

Familiarity crept around her, purring its welcome. This room had been a haven once. Somewhere to bring your friend to have buttered toast and hot chocolate after school. Somewhere to pore over homework after she'd gone, lying there on the rug, the warmth of the fire on your back. Somewhere to lay out your stamps before carefully sticking them in their album, counting them again, as though not knowing that the three you'd profited in the swap brought the total to three more than you had before. Somewhere to sit on a winter's evening, listening to a play on the radio, playing cards with Robert, Mother's knitting needles clicking softly in the background. Memories of being hastily ushered to bed before Father was due in from the late-shift, 'Quick, up the stairs before your father catches you!'... not that he'd have touched them, or even blazed at them, but displeasure would smoulder in his face and they would feel reproved without a word.

Sarah sat, letting the firelight warm her body as the memories warmed her heart.

Her father's paper rustled as he folded it away. "Well, what do you want?" he demanded again, his voice unsoftened by sentimental memories or firelight. "Why have you come?"

"How are you, Dad?"

"No better for seeing you!"

"Thank you."

He grunted, snatching up the paper again.

"I see you have a stick now. Arthritis, is it?"

He reopened the paper.

"Do you have a home help?" The room was hoovered and dusted by someone and she doubted it was him. "You could do with someone to see to your garden," she remarked. "The grass has a good year's growth on it, at least. Do you not qualify for council help getting it cut?" she asked, the hammer of her heart belying the casual enquiry.

"What's it to you?" he demanded.

She shrugged. "Nothing. I just wondered."

"Aye, well. It's none of your business."

"Sorry. Just wondered," she repeated. "Just making conversation."

"Aye." he grunted.

"Do you have to cook for yourself?"

"Look! I don't know why you're here," he said, throwing the paper to the side of his chair. "But it's a bit late to start takin' an interest in my welfare! If you want to tell me what you want, fine, get on with it. If not, you can see yourself out!" He reached for the television remote control.

Sarah almost laughed out loud at the empty gesture. The television was unplugged, always his careful habit on retiring at night. He had not yet plugged it in for today's viewing.

He threw the remote down impatiently.

"David died."

"David?"

"Your grandson."

He shrugged.

"I don't think you ever met David, did you?"

With some difficulty, he pulled himself out of his chair and shuffled over to the TV. Holding onto the mantel for support, he bent to plug in the set, fumbling, his hands arthritic now too and clumsy.

Sarah waited, pushing away the instinct to reach out and help him, swallowing the sympathy she felt for his pain and discomfort. He would not have wanted her help or her sympathy, would have been insulted by the offer. "Did you meet David?" she persisted. "D'you think you ever met him? David? Your grandson?"

"I have no such grandson."

"Well, no. Not now, I suppose."

"Never had."

Ice crackled in the space between them.

"And I had no daughter."

The ice entered her lungs with her indrawn breath. Its frozen sharpness stabbed at her heart.

He switched the TV on. "Just close the door as you go."

Silence arched its back, rising menacingly. The fire spat and hissed as she stumbled out of the house.

'Miserable old sod' was what David had called him. Miserable old sod was what he was. But more than that. He was heartless, cruel. She had been wounded by his indifference, but he had turned the knife with his hatred.

Yes, she had gone against his wishes by living with Tom. But that was so long ago, too long to allow anger to fester like that, to fester into bitterness and hatred. She could smell it on her clothes, taste it in her mouth.

She could hardly stand up, her legs felt so weak, her heart racing painfully in her chest. She leant against the fence, searching in her handbag for the little pills the doctor had given her.

"Are you all right, dear? It's Sarah, isn't it? I saw you go in to your Da's. Wondered how he'd be. He's a bitter old sod, isn't he?"

Hysterical laughter rose in Sarah's throat at the concurrence of opinion. It gurgled up and broke out as a gasping sob.

"Why don't you come and sit with me for a minute or two? Get your breath back. I'll make you a wee cuppa," offered the neighbour.

"Thank you, Mrs Cleat. That's kind, but…"

"You don't look fit for going for the bus. It's a good walk to the stop and you don't look as if you could get to the end of the street."

She'd watched her come from the bus stop, then. Watched her with neighbourly curiosity, no doubt. Had been a neighbour long enough to guess the reception she'd get.

"I'll be all right."

But Mrs Cleat was already pulling her in through her gate and Sarah had no strength to resist. She let herself be guided up the path and into the house next door to her father's.

The 'cuppa' was indeed welcome and reviving and, to her credit, Mrs Cleat made no effort to elicit the reason for Sarah's visit, choosing instead to chatter on amiably about neighbours and acquaintances they held in common.

"Old Mrs Bruce passed away shortly after your Mum," she said. "And Mr Ferguson not long after that. Street's not the same any more. No spirit. Nobody looks out for nobody but theirselves now. Nobody cares. Least of all, your Da. He talks to no-one, not even the postman. Just grunts at the home help. She keeps threatening to give up on him. He's already gone through three. At least he doesn't throw out the meals any more. At first, when he got meals on wheels… It was after he'd had an operation in the hospital, he couldn't look after hisself any more, so they got him the home help and the meals on wheels. Anyway, like I say, at first, when he got them, he'd just throw them out, dishes an' all, into the garden. It was shockin'. Many's'd be glad of that food! *And* I told him so. In no uncertain terms. 'Ungrateful, Mr Thompson. That's what you are,' I said. 'Ungrateful! Many's'd be glad of that food. Good food it is. Nourishing. You should be ashamed,' I told him. 'Ashamed!' After that, the doctor came and had a word and he stopped throwin' it out."

She paused for breath, offering Sarah a slice of cake.

"No, thank you," Sarah said. "What about…"

"Polite. You were always a polite little girl. Got it from your mother no doubt. She was a lovely soul."

"Yes," Sarah smiled.

"Gentle. Had a life of it with your Da though. Can't've been easy."

"No."

"Never complained though. Never a bad word to say about him, nor about anybuddy."

"I was wondering about the garden…"

"Disgraceful the way he's let that go!"

"Well, yes."

"Used to have a lad come. Work experience or something. Don't know what happened to him. Nice lad, he was. Quiet. Never much to say for hisself, but cheery enough when you spoke. Didn't ever get over the doorstep next door," she nodded towards her neighbour with a wry expression. "Never a thank you, a cup of tea nor anything. Don't suppose the old crab uttered two words to him. No wonder the lad stopped coming. Bit more'n a year ago now, I should think. Hisself's never done anything out there since. A disgrace I call it!"

"Well," Sarah rose. "Thank you so much for the cup of tea, Mrs Cleat. It really was so kind of you. And I did need it," she added with a glum smile.

"You sure you'll be all right going for the bus now? I could always phone for a taxi."

"No, it's okay. Thank you. I'll be fine."

"Got the phone in after my Len died. The kids thought I'd better, me bein' on my own an' all."

"Yes. I'm sure they're right," Sarah agreed, offering her hand. "Well, I'll say 'Goodbye' and 'Thank you' again." She shook the older lady's hand warmly.

"Any time. Just you remember, any time. If you need to see the old devil and he upsets you again, just you pop in here. The kettle's always on." The words floated down the path behind Sarah.

As she turned to wave to her benefactor, she couldn't help but notice that her father's door lay open as she had left it. She doubted she'd venture through it again.

Chapter 19

"...and you begin to accept your defeats
with your head up and your eyes ahead
with the grace of a woman, not the grief of a child..."
1971 Veronica A. Shoffstall

The rocking of the bus unnerved her, its constant throb beating out the unkind words that had wounded her.

'I had no daughter,' he'd said. 'Had no daughter.' What did he mean, *had* no daughter? Had she *never* mattered to him? Had he *never* cared for her? Even before Tom? Why hadn't he said 'I *have* no daughter'? Placing it after she'd gone against him, leaving the security of her childhood intact. Had he really *never* loved her?

The tender memories of Sunday walks, dressed in their best, his hand holding hers as she struggled to match his stride; her first day at school, when he sat her on his knee, promising that he would deal with anyone who called her names or tried to bully her. The kinder memories were few enough. Did these moments hold no tenderness for him? Even then?

Leaning her head against the window of the bus, she let it cool her flushed face, her heart heavy with sorrow, her tears running unchecked, mirroring the rain beyond the glass.

Cruel words, such cruel words. The bus drummed their rhythm. *'I had no daughter. I had no daughter.'*

He had chosen not to be a part of her adult life. It should not have been a shock to learn she had been so little a part of his. She should not have expected him to hold to the promises of her childhood. They were no longer binding. He had not stood in her corner to defend her from taunts and bullies for a very long time; nor had he held her hand to help her over obstacles or face the bleakness of life without her husband or her son.

The landmarks of the journey through life are often buried in layers of hazy memories. But some stand out clearly, untrammelled by the distortion time can wreak. This day would surely be another of the latter. She would never forget the way he had looked at her, through her, refusing to acknowledge her; the way he'd spoken, coldly, with spiteful clarity; the words he had said, disowning her, chopping away her roots.

She had always been sure that he would forgive and forget eventually, that, if she went to him, swallowed her pride, he would accept her back, allow the bonds of kinship to tighten, drawing them together again as family. He was her father, after all. Should that count for nothing?

But he had disowned her. He had made it clear there would be no forgiveness; there were no family ties.

As she looked back, the way she had come, there were no footsteps remaining to mark her journey. It was as though he had swept them away with an angry broom, wishing no trace of them on his path.

The finality of his cruel words had cut her adrift: she had lost her moorings.

As the bus raced through the wet countryside, she felt herself tossed in a torrent of memories and emotions. They rushed over her like wild water, her head bobbing helplessly in the spume. She thought she must drown in the subtle difference between loving someone and being loved by them.

The shilling Dad gave her every Saturday, teasing her that he didn't have one, then producing it from his pocket as she turned away, disappointed, became the treasure *she* had offered *him*, her love. Though it was *he* who turned away, it was *she* who was disappointed again.

The pain on her mother's face as she walked away from them. The pleading in her eyes, *'Don't go, child! Stay with me!'* Had her mother known she would not see her again?

Other memories, coming in waves, dragging her under. Things her father had no part in, waves he could have helped her ride.

Sitting at the kitchen table night after night, waiting for Tom to stride in the door, aching for his voice, his touch

Lying awake in her bed at night, wondering if he was with someone else, whispering, touching, making love. "I loved him." She shook her head, incredulous at her own weakness, amazed at how long it took her to stop missing him, to stop turning over in bed, seeking the warmth of his body. Sometimes, held in the moment before wakefulness dragged her from the hold of dreams, she thought he was there: her hand traced the ridges of his muscled stomach, felt the soft, down of hair that grew there, the responsive tightening as he turned to her. "I loved him," she whispered.

Waking to the empty bed, her hand tracing only the wrinkles of the cold sheet. That moment, lived a hundred times, a thousand, more. The moment of realisation, another day without Tom, that clench of pain.

Sitting in their bedroom night after night, touching the things he'd touched, reading his books, breathing the air he might have breathed, her face buried in his clothes, the last jumper he had worn, caressing the softness, inhaling the smell of him, a lingering scent that faded with the passage of time, until it was more in her imagination than her nostrils.

He had had the habit of putting on a clean shirt when he came home in the evening then putting it back in the wardrobe later that night. 'Don't wash that shirt,' he'd say. 'I'll wear it tomorrow.' But he never would. He'd end up with a row of once-worn shirts in the cupboard, like half-eaten biscuits. You don't want to waste them but they're never quite as appetising as when they're fresh.

After he'd gone, she found she couldn't bear to wash them, to wash away his scent, so they sat there getting limper and less appetising until she bundled them up and pushed them into a bin-sack, wasted after all.

When she examined photographs or memories of their time together, she could not decide which were real, which illusory. When he smiled lovingly into the lens of the camera had he really been happy to be there, on holiday with them? Had they really had fun that day? Did he really touch her with tenderness as he brushed the hair from her eyes for the photograph? The kiss he'd given her, the whispered, 'Perfect again!' had it been part of some elaborate game? Had none of it been real?

The tidal wave of finding David's diary, finding he'd broken the promises she thought were hers as a right, the right of any mother; that he would **love her** for ever. That *she* would be the one to leave, the one to **die first.**

The difference **between** loving and being loved.

She had no point of **reference,** no signpost. Memorial stones upturned, tossed about **as in a** tsunami.

If she wasn't to go **mad,** she needed something to clutch on to, a hope, a future, but, in order to go forward, she needed to know where she was.

The physical signs outside the window told her that summer was well advanced though it rained today. Once more the leaves would blaze in autumn glory; once more they would wither and die. Winter would follow autumn as surely as autumn prepared to end the summer. Hope would be born each spring, despair cling to each dark winter. Season after season, year upon year, whether she marked them or not.

Sarah took a deep breath, letting it out in a long sigh, fighting to rise above the waves of emotion that threatened to engulf her.

So, what next? How to go forward? Tom?

What did she know about Tom?

Only what he chose to tell her... and how reliable was that? Did she believe him? Could she trust him? She doubted it.

Chapter 20

David had described it as a tomb, but it wasn't like that at all. It was light and bright, much airier than she expected, with no particularly musty smell, no shadowy corners. Perhaps it was his mood reflected in the description. True, it was dome-shaped, filled with circle inside circle of filing cabinets like rows of mini mortuary drawers, but the dome was windowed and there was noise and activity under its umbrella, not the hushed silence of the grave.

Sarah paid for her search pass into the public rooms of New Register House, the General Register Office for Scotland, a part-day pass, because it was afternoon by the time she made her way there. Ten pounds, just as David said, a lot of money for her too, but a fortune for him with the little he earned and the load of demands upon it.

She walked along the corridor as instructed, wondering if he had felt as intimidated by his surroundings, knowing that he had never liked officialdom either, its impersonal efficiency, its uncaring formality. They were both 'people' people, not 'paper' people.

The lady at the reception desk had asked, "Are you a first time user?" took her money and issued the pass. She had to take a numbered ticket and "proceed to the waiting room until your number comes up on the screen there." She didn't have long to wait, hers being the next number displayed, and she was led further along the same narrow, carpeted corridor to one of the West Search Rooms, to seat no.25, at the end of a short row of desks.

She was beside a tall sash window, looking out to a narrow fenced area of grass and trees. The grass was well cared for and the trees were tall and well shaped. There were a few birds hopping and flitting about and she was sure she caught sight of a grey squirrel as it scampered into the branches of one of the trees. Taking a deep, steadying breath, she wondered how many others had gazed from that window, glad to see life out there, afraid to find death in here.

She was terribly conscious that, among the multitude of records held in this building, would be a slip of paper recording the death of her son, her David. And he had been here, before that slip of paper was written.

There was the muffled sound of traffic beyond the glass. People walked past the low iron railings that bordered the garden, unaware of, or unheeding the importance of, the lives forever recorded in the archives of this imposing building. She herself had walked by in the past, not thinking to enter, not curious then to delve into its stores.

But now she followed her son.

She looked around, wondering where he might have sat. He would have liked to be by the window, to see the life outside. But, perhaps he'd been too intent on his task to care where he sat, to notice much of his surroundings. Being more familiar with modern technology, he would not have been intimidated by the prospect before him, would not have procrastinated, as she did, examining views, studying the passing scene.

She pulled her attention back to the room.

There were other rows of desks, possibly a dozen at most, and on each one there was a computer and another screen, which she learned was a microfiche viewer. She had been handed a pack containing basic instructions and left to it.

The room wasn't very busy today and she was thankful there was no-one at the desk beside her to witness her lack of computer skills. With a deep breath, Sarah studied the instructions.

What did she hope to find here, among all these public records? And David, what had he hoped to find? Had he, like her, stared at the screen in front of him, hoping for inspiration, that flash of intuition that would lead him to the information he craved?

In the first instance, he had known that he wanted to see the registration of his birth, so probably that would have been where he started. She decided to do the same.

The screen displayed a list, inviting her to type in the relevant details on each line.

1.   Event type, she entered 'B' for birth.
2.   Sex, 'M'
3.   Year, 1983
4.   Surname, Reed.
5.   Forename, David.

Then she pressed 'enter' as instructed.

Immediately, an index appeared and there was his name. Her throat constricted painfully. It was only his name. But it was recorded here, stating that he had been born, he had lived.

Had she wanted, she could have then noted the Registration District and Number on the Orange Form provided and taken it to the archives, to the appropriate drawer to find a microfiche with a copy of his birth certificate on it. She chose not to, knowing already what it recorded, the information he had found, that *he* had been given his father's surname, but his mother had not.

She closed her eyes, imagining his puzzlement. In this more modern age, did it mean less to him than it still did to her? Perhaps many of his friends had 'partners' already. Perhaps it would not have shocked him, only surprised him. If he realised the significance of what he'd stumbled on, since what he really wanted to find was information about Tom, not her.

Did he then go on to search for a marriage certificate that did not exist?

She was engrossed now, needing to follow the steps he would have taken, craving the mechanical orderliness of the routine.

She typed again, this time entering the details of her parents' marriage, there being no point in trying to find what wasn't there, as David would have.

1.   'M', Marriage.
2.   'M', her father.
3.   1952, the year before Robert's birth.
4.   Thompson
5.   Gordon

And, once again, pressed 'enter'.

Once again, an index appeared, but this time, the information she sought was not there. She reread the entries. There was an entry for a Gordon Thompson, but it was not her father. This Gordon was married in Dumfries to someone called Elizabeth Murdoch, not her mother.

She studied the screen. There was an instruction at the bottom, inviting her to press the <F5> key if the entry she sought had not been found. She did this and was then invited to choose other search options. She pressed the no '3' key to search the entries for the year before. No, not there. The year before that? No.

Sarah sat back in the neat little typist's chair, regrouping her thoughts. Was this how David had felt. Bewildered. Unsure how to proceed. She had been certain her parents had married in 1952, yet there seemed to be no appropriate entry then. Perhaps she'd made a mistake somewhere in filling in the relevant information. She pressed <F5> and started again, typing even more slowly and carefully, then pressed 'enter' again. The same list appeared on the screen. If she hadn't made a typing mistake, then it must be an error of memory. She pressed <F5>, then '4', to search the year *following* the one already searched; nothing. The next year... and the next. Nothing. She didn't know what else to do but continue the exercise. <F5>, '4' for 1955... and there it was:

23rd October 1955.

1955. But she was born in December 1955, only two months later.

She cleared the screen. Yet again, she typed in details. This time those she was certain were on her own birth certificate.

Yes, there it was. 21st December 1955. Funny, seeing her own birth registered here among so many, making her feel important, worth taking note of, worth registering. Definitely 1955.

She went through the process that brought her parents' details up on the screen again. This time she did fill in an Orange Form:

Event; Marriage

Year; 1955

Registration District; 738

Entry No. 862

She completed the form with the details of her name, the date and her seat number in the West Search Room, knowing she was now supposed to find the relevant microfiche and pop the orange form in its place bringing the microfiche back to her desk to examine on the other screen beside the computer. That was the theory. She had no idea how to accomplish the task.

The lady who had shown her to her seat had said she'd be next door, if she needed help, but when Sarah wandered hesitantly into the next room, there was no sign of her. Only more rows of desks, with more computer screens and microfiche viewers, more searchers, each busy with their own searches. She looked around for some clue as to the next step.

"You look a bit lost. Can I help you?" someone asked from behind her.

"Oh, yes, thank you."

"First time here?" the man asked.

Sarah nodded. "You guessed it. I haven't a clue where to find the microfiche files."

The stranger patiently guided her across the corridor to an archway into the central area, the domed area surrounded by its circular corridors of miniature filing cabinets.

"What section d'you need? Births, deaths…?"

"Marriages," she supplied.

"Then it's through the central area, in the second corridor. Depending on which year you need, you go to your right or left. The years are marked on each drawer."

"Thank you. That's kind of you." But he had disappeared, intent on his own search, impatient now to home in on his own microfiche data.

She gazed around the round central area, filled with even more computers and screens, but this time there were also screens to view rolls of microfiche rather than the rectangles of film she was to find in the drawers.

People bustled about their business or sat at the desks studying the films, noting down the information they contained. There was very little chatter, only an occasional shared comment or two, not in whispers, but 'sotto voce' nonetheless.

She found what she needed in the '1955' drawer and took it back to her seat, slotted it into the viewer and searched for the relevant entry among the rows of copied certificates enlarged on the screen, pleased with her dexterity at the task.

There were a few things that surprised her.

The first thing she noticed was her father's date of birth. He was older than she'd realised. As a family they had never bothered with such 'vanity' as birthdays, by his decree, so she had assumed he would only be a few years older than her mother. He was, in fact, fifteen years older. He must now be eighty-two... and beginning to look it, she realised.

His status was recorded as 'widowed'.

He had been married before. There had never been a hint, never the faintest hint.

She checked the entry again:

checked the names... Mr Gordon Thompson, widower. Miss Martha Kelly; spinster.

checked the address... the home they lived in all their married life. Given as *his* address before the marriage. *His* house then, not *theirs*. The same home he had made for his first wife?

checked the date... 23rd October 1955. Definitely 1955. Could that be '52? No quite clearly a five... 1955... two months before her own birth date, 21st December 1955.

She closed her eyes, squeezed them shut with her fingers, tried to conjure up a picture, the picture of one anniversary they had held, their 14th. She had baked them a cake for a surprise, iced it with gaudy, pink icing, written 'Happy 14th Anniversary' on a piece of paper and stuck it on while the icing was still soft. Her mother had cried and hugged her. Robert had cried out too because she had punched his arm when he tried to scoop a finger-full of icing from round the side. Her father had asked where she'd got the money to buy 'such frippery'. It was the last time she'd tried to instigate a celebration in their puritanical household.

But how old had she been? Ten, nearly eleven. Definitely ten, but only two months off eleven. She was in Mrs MacPhail's class, Primary 7, one of the younger ones in the class, but nearly eleven, definitely Primary 7. She remembered, she had been to Helen's

153

house, saw the cake she'd made for her parents' anniversary, copied the idea. Helen was her pal in Primary 7, when she was ten, nearly eleven, and Robert was thirteen.

They had never made much of the date, she had had to prise it out of her mother, determined to do as her schoolfriend, to be 'normal', to do something special for her Mum. It had been a great success in Helen's family.

So, had they cheated? Told her it was their fourteenth anniversary when it was only their eleventh? Or had she just assumed it?

That was the only time there had been any attempt to mark the occasion and it had fallen very flat. She had supposed, as she grew older, that it had been because of her father's 'Wee-Free' Kirk upbringing, though he never went to church that she could remember. He had always been puritanical, pharisaical even, whiter than white, ever ready to cast the first stone.

But he wasn't without sin after all. They had *had* to get married. Mum was pregnant. For the second time. Well, well! They must have 'lived in sin' for years. More than two years. Perhaps until his first wife died?

She leant back in the chair, letting her breath out with a hiss of incredulity.

Forty-seven years! They had kept their secret well. But at what cost? She shook her head, remembering the pain on her mother's face, the sympathy registered there when he had dismissed the cake as 'frippery', choosing not even to acknowledge the sentiment that prompted its concoction, forestalling the intended congratulations. Her mother had smiled in understanding of her disappointment, had touched her cheek with tender longing.

Robert had demolished two huge slices of it after tea and stoutly declared the cake 'fandabbydozy', drawing a severe look from his father. She and her mother demurely ate one slice each before she rose from the table and ceremoniously scraped the rest into the bucket, ignoring mother's indrawn breath and father's 'tut' at the waste. She found it hard to forgive her father's lack of sensitivity and the incident still counted against him.

But she refused to drink from his bitter cup. She would let it go, taste the nectar of forgiveness again, as she did so often when these memories returned, acid in her mouth. She would not be like him. She would not spit all sweetness out of her life.

Had he no taste for happiness? What could make a man like that?

Had he felt trapped into marrying? Resented it, perhaps? Is that what he held over her mother? Blamed Martha for what surely takes two?

But who was she to stand in judgement? There was no marriage certificate here for her. She too had tried to keep her secret, hide her shame from her children.

Shame... Was it shame that had bowed her mother? Cowed her? Certainly she lived in a less forgiving era. When she fell pregnant, there was no sympathy, no help for an unmarried mother. She belonged to an Irish-Catholic family, living in Glasgow. She would have been cast out, spat upon for her sin, even then, in 1953, when Robert was born. There would have been little charity in the community she was brought up in, not for such as she. It was no like-minded boy of Irish descent she had fooled around with. No good, Catholic man she was 'shacked up with'. No, shame of shame, it was a married man, a 'proddie', the son of a crofter from the Western Isles, stronghold of the Scottish 'Wee-Free' Kirk. And he hadn't the decency to marry her till she bore him a second child.

Had her father earned that unconditional loyalty and gratitude because he didn't desert her, but accepted responsibility, married a 'foreign' woman, a 'papist', albeit belatedly and, no doubt, as much against the wishes of his own kin as hers? Is that what she owed him? The hold he had over her?

They had only each other. Their families both turned their backs on them. Sarah had always assumed that was because of religious bigotry, had deplored it since she had been old enough to understand it, but perhaps shame and perceived dishonour had had their parts to play too.

What bitter fare her father had supped in his upbringing. Her mother too, but she had swallowed it without digesting it. Sadness was her aftertaste, bitterness his craving.

Yet again, she studied the entry. 23rd October 1955. Well, well, well! Now there's a 'turn-up for the books', as her mother would have said.

Reluctantly, she removed the microfiche from the viewer, afraid that the facts would change again if she were to reinsert it, and again, and again, each time she looked. Her world had become shaky, the parameters hazy.

Such a tiny piece of film to contain so much. She slipped it into its envelope and carried it to the filing tray for return to its proper place, a task not entrusted to the public, understandably, if others felt as confused and incompetent as she did after perusing its disclosures.

And she had only been practicing! Locating her parents' marriage certificate to practice the routine, to follow the procedure David would have followed, to familiarise herself with computer usage. She hadn't begun the real work she had come to do: to 'investigate' Tom, to trawl for information as David had, seeking a starting point, unsure of how to go about 'investigation', not knowing what to look for or where to look.

She shuddered. What more was there to find in these archives?

There was no marriage certificate here for her, but there should be for Tom. Even before she did the search, she wondered what she'd find.

1.   'M'

2.   'M'

3.   1965. Tom said he'd been young when he'd married Mary. In 1965 he would have been eighteen. She'd start there. Or was it possible he could have married even younger? She doubted it, but decided to change the year to 1963, when he'd have been sixteen, old enough to marry in Scotland without parental consent. She'd work forward from there.

4.   Surname, Reed

5.   Forename, Thomas.

She pressed 'enter' and was not really surprised the search failed to bring up the entry she sought. She went through the process she'd learned, pressing <F5> then '4' again and again to search the succeeding years. There was no relevant entry, no record of a marriage between Tom Reed and Mary Somebody. She carefully studied each year's index as it came up on the screen, checking each Tom Reed that appeared, but they were all too young, too old, with middle names that weren't his or had married elsewhere in the country. Tom had told her he'd married in Paisley, where Mary lived, but, like everything else about his 'marriage', she knew now that that was a lie, a fiction. It was all fiction. A story he'd concocted to supply a reason not to have to marry her: to evade commitment. The liar! The pig!

Tears threatened her. Fatigue enveloped her.

So many lies. She was wearied by so many lies.

She searched for his birth certificate. More lies.

There was no record of one 'Thomas Reed' being born in Edinburgh, as he'd claimed, or anywhere else in Scotland, on the date he'd celebrated his birthday, or any date within ten years of it.

According to the computer, Tom Reed didn't exist.

She was exhausted. The search had taken a long time and a lot of energy. And it was fruitless: just more lies, more fiction.

The happy years, before he'd gone, floated out the window on a cloud of distrust. It had all been a sham, a charade. Some sinister game he'd been playing. She no longer trusted the memory of happiness.

Her whole life seemed to count for nothing. The record of her birth was here, but the only thing she felt sure of was that she'd been born. Living seems to have been some crazy dream. Nothing stood up to investigation. Nothing had been as she'd lived it. From that day, 21st December 1955, she had lived in the middle of a web of secrets and lies. Nothing had been real. It had all fallen apart in this room.

She closed her eyes, concentrating on the nearby tapping of computer keys, the rustling of papers, distant conversations, footsteps in the corridor, anything to drown out the crying in her head.

So many feelings crowded in upon her. Anger, humiliation, hurt. She felt betrayed, wounded, cheated. She was bereft.

She had no idea where else to look for information. Tom said he used an assumed name, but Tom Reed was not his real one either. She had no way of knowing under what name he'd been registered, in order to check further for a marriage certificate. But she doubted she'd find one under any name. He had lied, that's all there was to it. She had trusted him, committed her reputation and her heart to him and he had lied. He had let her down. He had never intended to be honourable.

What's in a name? 'A rose by any other name, would it smell so sweet?' Hadn't she read that somewhere? Well, Tom was no rose and he didn't come out of this exercise smelling sweet, no matter what his name.

And what of their children? They had been given their father's name, yet it was a fiction. Where did that leave them? Where were their roots? David had written that he might come back some time to trace his family tree. How would he have felt to find there was no such tree in the garden?

Someone was ringing a bell, one of those old-fashioned hand bells, like the old brass one they used to ring in primary school. Home-time, the dim memory of a notice informing the public that a bell would be rung fifteen minutes before closing time, then again ten minutes later. Time to tidy your desk, gather your things and head for home. She responded automatically, the habit ingrained many years ago. But there would be no comforting chat with Mum in the kitchen when she got home, to talk over the disappointments of the day, to share the humiliation and the pain. Mum was part of the pain.

It was a shattering blow to realise that so much had been withheld from her. Yet she had no right to the knowledge. That they had had an affair, had chosen to live together before marriage, was not really her business and she certainly had no freedom of speech to complain. But her father had held himself beyond reproach, the epitome of all that was 'proper'. Her mother had done nothing to correct the misrepresentation. She had allowed him to swagger in his self-righteous overcoat, to bully and threaten those who dared to sully the family reputation. It might have been easier to endure if they'd known how insecurely his coat was fastened.

They were locking up now, patiently waiting to see her off the premises. The second bell had long-since tolled, but she had been lost in the proverbial cupboard getting acquainted with the skeletons, and had heard it only dimly, its significance dulled by the heavy cupboard door she was locked behind.

She walked by the attendant as though in a dream, aware that he wished her 'goodnight', but unable to respond, not knowing how to empower her speech.

It was only four-thirty, still light, still busy outside, as she walked slowly from the building, and wandered the streets of Edinburgh, benumbed by her findings and, like David before her, seemingly unaware of their full significance.

Chapter 21

"Mum! Where on earth have you been? We've been worried sick!" Katie was waiting at the door. She'd been watching from the window and ran to open the door before Sarah had time to put her key in the lock.

"What? Have you dear? Oh, I'm sorry."

"Sorry? You walk in here at half-past eleven at night, without a word about where you were going, having been out all day."

"Is it?"

"Is it what, Mother?"

"Half-past eleven?" Sarah looked at her watch. "I had no idea."

"Where have you been?"

"Oh, just out and about, you know." She took off her coat.

"No, I don't know! And that's the problem." Katie took the coat and hung it on a peg in the hall. "I got home at six, expecting you to have the tea ready and not only…"

"Oh, dear! Sorry. Was it my day for tea? I forgot. Did you manage?"

"Of course I managed! That's not the point."

"Good. Sorry about that," Sarah said as she walked through to the living room. "I'll do tomorrow. Oh. Hi, Mike. You still here?" She smiled as she walked over to give him a peck on the cheek.

In return, he held her close for a moment before letting her go.

"You are a dear," she whispered softly to him.

Kate followed her into the room and flung herself into a chair. "Mum! You're infuriating! I don't care a toss about the tea! I was worried."

"Oh, you didn't have to be worried, dear. I was all right."

"I can see you're all right… now! But I didn't know *that* at six o'clock or seven o'clock… or eight, nine, ten o'clock!"

Sarah rubbed her hands together. "Mmm. Anyone else ready for a cuppa?" she asked as she sat down with a weary sigh, letting the cat jump onto her lap.

"I'll put the kettle on," Mike smiled.

"Thanks, love."

"Mum! We've been really worried."

Sarah stretched and rubbed the back of her neck, kneading the muscles gently, in an effort to release the weary tension that had built up during the day. "Yes, dear, so you said."

"So? Where have you been?"

"Well, it's a long story." She bent to cuddle the cat.

Kate sat back and waited.

"And I don't know if I'm up to it tonight," Sarah yawned.

"Mum!"

Sarah reached across and patted her daughter's knee. "I'm sorry, love. Really, I am," she sighed. "But I just had some things to do today."

"Till half-past eleven?"

"Then I had some thinking to do, so I went for a walk."

"Till half-past eleven?"

"Oh, don't keep on, dear. I'm not a child. I'm allowed to stay out late."

"But we didn't know where you were. You're *never* out in the evenings."

"True. Not like you, Mrs Tibbs," Sarah said to the cat as it purred on her lap.

"Anything could have happened!"

Sarah raised an eyebrow.

"Well, it could have. You could have been in an accident, taken ill somewhere, been mugged... anything!"

Sarah held her hands up. "Fair comment!"

"I wasn't sure at what point we should start the round of phone calls, you know, police, hospitals... "

"Oh, don't be silly, dear. This is getting *really* wearisome," Sarah sighed.

"Besides, now that I look at you, I'm not so sure you *are* all right. You look terrible!"

"Thank you, dear."

"Well, you do. Your clothes look as though you slept in them."

"I got caught in the rain earlier."

"And you're terribly pale."

"I'm just tired. Like you say, I'm not used to being out late. Or out much at all, in fact."

"Exactly! And that's why we were so worried!"

"Oh, please don't start that again." Sarah put her hand up, shaking her head wearily. "I've got a splitting headache and I'm very tired." She gently pushed the cat from her lap.

"Tea's up," Mike announced as he came through from the kitchen with the tray. "Your Mum's home now, Kate, obviously safe and sound." He gave her a 'loaded' look. "Give her a break, eh? Time to let the subject drop, I think."

"Thanks, love." Sarah smiled her gratitude both for the reprieve and the welcome cup of tea. "We'll have a chat tomorrow, maybe," she said to Kate as she made for the door.

Kate folded her arms and turned away with obvious frustration.

Sarah ruffled her hair as she passed. "Sorry, pet. Didn't mean to worry you."

Kate caught her hand and kissed it.

"And I didn't mean to nag. Just, I was so…"

"Worried. I know," Sarah shrugged. "I really am sorry."

"What have you done to your hand?" Kate asked, looking more closely at the hand she was holding.

Sarah pulled it away. "Oh, nothing. I grazed it against a wall or something."

Kate frowned at her. "It looks sore, more than just a wee graze." She got up and stood in front of Sarah, putting her hands on her shoulders, peering more closely into her face. "Are you sure you're all right, Mum?"

"Of course I'm all right!" she assured her, turning away to lift her cup of tea from the tray. "I'm just tired, and I've got a bit of a head."

"And that's all?"

"And that's all," Sarah said emphatically, sipping from her cup. "Mmm, lovely! Thanks Mike," she winked at him, receiving a warm smile in reply. "Now, I think I'll take this up with me and let you two say 'goodnight'. It's getting late, you know, and Mike should be getting on home. Don't forget, you've both got work in the morning!"

* * *

Sarah closed the door of her own little sitting room and leant against it, shaking, relief at being home and safe washing over her. It had taken a huge effort to keep her voice steady, her nerves controlled in front of Kate and Mike but now that she was here, closeted in her own wee room, the effort was too much. She crumpled against the door, her tea slopping over her clothes. She could feel her self-control ebb away, the strangled sobs fighting their way to expression.

With another gigantic effort, the last one needed, she hoped, she stopped her slide down the door, pushed herself from its support and staggered to the sofa, putting what was left of her cup of tea on the table beside her. Drawing her aching legs up to lie along its length, she curled into the cushioned comfort of the sofa and tried to still the trembling of her limbs, the fluttering of her heart.

It had been as she walked along Princes Street in a daze that she had seen him. She had still been sifting through the information she'd gleaned in the Registrar's, seeking to make sense of it, striving to come to terms with it, her mind on matters of the past, her heart aching with recent enlightenment.

He was standing at the corner of Princes Street and Hanover, leaning against the wall, holding out a copy of 'The Big Issue', the rest of his bundle lying at his feet.

Alan Hoddle, drug addict and spectre of her dreams. How often she had imagined herself following him, questioning him. 'Who is your supplier?' 'Did you know my son?' 'Did you show him where to get drugs?' 'Are you the one I can hate, the one I can blame?'

Rationally, she knew the odds were against him knowing David, having anything to do with him or his habit, but irrationally, he had become the focus of her feverish desperation to find someone to blame, someone to punish. He was the only link she had to the twilight side of addiction. Mike, Joan, Gary... all the others she met at Omega House, were seeking the daylight. Alan dwelt in darkness.

Looking around, she saw that, if she sat in the pizza place across the street, if she secured a window seat, she could watch him, unobserved. See who he talked to. If anyone gave him anything other than the price of the magazine. When he moved off, in which direction he went...

Mike had warned her against showing too much interest in the man. He'd called him dangerous, but she felt no danger. If she kept her distance, stayed out of sight.

The pizza she ordered tasted of nothing: she ate little of it, picking at it from time to time, making it last, accepting a second cup of coffee, and a third. She paid her bill before she had finished, returned to her seat, toyed with the cold coffee, the congealed pizza.

It was after six o'clock before he moved. He had hardly sold any copies from his bundle, no-one had spent more than a moment in his company, no-one had given anything into his hand other than the coins he dropped casually into his pocket. Her eyes stung from their unblinking vigil, her body ached with tension.

As he moved off, so she sprang into action, and was out of the shop too fast. He was crossing the street, coming up, past the doorway she lingered in, her face turned at the last moment to study the colourful menu posted in the window beside her, her breath held painfully against the instinct to cry out.

He walked past, his steps unhurried, his head down, shoulders hunched. She slid into step behind him, feigning a casual saunter, her head up, watchful, looking around as though the street were new to her.

When he turned the corner, so did she. When he crossed the road, she did too.

He stopped at a bus stop. She froze. What should she do? Could she boldly walk up to the stop too? Stand beside him? Wait for the bus? What if he recognised her? What if he spoke?

She hesitated, stepping backwards into the shadow of the building society entrance. Several others joined the queue before the bus came and she was able to sidle on behind him, unnoticed, at the last moment.

He went upstairs: she was about to follow, hesitated, torn between the fear of recognition and the need of close observation. What if he met someone on the bus? If she stayed downstairs she might miss the all-important moment, the secret hand-over of some little package, the exchange of money for goods other than 'The Big Issue'. But, if she followed him upstairs, he might see her, recognise her, sense she was following him. She didn't dare to climb the stairs: would have to take the risk of missing the moment. She sat facing them, watchful for his descent, waiting for the moment of disembarkation.

Not knowing her destination, and not hearing his mumbled exchange with the driver, she had no idea what fare to request, had paid as much as she thought likely and prayed that it would fit her journey. Now she sat trembling. What exactly was she doing? What did she hope to gain? And at what cost? This was all so crazy.

Surely everyone could see her agitation? Yet no-one paid her any heed. Couldn't they see the sweat that ran from her hairline, down the side of her face, the bridge of her nose, from her upper lip? She was so cold: cold with fear, chilled despite the warmth of the evening and the crowded bus.

The bus swung round corners and lurched across junctions, chugging up hills and coasting along straight roads. Minutes felt like hours and Sarah felt the numbing of time standing still. Every time the bus approached a stop, she readied herself for the sudden leap she must make if he disembarked here. Every time it started onwards again she sat back thankfully, glad of the procrastination, afraid of the daring of her impulsive plan.

Eventually, there he was, coming down the stairs. She recognised his boots, 'Doc Martins', old and scuffed, as dirty and neglected as the rest of his apparel, his old jeans and army-surplus coat, his unkempt, shoulder-length hair. He stood, leaning against the handrail, staring at nothing in particular. Casually, he mumbled something to the driver who grumbled his reply, bringing the bus to a halt without looking at the man who addressed him.

Sarah stood to follow him, then realised with horror that this wasn't a bus stop. The driver had stopped opposite a junction to oblige his regular passenger. If she also got off here, it would be obvious she was following him: he couldn't help but notice her. If she stayed on, she might miss where he went. Sickened, she hesitated too long to make the choice. It was made for her when the bus lurched forward again and travelled a further hundred yards or so down the road before stopping again at the request of an older lady, carrying two heavy bags of shopping.

"Thanks Erchie. Greta all right?"

"Aye, hen. Tam?"

"Aye."

"See ye then."

"Aye."

Come on, come on! Get off the bus. Get out of the way. I need to see where he's headed.

Knowing she should be offering to help, rather than desiring to harass, Sarah tried to contain her impatience as the woman grunted and groaned her way off the platform of the bus. At last, Sarah was able to get around her and run back towards the junction across the road.

She saw him immediately. He had had to wait for a gap in the traffic before he could safely cross and he was only just reaching the junction now. If she could get across herself, she could catch up, keeping a little distance between them.

"Terrible place this tae cross." The woman had hobbled her way to the same point before there was another opportunity to cross the road. "Should be a pelican here," she puffed, breathless from the exertion of hauling her burden this far. "Ye cin wait lang enough tae get over, ken. Mind, it gies me a wee breather," she coughed, putting her bags down at her feet while she caught her breath.

All of Sarah's instincts cried out for her to offer to carry the woman's bags. But she couldn't. If she took the time to help her, she would miss him. He was already turning the corner ahead. She mustn't lose him. She just mustn't!

Rudely, she ignored the woman's panting comments. If she stopped to answer them, she knew she would feel obliged to offer the assistance so obviously needed. Heedless of the oncoming traffic, she headed across the road.

"Watch yersel', hen!" the woman cried after her.

"Beeeeeep!" a car horn sounded.

But she was safely across, hurrying towards the corner, praying that the commotion would not cause him to turn round.

This part of Edinburgh was new territory for Sarah. The bus displayed a sign for Wester Hailles, but the bus had not reached its terminus. The streets here were all named things like Ladyburn Road, Ladyburn Gardens or Park or Grove, so she supposed the area was called Ladyburn, but she had never been here before, not having any need to come, not having any friend or acquaintance living here.

Her first impression was borne in upon her without conscious thought. Grey, concrete buildings, littered stairwells in shadowy tall blocks of flats, some highrise, some three or four storey. Blank windows watched her as she stole along, close to the walls, keeping as many paces behind him as she dared.

When he turned a corner, so did she. When he crossed the road, she did too.

Intent on following him, on keeping out of his sight should he turn round, she kept a wary eye for nearby shelter, paying scant attention to the path they took, forgetting that she would need to be able to find her way home at the end of this exercise. Her mind had not foreseen an end to the exercise.

A bicycle whizzed past close to her, startling her, so that she jumped against the wall grazing her hand. Another bike followed, missing her only because she hadn't moved. Neither rider so much as looked back to note her safety.

Shaken, she took a long breath, her eyes scanning the road ahead frantically.

He was still up ahead, exchanging curses with the uncaring cyclists, though he had fared better than she. He walked on, shouting after them, shaking his fist.

She put the side of her hand to her mouth to soothe it, staying where she was until she felt sure he would not look behind him: until it seemed safe to recommence the stalking of her prey.

He led her deeper into the scheme, the flats becoming shabbier and darker, with less signs of life. Windows boarded up, doors barricaded and padlocked, graffiti decorating them. Here and there limp curtains dressed the windows that had not been boarded: sometimes only one or two in a property. Surely a frightening place to live.

Some children ran, screaming across her path. Instinctively, she checked her watch. After seven o'clock, nearer half past. Surely time children so young were being called to bed?

They doubled back, their language that of the shipyard rather than the nursery playground, their manners non-existent as they jostled past her on the pavement. She shook her head in sadness, watching them as they scrabbled on the ground, fighting out some junior gang-land battle.

He was gone!

Her attention was diverted for a moment and he was gone!

Furious with herself for permitting the distraction, she rushed forward to where she remembered seeing him last.

But which way now?

She could go forward, round the next corner, across the next street... but he might not have.

He could have entered any one of the gaping entrances around her. She stood at a cul-de-sac, a sort of dilapidated play area surrounded by flats, each one the same as the next, each one the possible lair of her fox.

Suddenly, she felt very vulnerable. She was in *his* territory. Without realising it, she could become the hunted instead of the hunter.

She cowered in by the wall, her heart hammering, blood pounding in her head, not sure whether to seek him further or cut her losses. Still feeling exposed, she crept furtively along the wall and dodged into the first entrance to give herself cover, time to regroup, time to think.

"Aagh!" A scream was strangled in her throat.

The first she realised that he was there was when he grabbed her and pulled her into the darker recesses of the close, his voice hissing in her ears, his words fierce and dirty.

He demanded to know who she was and why she was following him, but there were so many expletives that she could barely understand his questions. He was holding her so tightly she couldn't get breath to answer him anyway.

Then he recognised her. "You're from Omega House," was the gist of it. "Mike's bird, or at least her mother. Ah ken you." His grip slackened a little. "So what d'ye want? Why're you followin' me?" he asked again, no more politely, with no fewer expletives.

She was still unable to speak. Her throat was constricted partly from the pressure exerted by his arm about her neck, partly by the fear that disabled her.

"Ach, yer as bad as yer wimp o' a son," he said, releasing her with a push that sent her reeling into the wall, a pipe burying itself cruelly in her shoulder. Before she could catch her breath, he was upon her. "*** fool. Should've kept his nose out o' where it didnae belang. Got nae mair'n he deserved." He spat on the ground at her feet. "An', here's your warnin' tae dae the same!"

He punched her hard in the stomach, then knocked her sideways with the vicious application of his knee to her side. She fell, wracked with pain and losing consciousness from the blow he administered to the back of her head. The last she remembered was him spitting again, but not at her feet.

* * *

She sat in her own little sitting room, sipping her tea, exhausted from the long day. Waiting…

When she heard Katie close her bedroom door, having completed her bed-time-bathroom routine, she waited another half an hour, then she quietly opened a drawer and took out David's diary.

It had been quite a while since she had dived into this pool of troubled waters and she wasn't certain she had learned to swim sufficiently to cope with its treacherous currents, but it seemed the time to try.

Alan Hoddle seemed to know who she was, who David was, and why and how he died. There must be a mention of A.H., or H.A. in the diary. David must have had dealings with the man. He would have recorded them.

The day had been filled with trauma for her, what difference could a little more make? A day that started with the mental brutality of her father and ended with the physical beating she took for her son.

She hadn't known how long she lay in that stinking, dark close. She became aware of the sound of rain, the feel of cool, dark air around her. How many people might have stepped over her, she could only guess, but it was when someone kicked her roughly and told her to get her carcass out of the way, that she came fully to consciousness.

Everything hurt. She had ended up curled in a foetal position, her handbag buried somewhere beneath her body, probably the only reason she still possessed it. Scrabbling to sit up, she felt inside it for the precious foil strip. Her heart felt weak and the tight band of pain around her chest must surely crush her, if the gripping pain in her stomach didn't get her first.

She turned to the side and vomited without care or caution, fortunately missing her clothes but not her own hand. Again, she scrabbled in her bag, this time, a one-handed search for tissues with which to clean herself up as best she could.

Having placed the blessed tablet under her tongue, she cautiously gathered her forces.

Testing her legs and her general balance gingerly, she got to her feet with the aid of the wall and the downpipe that had assaulted her shoulder earlier. Much earlier.

When she was able to focus on her watch face, by the light of the street lamp outside, when she dragged herself into its dim circle of light, she saw that it was nearly half-past ten.

She must have lain there for the best part of two hours, more, closer to three. And lain where? Where was she? What kind of place was it possible to lie unconscious and unaided for three hours? Were they so accustomed to drunks and drug users passing out on their doorsteps that another one could go unnoticed and uncared for so long? True, she saw as she limped away, many of the windows were boarded up, presumably defending empty houses from intruders: a weak defence for human charity, she felt.

Dusting down her trousers and straightening her jacket she moved away from the close entrance, glad to feel the light rain on her skin, eager for its kiss on her lips.

After getting on the move again, her next priority was to get herself to some kind of main road to find a phone-box or a bus stop, some link with the civilised world, some way of getting home. As long as she kept moving, surely this nightmare must eventually end.

Nothing was familiar. No landmark. no one street recognisable from another. Maybe this corner? Or that? It seemed inconsequential which way she went, just so long as she kept moving.

She was hobbling along, in considerable pain, not knowing whether she was heading in the right direction to get out of the scheme, when she saw a taxi draw up ahead of her. As it disgorged its passengers, she made a valiant effort to straighten up and catch the attention of the driver before he drove off again. Fortunately, just as she thought she'd failed and he had started to move away, he saw her and swung round to stop beside her.

With a silent, thankful prayer, she tumbled into the warm interior and gave him her address.

She used the time of the journey to do the best clean-up job she could manage with the limited resources of tissues, hairbrush and lip balm, all she had in her bag. Then, leaning back to rest, she worked out what, if anything, she should and could do about the assault she had suffered.

It would be difficult to prove the identity of her attacker without a witness and she was certain he would have an alibi lined up by now, so there seemed little point in reporting the assault to the police.

She tested her ribs and the back of her head gingerly. They were sore, probably badly bruised and certainly swollen, her shoulder too, but, as far as she could discern, nothing broken. Her stomach was very painful, but she wasn't bringing up blood or anything, so she had probably sustained yet another nasty bruise, but she would live, she decided, so didn't need urgent medical attention. If things got worse after a hot bath and a good night's sleep, then she'd go to Doctor Mitchell.

Getting past Kate without explanation of her dishevelled condition would be difficult, but she decided against recounting her adventures at this stage. Kate would only worry and become over protective, putting any further 'adventures' out of reach. not that Sarah sought any more of the nature she'd endured tonight!

Sitting in her room now, she was amazed she managed to pull it off, getting past Kate, getting up to her sanctuary without too much fuss. Tomorrow would be soon enough for explanations, if they could not be avoided. Tonight, she wanted some for herself.

In order to sort out a future, she was going to have to know what had been in the past. She had a need to see with clarity: a need to see through the murky waters, find what was important and decide how to act upon it. If she was going to drown, then she wanted it to be in clear water.

So, with better understanding of some of the feelings David may have had, she returned to reading his diary, confident that she would get better too at cracking his codes. The pieces of the jigsaw were already fitting together; like looking into a pool. Although the ripples of today had distorted the image, she was beginning to get the picture.

Chapter 22

When the phone rang the next morning, Sarah was still sleeping, having sat up very late, well into the night. After a while, she had taken the diary through to the bathroom and sat in a warm, soothing bath, generously laced with herbal crystals, reading through the last chapter of David's life. Her tears had added salt to the water: the soothing properties of the herbal essences failing to reach the pain in her heart. Dawn light coloured the bathroom walls, the water cooled around her and still she read.

Not long in bed when Kate's alarm sounded, she didn't heed it, only turned so that Kate would not see her tears if she happened to look in the room.

Sleep was a luxury that didn't steal upon her until much later, long after the front door closed behind Kate's rush to work.

The phone rang again, its shrill insistence calling her back from troubled dreams.

She looked at the bedside clock as she reached to lift the receiver. Eleven o'clock: the morning almost over: the few hours sleep not enough.

"Hello?" she answered hoarsely.

"Mrs Reed?"

"Yes."

"It's me, Mrs Cleat, your Dad's neighbour. Never thought I'd have to get hold of you so soon. It's your dad, he's been taken poorly. I've called the am'blance."

"But..."

"I know, funny, ain't it? You just seein' him yesterday an' all. I thought you'd want to know, what with your Robert being away and everything."

"Yes."

"Good thing you left me your number. Bet you didn't expect me to need it already."

"No."

"Good job my family had me get the phone in, wasn't it?"

"Yes."

"They worried you see, after Len died."

"Where?"

"The Infirmary, I should think. They'll probably take him to the infirmary. That's usual from here."

"Yes. Thank you, Mrs Cleat."

"That's where they took my Len, you know. Sudden that was too. Terrible. I was ever so upset. Sudden at the end, though he'd been ever so ill. I just didn't think it would really happen, you know. An embolism it was, in the end. Oh! That's them now! I can see the light flashing."

"Oh... I..."

"I'd best go. Make sure they..."

"Yes. Okay." Sarah was waking up now, beginning to function again. "Thank you, Mrs Cleat. Thank you for letting me know."

"Taken funny he was, out in the garden, your Dad, I mean. Silly fool was trying to light a bonfire. Burnin' old papers and things, photographs, boxes. Looked like he'd been up the loft 'n' dragged them down. Silly man. Should never've done it hisself. Not with his heart."

"Yes, thank you."

"Fire went out. Right after he..."

"Yes, thank you. I'll get over to the hospital."

"I'll just tidy it all back into the boxes for you. Don't want it blowin' about, makin' a mess. Private stuff too."

"Thank you."

"Right. I'll go then."

"Right. Thanks again, Mrs Cleat. I'll probably pop over later. Sort it all out."

* * *

He died in the ambulance. A massive coronary, his third, according to the doctor.

She asked to see him.

174

He looked at rest, at last. His had always been a troubled face, his carriage stiff and closed. Death had relaxed him as life could not.

His hands were placed on his stomach and she took one in her own. His was an old hand, veined and gnarled, misshapen with arthritis. Rigour mortis had not set in yet, so she could still wrap his fingers round her own and raise his hand to her cheek.

"Oh, Dad," she sighed, for after all was said and done, 'done and dusted' her mother would have said, he was her father and she had loved him. She kissed his hand and held it tenderly, remembering the strength it used to have. The fingers were blunt and work-worn still, but useless now.

Regret for all the wasted years washed over her. They could have been a comfort to one another after Mother's death and after Tom had gone. She could have eased his last years, made him comfortable, given him back something for the home and hearth he'd given her. He could have advised her, helped her in the business of raising a son. After all, he hadn't done too bad a job of Robert. Down-to-earth, practical and wise, qualities that would help her now, he had possessed when she was young.

"Oh, Dad," she sighed again, stroking the hand she held, conscious of the changes time had wrought in his hands as in his character, feeling the knotted veins, the arthritic nodules.

His wedding ring would never be removed, *could* never be removed, over the bent, swollen knuckle. She touched its smoothness, remembering her parents' marriage, a strange one, but a faithful one. Her fingers brushed over the engraving on its flattened surface. She'd never noticed it before, had certainly never been able to study it before, had assumed it to be a pattern. But now she saw it was, not a pattern, but initials. They were worn almost smooth, but she thought she could just about make them out. A capital 'G' and a capital... 'M', it should have been... but it didn't look like an 'M'. More like an 'A'. She frowned, looked more closely, then shook her head. It could be an 'M', she supposed, *must* be.

Gordon and Martha, an ill-assorted pair. Had they been happy? In their own way? It hadn't seemed like happiness, but perhaps she was unrealistic in her measurement. They had little to say to one another all the years she'd observed them, but is happiness only measured by communication?

She carefully placed his hand back as it had been, regretting that there was no answering squeeze for hers.

The rigours of death had eased from his face as he had succumbed to it, the lines and creases being the ones she could have expected of a man his age, no sign of the scowl she'd left him with yesterday.

The kiss she softly placed on his lifeless face was the one she'd saved nearly all her adult life, a daughterly kiss, of remembrance and love for the father he'd been in her childhood, the story-teller, the disciplinarian, the rock on which she'd leant. He'd never been one for kisses and affection, so this was one of a mere handful she'd ever been permitted to bestow, and it was given without his consent.

Sadness engulfed her.

So it had indeed been the final 'goodbye'.

When she'd stumbled out of his house yesterday, it was his last words that rang in her ears. 'I had no daughter,' he'd declared.

"Well, you're wrong, Dad," she whispered. "Like it or not, I *am* your daughter, and I loved you despite your indifference."

Chapter 23

She would have to phone Robert, find out what was to be done. He would probably come over and she would be glad to see him, needed to see him. So much had happened in so little time: so much to tell him; so much that could never be told over the telephone or in the pages of a letter.

But meanwhile, she'd better go over to the house, *his* house, tell Mrs Cleat, see to the boxes, lock up the house.

"Oh, I'm sorry, dear. He was a miserable old man, but he was your dad, after all. I'm sure he wasn't always so miserable. Certainly got worse after your poor mum died. Now, she, on the other hand, was a dear soul." Mrs Cleat smiled her sympathy, more for the older, harder loss of years ago. "You must let me know if there's anything I can do," she added, turning to the boxes lined up in her hall. "Mostly old bills and stuff, and photographs and old letters. Must have wanted to clear them out. You'd best take them next door. You and your Robert'll probably want to go through them."

"Yes, thank you, Mrs Cleat. You've been very kind."

The neighbour waved her hand dismissively. "Couldn't leave th'm blowin' about out back, dear, not private things like that." She drew herself up. "Mind, I didn't read anything!" she said.

"No, no. I'm sure you didn't."

"I'm not like that, you know."

"Yes, I do know, Mrs Cleat," Sarah reassured her.

"Oh, I like to know what's goin' on just like anybuddy would. But I'm not nosey. Wouldn't like neighbours pokin' into my business. Keep meself private, always did, even when my Len was alive. Here," she said. "Let me help you with them boxes."

Another funeral, more than a year after David's, but in the rain this time, nowhere dry to sit in the gardens even if she had wanted to, which she didn't.

She felt no reluctance to leave this place today. There was nothing to keep her here. David's memories belonged in better places and her father's were best forgotten.

Her mood had changed since seeing him in the hospital. She had had time to reflect, time to remember without the pathos of his lifeless body to tug at her heart. Tender memories of him were few in comparison with the flood of memories, just being here in this sad place unleashed of David.

The pain revisited in full intensity and made her harden her face for her father's funeral.

So, yes, another funeral, even smaller this time: only herself, Robert, Kate and Mike, and Mrs Cleat along with a few neighbours. The same minister intoned the same pious nonsense, and charged for his services. The same organ droned out the same dirges. This time there were no tears, with even Robert dry-eyed and business-like.

"Not exactly a popular man, was he, Dad?" Robert asked ruefully, after they had shaken the few hands that were proffered and were walking back to the car.

"Are you surprised?"

"No. He made no effort to be nice to anybody. Especially after Mum died."

"And he made no effort to be nice to her while she was alive."

"No."

"You can't help wondering why he cared when she did die."

"Missed her, I suppose."

"Yeah, missed his skivvy!" Sarah said, in a rare moment of bitterness.

"I think he probably loved her, in his own way."

Sarah stopped walking to stare at Robert. "Loved her! Loved her? I don't think so! He never had a tender word for her, a look even."

"In his own way, I said."

178

"In his own way? And what way d'you suppose that was? In the same way he loved his working boots? He lavished more care on them."

"Okay! Okay! Just trying not to speak ill of the dead."

"Yeah," Sarah sighed. "You always were too nice. Must take after Mum."

Robert walked on thoughtfully, frowning. After a moment or two, he stopped and turned to Sarah. "You do know, don't you, that Mum was not *my* Mum?"

Sarah spun round to stare at him. "Pardon?"

"Not my real mum."

She swallowed. "What d'you mean, not your real mum?"

"Not my real mum."

"Mum?"

"Yes. Mum was *your* mum, not mine. I thought you knew."

"But you never... you always..." The world tilted a little around her. The sound of the rain on her umbrella seemed very loud.

"She was my 'Mum', as good to me as any mother could have been, and I loved her to bits, but she wasn't my birth mother."

"Wasn't?" The ground sank away from her. She had to put her hand on Robert's arm to steady herself. "She wasn't?"

"No."

"I don't understand."

Robert allowed time for her to absorb the revelation.

"Who?" She swallowed. "Who *was* then?"

"I don't know. Apparently she died when I was young."

"Died?" Sarah looked round at the rows of gravestones, almost expecting a woman to rise from among them. 'Oh, there she is,' Robert would say. She stared at him. "How do you know all this?"

"I sort of knew all along."

"Sort of?"

"I must have been about two when she died. I have vague memories of someone, nothing very real. Then, when I was fourteen, I needed my birth certificate for something... school trip or something." He gestured the event's unimportance. "Mum

179

must've seen it coming. She was all prepared with the answers to the inevitable questions."

"Wait!" Sarah tightened her grip on his arm. "I don't know if I can take this in. Mum was not your 'Mum'?"

"No."

"But you never said. She never told me."

"It wasn't your problem. It was mine, and I was cool with it. She had been the only mum I could remember. She was great. Cool," he shrugged.

Sarah couldn't move her feet. She felt 'rooted to the spot'. She could feel herself bed into the soil, there, in among the gravestones, her life ebbing out through the soles of her shoes. "Did it not occur to you that it might matter to me? That I might *want* to know?"

"No. It didn't alter anything. You were still my sister."

"But I'm not! I wasn't!"

"To me you were. Besides, at the time, Mum asked me not to say, thought it might upset you. I thought she might've told you later."

"Darn right it upsets me! Did it not upset you?"

He had resumed walking, making her uproot her feet, making them move one after the other... one, two, one, two... left, right, left, right... They were at the hired car now. Robert unlocked it but Sarah made no move to get in.

"Yes, it upset me a little at the time. It was a bit of a shock to realise that my real mother was dead, I'd never be able to meet her. But then I sort of forgot."

"Sort of forgot?"

"Yes," he shrugged again as he sat in the driver's seat. "Chose to forget, I suppose," he continued after she at last lowered herself into the passenger seat beside him. "It just didn't matter. I loved her, Mum, I mean. Possibly even more, knowing she loved me though I wasn't her kid. She'd always cared for me just the same as she cared for you. I never felt second best."

"I always thought you were her favourite."

"There you are then. It didn't matter, did it?" He started up the engine.

"You should have told me," she said, weariness making her voice hoarse.

"Why? What difference would it've made?"

"I don't know. But you should have told me."

"I wanted her to be my Mum. No point wanting anything else, I suppose," he said with a shrug, checking the mirror, driving off. "So she *was* my Mum. And you were my sister. I didn't want, didn't *need* anything to change." He glanced across at her with a schoolboy grin. "If I'd told you, you might not have wanted to be my sister any more."

"But I'm *not* your sister."

"But you are! In every way that matters, you are my sister."

"Except by blood. By blood I'm only *half* your sister. Your half-sister."

Robert stopped at the end of the crematorium driveway. Before attempting to join the stream of traffic on the main road, he turned again to look at her. "Does it matter? Does it really, really matter, Sarah?"

She swallowed, looked down at her hands then closed her eyes. "I don't know." She looked up at him, seeing the anxious pleading in his eyes, the love in his face. "Probably not," she agreed quietly, reaching out to touch his beloved face. "Probably not."

"No. It doesn't matter. What matters is family. We're family. That's it. Bottom line. We grew up together. We played together, we ate together, we laughed together, we cried together. We looked out for one another. We were, we *are* brother and sister. We're just 'family'. That's what matters."

He put the car into gear and eased out into the traffic.

Sarah sat back in the seat, her eyes closed. It certainly helped make sense of their marriage certificate. They must have met after Robert's mother died, then, when Mum became pregnant, his Dad, *their* Dad, married her. But he should have told her. *Someone* should have told her.

She was drifting, floating, not quite in control of her life, not knowing in which direction this current was taking her, more points of reference swept away.

181

Chapter 24

They had sent Katie and Mike on home to prepare something for tea. They had explained their intention of going to Dad's to sort through some of the boxes, look for any paperwork needing attention, any loose ends needing tied up.

Sarah had waited for Robert, having no desire to look through the boxes and drawers on her own. She hadn't wanted to come today either, but Robert had only flown in yesterday, hadn't had a chance to go to the house yet and was keen to get it over with.

"Ah! The ancestral home," he sighed as they stopped outside it. "Bit run down, isn't it?" he added with distaste.

"He seems to have let things go a bit, especially outside."

"You can say that again."

"He seems to have let things go…"

"Ha, ha! Very funny." He cuffed her gently round the head. "Not so bad inside, you say?"

"No. He had a home help."

"Yes. I knew that. I set him up, at one time, with a gardener as well. The garden was obviously getting too much for him even back then."

"Well, if he had as much trouble keeping gardeners as he seems to have had keeping home helps…" Sarah shrugged.

"Suppose so," Robert agreed wryly. "Let's get in, then. See what's what."

When Sarah had taken the boxes in, the day he'd died, she had left them in the hall, not wanting to be in the house a moment longer than she had to be. Now she looked round with Robert. Their father had obviously been intent on a good, old-fashioned clearout. Cupboards and drawers stood open, their contents piled up on the sideboard and table in the living room. There was a bin-sack beside the sideboard, filled and tied, ready for removal. Another half-filled. One open drawer seemed to hold any current papers, things he must have decided were to be kept. The boxes Mrs Cleat rescued were obviously headed for more certain destruction than the dustbin.

"I never realised he was such a hoarder," Robert said, looking round helplessly at the task before them. "How on earth are we going to sort through this lot. I've got to be back in the States next week!"

"Prioritise. We need to prioritise," Sarah decided. "The bin sacks should go straight out... they can't contain anything he considered private or important."

"Yes," Robert agreed.

"We should check this drawer first. He deemed these the important documents, the ones worth keeping." She indicated the one whose contents had been sorted and replaced. "As for this lot," the boxes, "I don't know," she sighed. "He must have wanted them burned because he didn't want them found after he was gone. They must be private. Perhaps we should just do as he intended and burn them?"

Robert shook his head. "There might be photographs, things we'd like to keep, things of Mum's."

"Things of *your* Mum's even," Sarah suggested.

Robert sat down heavily in his father's chair. "Phew! I never thought of that." He rubbed a hand across his brow. "I don't know if I'm ready to cope with that."

"Let's go through the drawer first then."

"Yeah," he nodded. "Best idea. Yeah."

The unpaid bills, in their envelopes, the payments tucked in beside each one, ready for the home help to take to the post-office or the bank, they were easy enough to deal with. And the insurance policies, one for the house and its contents, one for Gordon himself and, strangely, one for Robert, presumably so that Dad could have afforded the trip to his funeral should his son have predeceased him. No policy for Sarah, but that was no surprise. Those they found, Robert put aside to deal with. Bank books, Birth certificate, National Insurance card, TV License, Driver's License, no surprises in the drawer. While Robert checked through it, Sarah went to the kitchen to make them a cup of tea.

It had hardly changed. In all the years since she had last lived in this house, the kitchen had hardly changed at all. Her mother's apron still hung on the hook behind the door. The same cups hung on the same hooks under the same top unit. The same cutlery was still in the same drawer, in the same order, knives to the left, then forks then spoons, the teaspoons along the bottom, the sharp knives, tin opener and other assorted instruments to the far left. The kettle was different, a newer version of the same model.

The tea caddy stood in the same corner of the worktop beside the teapot, its 'cosy' loosely on top, ready for service, the same hand-knitted one her mother had lovingly made. Picking it up, holding it in her hands, feeling the old, soft wool, she caught her breath in sudden memory, the clarity of the moment stunning her.

She could see again her mother's hands working the needles, the wool flying through her fingers, the ball rolling at her feet. She had taught Sarah to knit too: the happy hours together; her mother's endless patience; the feel of the wool; the growing masterpiece, the pride in accomplishment, they were all here in her hands. She could hardly breathe. This was still her mother's kitchen. Sarah ached with longing for her. She sat at the kitchen table and wept for her mother.

"What's happened to that cup of tea?" Robert shouted through at last. "Can you not find anything? Last time I was here, it hadn't changed much."

Sarah dried her tears and took a deep, steadying breath. "Still hasn't," she tried to shout through.

"Getting nostalgic, are you?" Robert said softly from the open door. "Here." He opened his arms to her. "Catches me the same way every time," he admitted. "It's still Mum's kitchen, isn't it?"

"Oh Robert. I missed her so much. I wish she'd let me see her, stay in touch after I left."

"She couldn't, pal. Dad forbade it."

"But…"

He shook his head. "No. She couldn't overstep his authority. It was just the way they were. She didn't have the strength to go against him."

"I don't think she ever tried."

"Don't be bitter, Sarah. Mum loved you."

Sarah shook her head.

"Yes, you know she did. It must have broken her heart not to see you, not to share your life, her grandchildren. He deprived her of all these joys." He shook his head sadly. "But, it was just the way they were."

"You said 'family matters'," she sniffed.

"It does matter," he reaffirmed. "To me, to you."

"But not to Mum."

"Yes, to Mum."

"But not enough."

"Perhaps not," he had to agree. "But I think it did. It was just that she seemed to feel her first loyalty was to Dad."

"He didn't deserve it."

"No, I don't think he did. But something compelled her to give it."

They made the tea and sat in the kitchen to drink it, surrounded by memories of their mother, her gentle kindness, her loving care, her wisdom in their difficulties, her comfort in their trials. They felt that *hers* was the life they mourned today, *she* the focus of their grief.

After a while, the memories became lighter, filled with the laughter they had shared in this kitchen, and it was in that lighter mood they went through to tackle the boxes their father had meant them never to see.

One was filled with official letters, business letters, all the printed, private correspondence common to any household. Two of them contained old bills and receipts, the accumulated notification of services rendered, items purchased over all the years of Gordon's adult life. Nothing vaguely official had been discarded. There was a certain fascination in noticing the changes in form and presentation the passing years had brought.

"Good grief! These should probably be in a museum!" Robert exclaimed. "I didn't know anyone kept all this sort of 'bumf'!" He looked at Sarah's face. "Tell me you don't!"

"Well, you never know when you might need to produce..."

185

"But you don't keep everything? Please tell me you don't keep everything!" he pleaded.

"Well…"

"You're as bad as Dad!"

"Clearout scheduled at home. Tomorrow!" she determined.

Robert laughed. "Well, I suppose you'd have to be like him in something."

"Ugh!"

There weren't many photographs; Dad felt uneasy with the vanity of them. They remembered most of them, when they were taken, where they had been that day, what they had been doing. Again, the memories mostly happy, because it was only when father was in a particularly good mood they dared to bring out the camera.

There were a few unfamiliar to them.

With a sigh, Robert gazed, at last, into the eyes of his birth mother. The photograph was dated three weeks after his birth and captioned on the back, 'Gordon and Annie with baby Robert." She was seated, the baby in her arms, her husband standing proudly behind the chair.

"She's beautiful," Sarah whispered.

He nodded, too full for words.

"And Dad! Just look at him! He looks so different. He actually looks happy!"

"And young!" Robert added.

"I can't remember him ever looking like that."

"Me neither."

"And Annie, your Mum…. Annie! On his ring!" Sarah pulled at Robert's sleeve. "His wedding ring, his and Annie's! 'G'&'A'. Not his and Mum's. All those years. He wore it all those years."

"Poor Mum!" said Robert, understanding immediately.

"Oh, poor, poor Mum!" Sarah covered her face with her hands, tears stinging her eyes. "How awful for her. She must have known he still loved Annie. Oh, it's too, too sad," she wailed.

Robert shook his head. "Heartless, cruel man."

Sarah rocked on the chair, her arms wrapped tightly about herself, grieving for her mother.

After a while she saw that Robert was still gazing at the photograph he held in his hands, so she dried her tears and set aside her pain. "How does it feel to see her photograph after all these years?" she asked him.

"Strange, really strange."

"Had you seen a photograph of her before?"

"No."

"Not ever."

"No. I didn't know there were any."

"If Dad had had his way, you never would have either!" Sarah waved her hand, indicating the boxes stacked around them where they sat at the table in the livingroom. "Typical!" she sniffed her indignation. "He was going to destroy them!"

"Hard to imagine he'd kept them this long."

"Not a great sentimentalist, our Dad."

"But perhaps more than we'd realised, what with the ring and since he did keep these things."

"More likely Mum kept them and he just didn't bother throwing them out before," Sarah guessed.

"Makes you wonder why he decided to now."

"Probably after he saw me that day. Maybe something he'd been meaning to do before he died, then me turning up made him more determined. He must have known he couldn't have that many years left."

"Possibly," Robert agreed, turning over another photograph of his mother, this time on her own, younger in this one, her long hair falling around her shoulders, her smile sweetly innocent, 'Annie, aged 16' the information on the back.

"She really was lovely," Sarah reaffirmed.

"Lovely. But she was not 'Mum'. In my head I know she was my real mother," Robert explained, putting the photograph down again. "But in my heart, *this* is my Mum." He picked up a different photograph; one they knew so well, a photograph of Martha with one of them at each side of her, laughing into the camera, holding her there, forcing her to allow her picture to be taken, her face betraying her reluctance but smiling despite it.

187

A few more photographs of people they didn't know and whose identity they could only guess at unless it was revealed on the back, then they were ready for the next box.

Before he opened it, Robert reached out and covered Sarah's hand with his. "I found his will," he said softly. "In the drawer."

"Oh, I didn't expect him to have one," she said with surprise.

"No. I didn't either. I didn't think he'd have much to leave." He squeezed her hand. "Sarah," he said gently. "I'm sorry. He has made no mention of you at all."

"I don't want anything."

"I know. There isn't that much anyway. But there's been enough misunderstanding and too little communication. I didn't want you to find out later."

"It doesn't matter, Robert. Honestly, it doesn't."

He shook his head. "It's not that. Anyway, half of everything is yours. I'll share it with you."

"I told you, I don't want anything."

"Neither do I. We'll share it and that's an end to it." He silenced further protest with his look. "The thing is, what I want to tell you, what I don't want to tell you…"

She laughed. "Come on. Make your mind up. Are you telling me or not."

"It's just, you see…"

"My father cut me out of his will. There! That's it! I've said it! It's not so hard to say." Bravado hiding her hurt, wanting Robert not to be upset.

Robert left his seat and walked over to the window. "He claims I was his only offspring. Not just his only son. His only child."

Sarah swallowed. "I knew he felt like that. He said as much the day before he died."

"But it's cruel. It's a terrible thing to do, to not only disinherit one of your children, but to disown her. To pretend she was never born. Insufferable man! He disgusts me."

"Thank you, Robert, for caring," she said quietly, "but it doesn't matter."

"Of course it matters!" He put his hand on her arm. "It's hideous. Unnatural."

"He was angry."

"And he nursed it long enough. You married, when? Twenty-odd years ago?"

"Twenty-three, twenty-four, and that was the problem. I didn't marry. I lived 'in sin'!"

Robert turned away with a grunt of disgust. "He was no angel himself according to what you found on his marriage certificate."

"But he put it right."

"He covered his 'sin', hid it in respectability. He was a hypocrite!"

Sarah shook her head. "It doesn't matter now."

"I wish I'd known when he was making this will."

"And what would you have done? What *could* you have done?"

"I could have spoken to him, reasoned with him. It's disgraceful!" Robert clenched his fist. "He should have been made to see that it was a shameful thing to do."

"And he would have listened?"

"At least he'd have heard it. Hypocrite!" Robert was pacing now, his hands gesticulating wildly, like those men who take their soapbox to Speakers' Corner. "He was the one used to tell me, '*Family*, boy, that's what matters. The family reputation! Its good name! Loyalty! Never allow anyone to run this family down. We walk tall in this community. You make sure it stays that way. Family, boy, family! That's what matters.'"

"But don't you see?" Sarah pointed out. "That's what I did. I sullied the family name."

"So, in other words, it was the family's 'good' name that mattered, not the family, not the living, breathing family!" He kicked one of the boxes. "Well, he was wrong, Sarah! He was stubbornly, hypocritically, wickedly wrong! *We* should have mattered! You, me, Mum, we were his family. We were the ones he should have cared about. Not his precious family name! Well, stuff his mean, selfish, unnatural will," he shouted. "He can 'stuff it where the sun don't shine!'" He accompanied the ripping up of

189

the will with a string of oaths and obscenities, both verbal and signatory.

"Stop it, Robert! Have you no respect for the dead?"

"No!" he shouted back at her. "And he deserves none!"

"Oh, Robert," she sobbed.

"Listen, sis!" He knelt in front of her. "You and I, we are family. And we do matter! That old..."

"No more Robert," she pleaded, putting her hands over her ears.

"That old so-and-so," he compromised. "Can do nothing about it. He had his day and he blew it. He died lonely, unhappy... and unmourned. We're not going to waste any tears on him. Let's check this last box and get out of here. Better still, let's take it with us and look through it tomorrow. I've wasted enough time on the old..."

"Robert!"

"Yeah, well, you know. Come on, sis, let's go home."

And so, they left their father's house, unaware of the mixed treasure they carried with them.

Chapter 25

"…and you learn to build all your roads on today
because tomorrow's ground is too uncertain for plans
and futures have a way of falling down in mid-flight."
1971 Veronica A. Shoffstall

"Dad phoned," Kate informed them when they got home.

"What did *he* want?" Sarah asked, hanging her coat on its peg in the hall.

"It was kind," Kate defended. "He wanted to say how sorry he was about Grandad."

"Oh, did he? That was nice."

"No need for sarcasm, Mum. It was nice. He didn't have to."

"No, I suppose not," Sarah relented.

"So Tom's back, eh?" Robert shook his head as they went through to the livingroom. "I really thought he was dead, you know?"

"Didn't we all?" Sarah said as she flopped into the chair.

"No, I mean it. I *really* thought he was dead. I was sure that was the only explanation there could be."

"And you were right. It was the only acceptable one," Sarah said, as much to herself as anyone.

Robert sat opposite her, his elbows on his knees as he leant towards her. "Any chance I could see him?" He turned to Kate. "Did you tell him I was over? Staying here this week?" he asked her.

"Yes. He asked after you very kindly."

"I liked Tom, y'know," he said to Sarah.

"I do know. I liked him too. Look where it got me!" Sarah lamented.

"But he did have a reason for disappearing. It wasn't planned or anything."

Sarah could feel anger rise in her. "But he could've let us know he was alive, saved a lot of pain and heartache," she said, "to say nothing of the time and effort of searching for him."

"I know, I suppose. Still, it'd be nice to see him again."

Sarah threw her hands in the air. "I give up! You've got as short a memory as Kate."

"He was wrong, Sarah. I know that. Everyone makes mistakes."

Sarah was out of her seat, punching cushions, straightening furniture. "Mistakes! You call that a mistake? To abandon your wife and two kids for eleven years?"

"And he has apologised."

"Then turn up out of the blue, 'Sorry dear. I got detained. Hope it hasn't been too difficult for you, eleven years as a single parent.'"

"I suppose," Robert reluctantly acquiesced.

"Yeah, you suppose right." She walked over to the sideboard, rearranging photographs, dusting them with her hand. "That was some 'mistake'!"

"Sorry, sis. You're right. He was way out of line."

"*Way* out!"

Robert was beside her. "Yeah. It's okay," he said gently, putting his arms around her. "I'll not see him."

She leant against him, tired of the fight. "Oh, I don't mind. I know you liked him. It wasn't you he abandoned," she relented.

"But it was you, and you're right, it was unforgivable."

"But see him anyway, if you like."

"Good," said Kate. "'Cos I invited him over for supper!"

"You what?" Sarah exploded.

"Only kidding, Mum," Kate held her hands up. "Only kidding! D'you really think I'd dare invite him here without your consent?"

"I sincerely hope not, because I do not intend him to cross this threshold!"

"I thought you were going to try…"

"I know, I know. It's just, it's been a trying day." Sarah put her hand to her head, her eyes closing with sudden weariness.

"Let's have some supper and get some rest," Robert suggested.

"What about the last box?"

"Time enough in the morning," Robert told her. "You've had a rotten day. You look shattered."

And that's how she felt. Shattered. Her past, everything she thought was fundamentally solid, was crumbling in the repeated shockwaves of discovery. Any plans she might make could only be tentative, uncertain; at any time some new revelation could shake them, shattering her future as surely as her past. The way forward seemed hidden from view, obscured by the dust and debris of the collapse of what she had thought were unassailable truths.

Yet she knew she must move forward if she were to survive. She must pick her way through the debris and recover her identity. The thought of the journey made her weary.

Today had been a 'rotten' day and she was glad to pull her duvet over it.

But, though she may have finished with the day, it had not finished with her and her sleep was troubled, with dreams of shooting galleries, all her so-called 'family' the targets, being shot down one by one. *Ping!* There goes her father. *Ping!* Her mother too. *Ping!* No brother. *Ping! Ping!* David and Tom. Where was she? Running through the dark fairground, her own screams loud in her ears, falling, falling... lost... lost... falling... falling...

She woke up sweating, a weight on her chest, her breath coming in gasps, her heart thumping erratically. Tablets. The little tablets the doctor had given her. She turned on the bedside light, felt around on the little table, snatching up the foil strip, then she lay back down, the tablet under her tongue, breathing slowly, calmly, willing her heartbeat to settle, waiting for the dizziness to pass.

After a while, she crept downstairs to get herself a warm drink, expecting the house to be in darkness, everyone asleep.

"Hey!" Robert greeted her softly. "Couldn't sleep?"

She shook her head. "Bad dreams."

"Need a drink?" Robert offered, getting to his feet, moving towards the kitchen.

Sarah nodded. "Thanks. Something warm and soothing."

"Camomile?"

"Yeah, fine, thanks, Robert." She sank down wearily into the sofa. "What about you?" she called through softly. "Couldn't sleep either? Bad dreams?"

Robert appeared again in the doorway, the kettle hissing gently in the background. "Bad thoughts," he admitted. "Two things. Keep thinking of Dad's inhumanity to you..."

She shrugged her indifference.

"Not just the will, which, by the way, I hope the lawyer's got a copy of, since I probably won't be able to access his bank account without it. But the way he treated you, both years ago and now, last week." He shook his head in disbelief. "That any father can tell his daughter, under any circumstances, that he 'has no daughter', worse, '*had* no daughter'. It's unnatural!" The kettle was boiling. He returned to the task of making her drink. "Unnatural and gross," he repeated as he carried through the mug. "Shall I leave the bag in?"

She nodded, taking the drink from his hands.

"I'm finding it hard to forgive the old man," Robert said as he sat down in the armchair. He leaned back and closed his eyes for a moment, taking a long, deep breath. "It's new to me," he said at last, "all these feelings of disgust, loathing. I'm not used to feeling like this. I've been away so long. Only occasional trips back. I'd forgotten what a twisted old..."

Sarah looked up with a cautionary stare.

"...a twisted old so-and-so he'd become. In fact, I think I'd forgotten what a mean spirit he always had. When you're away from home, it's easier to forget, to paint memory with a rosy glow. Nostalgia, I suppose. Even when you told me what he'd said to you I don't think I really took it in. Not that I thought you'd made it up, just that it's full significance didn't hit me till I saw it in raw print."

"Cold print."

"Pardon?"

"'Cold print', I think the expression is. More appropriate, anyway," she added quietly.

"Yes. It was cold," Robert agreed. "And you must have thought that *I* was cold."

"You? You were anything but cold!"

"No, I don't mean when I read Dad's will. That he 'owned only one offspring', no. Heaven's no! I was furious! Burning with it! But I mean, after that. When we got home. I talked about wanting to see Tom. You must have thought me an insensitive fool."

Sarah shrugged her shoulders. "It's okay."

"No, it's not okay. It *was* insensitive. When I think what he put you through! I remember when I came over. We checked everything we could check. You were frantic. It was a dreadful time, so much pain. Then all the years of struggling on your own. And David. Who knows? If Tom had been around..."

Sarah jumped to her feet. "Don't even go there, Robert! I've thought of that, can't cope with it."

"Okay, sis," he soothed her, drawing her down on to his lap. "I'm sorry. I should have thought. I'm so stupid sometimes."

"You're fine," she assured him, stroking his face. "You're a great 'big bruv'."

He gazed deep into her eyes. "Love you, Sis," he whispered.

"Love you too, Robert."

He held her close against him while they both relaxed into the security of their familiar relationship, one of confidence and trust.

"I would never want to hurt you, Sis."

"I know that," she said, getting off his knee, going back to the couch to sip at the warm drink again. "You just weren't thinking."

"But I should have thought."

"We'd had a harrowing day."

"No excuse."

"Anyway, I've been thinking. You *should* see Tom."

"No way!"

"Yes. We both should. There are some things I need to check out. You can help me."

"How?"

"I'll tell you in the morning. Meantime, if you're not sleepy yet, d'you fancy getting the last box out of the way?"

"Are you sure you're strong enough? You look a bit pale."

"No, I'm fine. Anyway…,what could it possibly contain that would upset me more than what I've already found out today?" With a huge sigh, she looked over at Robert. "I just can't believe you're not really my brother."

"I told you," Robert insisted. "I *am* your brother. Half-brother on paper, all brother in heart."

She ruffled his hair. "Soppy ape!"

Robert brought the box to the coffee table in front of them. This was the only one that had been carefully sealed up with sellotape, sellotape that had become brittle with the passing of time, indicating that their father had not opened it before consigning it to the bonfire pile. "He must have know what was in it," Robert remarked.

"*And* that it was Mum's things," Sarah breathed, once it was opened. "Look! Letters. I thought it was only the heroines in romantic novels who tied up their letters with pink ribbons."

"And kept dried flowers and baby teeth," Robert added, lifting things out. "Look! This was your hair." He showed her the baby curl, carefully placed in a tiny envelope with her name written on the outside.

"Mum's writing. I'd forgotten how beautifully she wrote. Almost copperplate." She traced her name, her fingers lingering on the envelope, her heart aching for the touch of her mother's hand.

"And mine." He showed her.

"I had no idea Mum kept all these things."

"Me neither. Jewellery. I didn't know she had any, did you? She never wore it."

"Well, she wouldn't, would she? Not the way Dad frowned on such 'vanity'! But I remember that ring. She used to wear that on a Special Occasion."

"Like?"

"She wore it to my school prizegiving."

"Yes, you're right. With a brooch, she had a matching brooch. Look, here it is!"

Sarah nodded, still examining the ring, turning it over in her hands, slipping it on her finger, her eyes misting. "Oh Robert, what treasure. To find mum's things." She took the brooch from his hand.

"And to think the old..." he caught her glance. "The old so-and-so..."

"Thank you!"

"...was going to throw it all out!"

"I'm amazed he hadn't long ago."

"Perhaps he did have a sentimental bone in his body."

"Doubt it. Look at the sellotape. This box hasn't been opened in years. Probably since Mum sealed it all up before she died."

"But why would she do that?" Robert wondered.

"Probably kept these things, her precious things, in this box for years. Gathered them into it, hid it away from him, from his prying eyes. She probably sealed it and resealed it each time she went into it to add a momento, or to look at the old ones. I bet he had no idea what was here. He'd just know it was her box and he had no use for it."

"And didn't want us to have it, mean old..."

"Maybe he would have opened it before burning the letters and things."

"But didn't get that far." Robert agreed.

"Anyway, under the terms of his will..."

"Which I tore up."

"Which you, in a fit of pique, tore up."

"Fit of peak! Convulsion of rage, more like."

"Anyway, this is all yours now. Mum's treasure. For you to cherish for her."

"No. I think she'd have wanted you to have it. Especially things like the jewellery. Her ring wouldn't fit me anyway. Nor would it look so good," he laughed.

"No." She held up her hand, smiling as much at the warm memories the ring evoked as at the beauty of its filigree. "It's pretty, isn't it?"

"Lovely. It suits you."

"Anyway, I know where *I'm* going to get *you* a ring," Sarah decided.

"Where?"

197

"Tomorrow. I'll tell you tomorrow," she said. "Now, back to Mum's box."

"Okay, but you know you're a tease, don't you?"

"D'you think it's okay for us to look at these letters?" Sarah asked. "I mean, what if they're from old boyfriends or something?"

"So? Wouldn't it be lovely to know that Mum had had a lover? Someone who treated her right?"

"Yes, but I doubt if she had, not under dad's watchful gaze. Anyway, these letters seem mostly from her sister, Auntie Mary." Sarah looked through the bundle she had in her hand.

"Auntie Mary? Auntie Mary? Remind me...." Robert closed his eyes, searching his memory.

"She was Mum's oldest sister. She had four sisters, I think, and a brother or was it three sisters and two brothers? Yes, I think that was it. Mum was one of six. Four girls and two boys. Mary was the one Mum took us to see when you were about, oh, I don't know, I think you were about seven. I must have been five. It was when their mother died. Mum sneaked off to the funeral. Dad was furious, said they had agreed it wasn't 'fitting' to see her folks. Though what he meant by that...."

"This all went over my head. I have a vague memory of someone. We were in an old sort of waiting room?"

"Mary's sitting room."

"With not much furniture in it?"

"Just two cottage-style chairs and a wee two-seater sofa. There was an old sideboard too, I think."

"There was another boy."

Sarah nodded, remembering. "Wee Patrick, her son. He was younger than me. Thought you were the 'bee's knees', a Big Boy."

Robert closed his eyes, searching out the memories. "We played with his toys, a couple of matchbox cars and an old wooden garage his dad had made him. I remember I was dead jealous of that garage. It was painted red and had two stories. But it wasn't that, it was because his *dad* made it."

"And we had home-made scones and wee sandwiches."

Robert laughed. "I remember."

198

"And Mum cried a lot," Sarah remembered with sadness.

"I don't remember that but I suppose, if it was her mother's funeral."

"She seemed to have been close to Auntie Mary before, well, before she married, I suppose," she shrugged. "These letters are all dated after." She browsed through them. "Keeping her up to date with family gossip, by the look of it. Oh, and here's the one telling Mum her own Mum had died. Sad, really. Sounds like she'd wanted to see Mum. Listen...

Why didn't you come, Martha? She wanted so much to see you. Father O'Brien was with her at the end, heard her confession. He asked where you were. I told him I didn't get word to you in time, but I had Martha. Plenty of time. So where were you? Would he not let you come? Was that it? Will you not stand up to the man, Martha? I'd like to see the husband who'd try treating me like he treats you!'

Oh, that's sad!" Sarah said, putting the letter back in its envelope.

Robert nodded. "Mind you, I like the sound of Mary! A real 'stand-no-nonsense' aunt. Yes, I do like the sound of her. Mind, she sounds someone to stay on the right side of, though! I wonder if there's any photos of her." He rummaged through them.

"And here's one extolling your virtues!" Sarah waved the letter at him. "'*Such a sweet boy, a polite child, a fine little fellow. Patrick has not stopped talking about him even yet. It's not often a bigger boy gives him such attention. He's not much like his father, is he?' '*Sweet boy!' 'Polite child!' She obviously only met you the once, then! You 'fine little fellow'," Sarah joked, reaching for another of the letters.

"That must've been after we went that time."

Sarah sat back. "Wow! What a brain! It's impressive!"

He cuffed her head playfully.

"This is an earlier one, much earlier, dated before I was born," she said, ducking his hand. "August 7th 1955 , more than four months before I was born." Sarah started reading the letter while Robert continued to dig through the assorted treasures of the box.

"Hey, I'm sure I remember this hair-slide-thingy. Did Mum not used to… "

"Oh, no! Oh no," Sarah gasped. "Oh, Robert, no. This is awful."

He took the letter from her and read it aloud:

'Dad has forbidden any of us to contact you, so I don't know if I'll be able to write again. You know what he's like! If he's got a drink in him when he finds out I've written to you, there'll be hell to pay.

Anyway, I've found out what you asked. Father O'Brien says the man's a widower who's looking for a house-keeper and says he'll marry for appearances sake. Seems his wife died in childbirth so he's got things all ready for a baby and he says he wants a mother for his two-year-old son.

He's a mining engineer, a gaffer, and has his own house. The only problem is that he's not RC, so Father O'Brien isn't happy with me passing on the information, but he says he understands your predicament. He's not such a bad sort. Not bad-looking either. Pity he's a priest! Anyway, don't know how you'll get on with that, it's up to you.

Don't suppose it matters much now, since Dad says you'll burn in hell for your sins anyway! Nice one, eh?

So here's the address. Good luck with the 'interview'. God, I'm glad it's not me!'

"Robert! Do you know what this means?"

"I'm not sure," he replied. "You've gone ahead of me. Let me catch up a minute. Now, this letter was written four months before you were born, so, Mum was pregnant. Sounds like her father must have thrown her out."

"Don't you see? That's it! She hadn't met Dad by then. She was going for an 'interview' with him. That means…"

Realisation dawned on Robert. "It means he's not you father."

"He's not my father." Her voice was dull and toneless. "He said he had no daughter," she remembered, "and he hadn't," she whispered. "I was not his child!"

"Wow! That's a bit of a shocker, is it not?"

"He wasn't my father." The room began to lurch. "Dad wasn't my real father." She felt herself slipping.

"We're not even 'half' related."

Sarah looked at him with new horror, the room swinging back sharply. "But that's awful!"

"No! It doesn't matter," Robert insisted urgently. "We are *family*. You and Me, we're Family!" He waved the letter in front of her. "This changes nothing."

"So that's what he meant." The room lurched again, her balance going, darkness threatening.

"Do you hear me, Sarah? This doesn't matter! It changes nothing!"

"It changes everything," she intoned, as though in a trance. "I don't know who I am any more. Everything has changed. It feels as though the ground is falling away from under me. It's like my dream. I'm falling again, falling, falling…"

She slumped over on the couch, unconscious, the dream bursting in her head like a firework, then… darkness.

Chapter 26

"Sarah, Sarah! Oh, God, please let her be all right," Robert prayed. He ran to the livingroom door. "Katie! Katie! Wake up!" he shouted. "Wake up! It's your Mum. We need a doctor. Katie! Katie!" Running back into the kitchen, he grabbed a cloth, plunged it into cold water and ran through to place it on Sarah's brow, squeezing some of it over her face. He felt for her pulse. Still strong. Breathing, fairly normal.

"What's happened?" Katie asked breathlessly, as she ran into the room.

"She passed out. Just a faint, I think. I hope. You'd better call the doctor anyway. Does she still have heart pills?"

"Yes." She held them out to him. "I grabbed them as I ran past her room. Thought it might have been another attack. It's not, is it?"

He put the little tablet under her tongue. "I don't know. I don't think so."

She had started to dial Doctor Mitchell's number. "You don't think I should call an ambulance instead of the doctor?"

"Ask him. Tell him she's starting to come round." He wiped the cool cloth round her face. "It's okay, Sarah. Don't try to talk. You fainted or something."

"Hello! Doctor Mitchell. It's Kate Reed. It's Mum. She passed out again. No. Yes, straight away. Yes. Robert's here. Right. Thank you." She put the phone down. "He's coming round. He says since she's coming round and we gave her the tablet she should be all right. Probably not need an ambulance. He'll check her out when he gets here." She knelt beside her mother. "Oh, Mum. Are you all right?"

"Yes, love. I'm fine." Her voice was weak, hardly more than a whisper. Things were a little hazy, and moving, this way and that, but she tried to sit up... for Katie, she tried to sit up.

"Hardly fine," Robert remarked, helping her, putting his arm round her shoulders, steadying her, holding her against the sway of the room. "You gave me a hell of a fright!"

"Language please," Sarah said in a whisper.

"Well, you did."

"What happened" Kate asked. "I mean, before you fainted or whatever it was?"

"We were looking at some of…" Robert began.

"Just talking, dear." A little stronger now, her voice a little stronger. "It's just that it's been a stressful day."

"And what were the pair of you doing down here in the middle of the night?"

"We were…"

"We were just talking," Sarah said quickly, her voice breaking. She cleared her throat. "Like I said, just talking. You go back to bed, Katie dear. I'm fine now. Really, I am."

"So what's with all the letters and stuff?"

Taking his cue from Sarah, Robert leant forward, gathering everything up quickly, putting it all back in the box. "Oh, just some stuff we were looking at." He got up to take the box out to the kitchen.

Sarah smiled her gratitude.

"What stuff? From Grandad's?"

"I'll tell you about it another time, Katie love." Sarah had managed to sit up and was sipping a glass of water Robert brought her.

"Have I seen that ring before?" Katie asked suspiciously.

"Oh, it's an old one. I think I hear Doctor Mitchell's car. Could you let him in, please dear?"

"What's the big cover-up about?" Robert hissed in Sarah's ear while Kate was out of the room. "She's a big girl. Aren't you going to tell her?"

"Not yet," Sarah hissed back. "I've got to come to terms with it all myself first. I'm shaking all over. Feel as though I fell out a ten-storey building."

"You're probably in shock."

"Dead right I'm in shock. My whole life has tilted on its axis."

"Try not to talk for a bit. You're still a hellish colour." He ignored the reproving look. "I don't fancy another funeral already."

"Gee, thanks!"

"This is all going to take a bit of coming to terms with, right enough."

"Everything in the last year or so, ever since David..." She started to weep. "I wish I could wake up out of this nightmare," she sobbed.

But she knew the nightmare wasn't over yet. She had dealt with the pain and grief of losing David, had thought she was getting over his death, the fact of it, if not the manner of it, then she found his diary. She had thought she could cope with that, then she visited her father, felt his indifference, his coldness and the last of her hopes of family reconciliation were crushed. Robert was not her brother, a terrible shock. Her mother was not his. His father was not hers. So much had shaken her. And she still had to deal with Tom.

In all of this, she was getting to know herself better. When David died, after the initial numbness, the anger, the pain, after all of that, she had tried to take stock, the realisation coming to her gradually that she had been living for her children, and only for her children. Ever since Tom had abandoned them, she had put her life on hold and only lived for the children.

When David died, there seemed no point in going on. Except that Kate needed her. But for how long? She would marry soon, make her own life, a life her mother would have only a very small part in, and rightly so. Sarah had no desire to intrude in Kate's married life.

Going even further back, she had lived for Tom. not just *with* Tom but *for* Tom. When he had two-stepped into her life, she thought she had danced free, but she had only changed partners. Instead of dancing to her father's tune, she danced to Tom's: instead of seeking her father's approval, she sought Tom's. Because Tom gave his more readily, it felt like freedom.

So why should she put on her dancing shoes now that the music had stopped?

She desperately sought rest. But not yet.

There were things to be sorted out with Tom, nothing to do with this nightmare, yet part of it too, in a way.

Strange, she was sure of very little any more, yet she was sure of so much! In the middle of the thick fog caused by the years of deceit, she saw with a new clarity what she must do.

But not until she had the dreamless sleep induced by Doctor Mitchell's prescription, not until she was rested, had time to take it all in, sort it all out. Find out who she was, hear her own music.

Chapter 27

It was well into the next afternoon before she woke up, refreshed and hungry. But she didn't go downstairs to get something to eat, not at first. Instead, she lay back on her pillows, evaluating all that she had recently learned.

So, Mum was her Mum, but not Robert's. Dad was Robert's Dad, but not hers. Robert was not her brother. A real 'bummer', that, but not much to be done about it. She didn't feel any different about him, and he didn't seem to feel any different about her, so that was okay.

At least she didn't need to make herself love 'Dad' any more. He certainly had not loved her. So that was okay. She could let go of that hurt.

She tried to feel good about it, but couldn't. Pain clutched at her heart. She *had* loved him. Despite his harshness, despite his coldness, she *had* loved him, she *did* love him. He had been her 'Dad'. There was just no other way to remember the past. He had been her Dad, like it or not. She would have to learn to live with the pain of knowing that her love for him had never been reciprocated, but she knew that she couldn't pretend, wouldn't pretend, that she hadn't loved him. He would always be her 'Dad'.

No, she would not allow her father's cruel words to douse the love she had stoically borne him over the years of her childhood. He had never loved her in return: she now knew what she used to wonder. His indifference had not thwarted her before, why should it now? No, it would be his epitaph: 'That he was loved *nevertheless*'.

And dear Mum, what of her? No wonder she was so loyal. He had taken her in, married her without love, for the sake of his son and her unborn baby. He had given her respectability, something she seemed to need, a name for her and her child. Sarah understood better the gratitude Martha must have felt. She had obviously never expected love from him, so would not have been surprised or upset when it wasn't forthcoming. She had made a contract and she kept to its conditions. A remarkable woman.

Sarah found that she could forgive her father. He had kept his side of their bargain too, it seems. The love she had for them both could lay undisturbed in her heart. They had been her parents; they had done their duty as they saw it.

Love is such a funny thing: given, even when unearned and undeserved; taken for granted, abused, turned away. Yet resilient, a fragile candle burning with the intensity of a furnace. Not to be snuffed by indifference; love born of duty rather than sentiment, of honour rather than affection.

So, what of Tom? Her love had burned for him too. Could she find the same magnanimity for Tom?

Ah, but this was different! The kind of love she had had for Tom was born from something quite different. It had been 'eros', as the Greeks would have it, not purely physical, though that had been the initial attraction. Then it had grown into a mixture of 'eros' and 'philia', the love of affection, nurtured by shared moments of pleasure and pain. Not a love born from duty.

There was a light tap on her door. She hastily wiped her tears.

"Hey!" It was Robert. "Thought you might be awake by now. Hungry?"

"Starving!"

"Good. Doctor Mitchell said you might be, so I've got some afternoon tea. Very English!"

"Well, I'll have to go to the loo first!"

"Then I'll bring it up. We'll have it together in here, okay?"

She smiled. "That would be lovely."

"Like…"

"Yes," she agreed. "Like we used to." She smiled, remembering the 'invalid teas' Mum used to make when one of them was recovering from illness. She would bring it up to the bedroom on a tray: a pot of tea, some bread and butter, perhaps a boiled egg each, or some scrambled eggs. Maybe some grapes, or even cherries. The three of them would sit on the bed. Whoever had been ill, tucked up under the covers, the other two on top of the counterpane. It was their special treat. A magical, healing thing.

Sarah closed her eyes. *Oh, Mum. I miss you. More now than ever,* she whispered. *I feel so lost. So lost and alone.* But she wasn't alone. She could hear Robert whistling as he came back up the stairs. She had Kate and she had Robert. For a little while anyway. Until he went back to his family, his real family.

"Have you not even been to the bathroom yet?" he complained, seeing her get out of bed and reach for her housecoat. "Hurry up, or it'll get cold," he scolded.

"Sorry."

"I should think so! Been slaving all morning."

"Mmm! Smells good!" She gave him a peck on the cheek as she passed. "Back in a mo'."

"So, we know who my mother was," Robert said, through a mouthful of toast. "What about your father? How are we going to find out who he was?"

Sarah shrugged. "Hadn't got to thinking about that yet."

"But you'll want to, I suppose?"

"Probably. Though I wouldn't have a clue where to start."

"Birth Certificate? Seems to be your preferred method."

"No use. I've seen it. Dad is named as my father."

"Big of him!"

"Yes, I think it was," Sarah replied seriously. "He took Mum in when she was cast out by her family, gave her his name, respectability, a name for her child. I think that was generous, especially in those days."

"Hmm, s'pose so," Robert agreed reluctantly.

"And, in return, he got a housekeeper and a mother for his son."

"Happy family!" Robert declared. "And now, have you got Master White, the painter's son?"

"No, but I'll have that last piece of toast, if you don't want it! And then I really must get dressed. I want to buy you a ring, if I can. If it's there," she muttered under her breath.

Chapter 28

> "After a while you learn that even sunshine burns
> if you get too much.
> So you plant your own garden and decorate your own soul
> instead of waiting for someone to bring you flowers."
> 1971 Veronica A. Shoffstall

"You're a liar and a cheat!"

"But you knew that. You always knew that!"

"No, I didn't *always* know that, Tom. I found out when it was too late to do anything about it. We were committed. We had two kids before I found out what you were really like."

He sat at his desk, fiddling with some papers. "So? You chose to hang around once you did know."

"And what else was I supposed to do? Where could I have gone? I had no family to go to. You'd made sure of that. I had no job, no means of support."

"Okay! Okay!" Tom held his hands in the air.

"And I loved you, dammit! I loved you. I trusted you. Even after I knew you were no good, I loved you. I didn't think you would ever lie to me. I didn't know you already had."

"But I hadn't, Sarah. Not really." He got up and came round the desk towards her but she moved away, out of reach.

"You told me you were married!"

"Well, I know, but…" He leant on the edge of the desk.

"That was a lie!"

"No. No, it wasn't exactly." Tom started fiddling with papers again, tidying the desk beside where he sat.

"What's that supposed to mean? It wasn't *exactly*?"

"Well.," shuffling papers, tidying again, not quite looking at her.

"Either you were married or you weren't."

"I was."

"Then why could I find no trace of it in the records?"

"Well that would depend…"

Sarah stood, hands on hips, glaring at him. She had come to tackle him about these issues and she had no intention of backing down till she had some answers. His obvious reluctance to discuss matters was not going to put her off. They had come into his 'inner sanctum', as he liked to call it, leaving Robert browsing around the shop. She knew she had the advantage, having taken him unawares: he was still smiling from the warmth of Robert's greeting and his own delight in seeing him again when she struck.

"That would depend on what?" she demanded.

Tom looked round furtively. "It would depend which name you looked under."

"I beg your pardon?"

"I said…"

"Yes, I know what you said, Tom." She stood in front of him, making him look at her, "Or whatever your name is," she said. "Harry, is it?" She picked up a pile of papers from the desk. They were addressed to the shop, the name 'Fame's Furniture' printed boldly. "Harry Fame, perhaps?" She tossed the papers down, knowing from his expression that she had guessed correctly. "Huh! Tom, Dick or Harry. Take your pick. It doesn't seem to matter."

"Sarah…"

"Let me get this right. What you're saying, is that you had already assumed one of your false names before I met you. There never was a 'Tom Reed', just like there is no 'Harry Fame'! Is that right, Tom?"

He didn't have to answer. She knew it was true, having worked it out at the Registrar's Office. "That's why I could find no trace of you, your birth, death, marriage, imprisonment, you name it, you had a persona for everything."

Tom shrugged.

"So, were you married? Under whatever name you chose that day? If I went back to Register House, would I find an entry under the name you'd give me now?" But before he could answer, she held her hand up. "No, don't tell me," she said with a sigh. "I won't believe you anyway."

He shrugged again.

"Like I said, Tom. You're a liar and a cheat!"

"I don't know what to say."

Sarah held her hand up again. "Just don't say anything. Like I say, I wouldn't believe you anyway."

"Sarah, I'm…"

"And please don't say you're sorry!"

"But I…"

"No, Tom. Don't! I mean it. I don't want to hear that."

"Okay. So what d'you want from me?" He sat down behind his desk again, leaning back in the chair, challenging her.

"From you? Nothing." She leant across the desk, taking on his challenge, ready for the head-to head. "I want nothing from you." She walked to the door. "I want you to disappear again. To stop existing. To stay out of my life. And, especially, to stay out of Kate's life."

"I don't think I can promise you that."

"Why not? I think you *owe* me that!"

"Possibly, Sarah. But I think you'll find that that's not what Kate wants. And it's not what I want."

"To hell with what you want!"

"Maybe. But what about Katie?" He was up, out of his seat, over beside her at the door in two long strides, his face close to hers. "She's found her father. She's happy I'm back in her life. Are you really going to take that away from her? Do you really think you have that right? She knows what I am. You made sure of that. She told me you told her all about me. But she still wants to see me. Family you see. Blood's thicker than water, Sarah. I'm her father. She forgives me."

"We'll see about that."

"I don't think there's much you can do." He held the door open for her, inviting her to join Robert again as he approached them through the shop.

"You've got one or two nice pieces here, Tom," Robert called over. "Business good, is it?"

"Not bad, not bad. Could be better, but it keeps me in biscuits."

"Choccy ones, I imagine!" Robert laughed. "Finished your cosy chat?" he asked.

"Yep! Think so." Tom looked at Sarah for confirmation.

Sarah took a deep breath. "Yes. Anyway, Tom, that was not the only reason we came today. We've some business for you."

"Business, I like." Tom gave a Shylockian chuckle, rubbing his hands together.

"Telling you, Robert. He's a bit of an 'Auntie Wainwright'. Not that that'll mean much to you, I suppose. You've probably never seen 'Last of the Summer Wine'."

"Wrong! I have actually. Angela's mum is a great fan. She brought us over some tapes a few years ago. We enjoyed them. Now, Auntie Wainwright...."

"She's the one with the junk shop."

"Oh, yes."

"When you've quite finished insulting me and my shop."

"Yes," said Sarah. "I'd like to buy a ring for Robert. Something second hand, gold, with a bit of character. A bit like yourself, darling," she winked.

Tom had been taken by surprise by the sudden change from all-out-attack to matey-banter. He wasn't sure if Sarah was serious or what. He was flustered for a moment. "Rings?"

"You said you sometimes have rings and things?"

"Yes..." he faltered.

"Same conditions apply? Good discount, but I *do* pay, you give me a receipt, etc., okay?" She smiled sweetly, confusing Tom further.

"Well, yes, I suppose."

Sarah linked arms with Robert and giving Tom another sickly smile, drew them all back into the office. "Robert, darling. Tom sometimes has a few bits and pieces of jewellery. I'd like to pick you out a ring."

"Oh, didn't realise you dealt with jewellery," Robert said to Tom.

"Well, I don't really. Just sometimes a customer asks me to, well, sort of, payment... sort of as payment."

"Oh, you mean a sort of *barter* system," Sarah said archly.

Tom was beginning to recover his composure, beginning to regain the control he'd lost by her deliberate pendulum swings of attack and retreat. The whole encounter had been sprung on him. His surface joviality had been scratched away and his scheming underpart revealed. But no more. He was getting back his 'cool'.

"What she's trying to infer," he informed Robert, "is that the jewellery might be stolen. But I can assure you it is not." He drew out an array of rings from the same set of drawers the watches had been stored in. "All legal and above board, bought and paid for!"

"In kind, if not always with money," Sarah supplied with that same sweet, innocent smile. "Oh, we believe you, Tom. We wouldn't be buying if we thought for a moment…"

"Look, do you want to buy one of these, or not? 'Cos, quite frankly, I'd as soon you didn't, if you have any doubts."

"D'you resell many of them?" Robert asked.

Tom shrugged. "Occasionally. If they're worth anything I sell them direct to a dealer. Most of these I've had for a while, not great quality, wouldn't fetch much. Some of them are nice though, if you're not particularly looking for an investment."

"Just a nice ring," Sarah said casually, turning one or two of them over, checking for inscriptions, looking for that special one. "Like this one," she said to Robert. "Oh, do try it on, dear. See if it fits. Perhaps on your pinkie? Yes? Oh good. That's the one I'd like to buy," she declared.

"Not anything great, that one. Been here a while. Would you not rather have something a bit fancier?" Tom asked, offering one or two more elaborate rings, with stones set in them.

"No. No, this is the one we want, isn't it Robert? Nice and plain, not too flashy."

"Yes," Robert concurred. "Perfect. How much?"

"No, darling. My shout. My present. Anyway, Tom and I have an arrangement. Good discount." She nudged Tom with her elbow.

"Sure, sure," he agreed, his discomfort and confusion showing again. "And a receipt. Yes, I know, I know. These awkward customers," he joked to Robert.

With the ring bought and paid for, Sarah saw no reason to linger in the shop. "Okay then, boys? See you around, Tom. More shopping to do. Come along, Robert."

"What on earth was all that about?" Robert demanded, when they were outside the shop and out of earshot of Tom.

"Tell you later. Fun, wasn't it?" she laughed. "Did you see Tom's face? Didn't know if he was coming or going, did he?"

"Poor soul didn't know what'd hit him. But what was it about? You're up to something."

"Like I said, tell you later. Come on, we've a couple more things to do before you've earned your supper!"

* * *

"I think we should invite Tom out for dinner tomorrow night," Sarah announced later, as she, Robert, Katie and Mike sat round the supper table. They had enjoyed a good meal and had been sitting chatting amiably over dessert.

"Wow! That's a bit of a change of heart, is it not?" asked Kate. "What brought that on?"

"Well. He's right. He is your father, after all. I know you want to see him and I know Robert wants to see him again before he goes home."

"Only if it doesn't upset you."

She patted his hand affectionately. "It doesn't upset me. I think it's time I forgave and forgot. The past is past. Tom's paid the price for his crimes, if not for his stupidity. I think it's time I let him off the hook. Just a little bit," she added hastily. "I don't want him back in my life. Just a truce of sorts. So Kate can have her father, if she insists, without having to resort to subterfuge to see him."

"Oh, I wouldn't, Mum."

Sarah patted her mouth with her napkin, put it down and started to rise from the table. "You can phone him, if you like. And make reservations somewhere nice, will you, dear?" she asked as she carried some dishes through to the kitchen. "You and Mike can choose. You'll know where would be nice." She came back for more plates. "Make reservations for six. Tell him he can bring a 'friend', if he has one."

"Mother!"

"Sorry! Okay, just for the five of us."

"Are you sure, Sarah?" Robert asked, stopping her as she lifted his plate, his hand on her arm. "I thought you hated the guy."

"Whatever gave you that idea? No. I don't hate him." She gathered the rest of the plates onto the tray she'd brought through. "I hate what he did to us. I don't approve of his lifestyle. But, no, I don't hate him."

"Why do I get this uneasy feeling that you're not being totally honest with us?" Robert narrowed his eyes. "You're too brittle, too, I don't know, sure of yourself, all of a sudden. As though you have a plan afoot. It reminds me of when we were kids and you had a 'scam' on."

"A 'scam'? Who? Mum?" Katie asked with delight. "What kind of things did she get up to, then, Uncle Robert? Do tell. From the way Mum tells things, she was a model child, incapable of anything so devious as a 'scam'!"

Robert laughed. "Oh, I could tell you a thing or two."

"Not if you want your coffee, you can't!" declared Sarah as she headed for the kitchen.

* * *

When they all met the next evening, Tom was very guarded and his unease seemed to grow with each teasing phrase, each familiarity Sarah tossed his way.

Realising this, Robert and Kate went to great lengths to put him at ease, turning the teasing back on Sarah.

But she didn't mind. It was better if Tom thought they were on his side, that he only had to win her over. And she would let him. In her own time, she would let him break through the barriers she had erected, would let him charm her round. He would have his victory, at *her* price.

"And so," Katie was saying. "Since you're all here, all my family and loved ones," she added, giving Mike's hand a squeeze. "Mike has an announcement to make, don't you, Mike?"

"I do?"

"Yes," she prompted, giving him a nudge.

"Oh, yes," he grinned. "I remember now. Katie wants me to tell you…"

"Mike!"

"Sorry! Got that wrong," he teased. "It's my pleasure to announce… is that better?" he asked her in a stage whisper.

"Mike!"

"We're going to get married… if no-one has any objections!"

"In April," Katie prompted.

"Yes! In April. Whether there are any objections, or not, actually. Okay?"

"Oh, that's lovely. A spring wedding! I could wear a dress and coat, and maybe a hat," Sarah teased. "A silly, fussy sort of hat."

"Oh no, Mum!"

"Only kidding, darling." She blew her a kiss. "April will be lovely. I promise to behave perfectly as 'mother of the bride'. You can help me choose my outfit, so's you're not embarrassed by me." She raised her glass. "Congratulations, both of you!"

"Congratulations!" they all chorused.

"And we hope you'll *all* be able to come?" Katie looked enquiringly at her mother, holding her breath, waiting for the reaction.

"Why that would be lovely. You will come Robert, won't you, with Angela and the children? Whatever money Dad's left could help with the fares, couldn't it?"

"Of course we'll come, all of us." He went round to Kate's chair to give her a huge hug and plant a kiss on her cheek. "Wouldn't miss it for anything! Congratulations, Mike!" He shook Mike's hand enthusiastically. "You've made a great choice, as the cliché goes."

Kate was still waiting, her eyes never leaving Sarah's face.

"And you, Tom," Sarah relented. "You'll come too, won't you?" she asked softly. "After all, it will be your privilege to give the bride away."

"Oh, thank you, Mum." Kate leant across to kiss her mother's cheek. "You will come, Dad, won't you? You will give me away, won't you?"

Tom nodded, unable at first to speak, uncertain of what was happening between him and Sarah, but delighted at the turn things were apparently taking.

"That would be my greatest pleasure," he said huskily when he found enough voice.

"Oh it's going to be the most beautiful, perfect wedding," Kate crowed excitedly.

"Not if my lot are coming to it," Robert joked. "Little boys have a habit of wreaking havoc at weddings and such occasions!"

"To say nothing of my nieces and nephews," Mike added.

"They'll all get on famously and we'll have such a good time." Kate's excitement was not to be subdued.

Tom looked across the table to Sarah, seeking to catch her eye, searching for an indication that this really was to be a truce, something lasting that they could build on, but she had turned to Mike, to give him a congratulatory kiss.

The rest of the evening in the restaurant was filled with questions and plans, arrangements and jokes about the coming event. A happy time looking forward to an even happier time some eight months ahead.

* * *

"Now, Uncle Robert, you must promise that you'll bring Angela and the kids over in plenty of time before the wedding," Kate demanded. "I want some time with them before I go off on honeymoon, not just a day or two, mind. At least a week."

"You'll be sorry!" Robert warned.

"No I won't," she punched him playfully on the arm. "You know I won't. I mean it. At least a week!"

"Okay, bully. We'll see what we can manage."

"Good. Kiss the kids for me when you get home and tell them to keep writing. I love their letters."

"Me too," Sarah said, giving him a hug. "Take care, 'bruv' and thanks… for everything. You were great."

"Love you, 'Sis'," he said, tears making his voice husky. "Please be careful," he said into her hair. "You're so precious. All the family I have over here. Please don't do anything silly."

"As if!"

"Yes, as if," he returned. "I know what you're up to. Be careful!"

"I will. Truly!" she assured him. "I will."

"That's your last call, Uncle Robert."

"I have to go," he agreed. "Take care of your mum, Katie. See you in April!"

And with a last clinging hug, they let him go back to Canada.

"I shall miss Uncle Robert," Kate said sadly.

"Me too. Still, April is not too far away, only seven and a half months, and we have lots to do." Sarah hugged her daughter. 'And you don't know the half of it,' she added silently.

Chapter 29

Tom decided to go along with whatever Sarah was 'up to', since it seemed to include seeing more of him. She had phoned him up after their dinner with the others, to ask if they could meet for lunch to talk over wedding plans.

In the event, they didn't really discuss the wedding much, apart from him making an offer to pay for it and her refusing. He decided to wait a while and make the offer again, once she had had to start paying for things and saw how much it was all going to cost.

Meanwhile, she met him for lunch a few more times and they were getting along pretty well. They always did have the same sense of humour and he enjoyed seeing her laugh. He watched her as they walked and talked and knew that he was still in love with her, had never stopped being in love with her. Tom felt her softening and was hopeful that they could, after all, make something of a future together.

Kate was delighted that her parents were 'seeing one another'; that they were 'courting' again, as Tom joked. 'Building bridges', her mother called it.

It would please Kate greatly if they chose to stay together, or rather, to get together.

"What do you two talk about?" she asked Sarah one day after she came home from a 'date' with Tom, flushed like a school girl after her first kiss.

"Oh, this and that," Sarah laughed. "Mostly that."

"Oh? And what's 'that', may I ask?" Kate grinned.

"Never you mind," Sarah said, blushing at the memory of Tom's endearments. "Anyway, we mostly talk about you and David."

"Oh you do, do you?"

"Yes, we do, madam, since you ask. We talk about when you were little. The things your Dad remembers. And he wants to hear all the stories I can remember about you, from the years he was away. He regrets that he's missed you growing up," Sarah said wistfully. "I don't suppose it was a bed of roses for him either, being in prison, separated from his children. He always loved you both, you know."

"I know, Mum."

"I think it really hurt him to leave you."

"He said."

"He gets very choked up when we talk about David."

"Yes, he asked me for a photograph."

"You haven't given him one, have you?" Sarah demanded, jumping up from her chair, knocking over the little table beside it.

"No. Why? You wouldn't mind, would you?"

"Yes. I mean, no. Yes, I would mind," she said as she righted the table.

"But why?"

"I'm not ready yet. Not ready for that."

"For what, Mum?"

"Nothing. It doesn't matter. Look, would you mind just forgetting about a photograph just now? If your dad asks again, just say you forgot. There's something I need to sort out first."

"Okay."

Sarah looked flustered, bothered again, fussing with cushions, tidying the already tidy room.

"So you talk about David and me?" Katie tried to backtrack a little to regain the happier mood of a few minutes ago.

"Yes." Sarah folded the discarded newspaper.

"All the time?"

"Most of the time." She took the newspaper through to the kitchen, putting it in the bag labelled 'paper for recycling'.

"And what else do you talk about?" Kate pursued impishly, calling through to her. "When you're not discussing your children?" she asked as her mother reappeared.

"Ah, then we talk about us," Sarah blushed again.

"Yes?" Kate prompted.

"And that's none of your business," her mother chided playfully as she sailed out to the kitchen again. "Have you had supper?"

Kate watched as her mother moved about making a pot of tea, pleased to see Sarah looking younger and fresher than she had looked for a very long time, even before David's death. She seemed to have more, more sort of *purpose* about her. As if she was *going* somewhere, had a life-plan again. Kate guessed she was enjoying the attention Tom was lavishing upon her: she seemed to look forward to their times together. The good days were becoming more frequent for Sarah, and Kate was relieved.

"Mum?" she asked casually as Sarah buttered the toast. "When are you going to invite Dad back to the house?"

"Soon," Sarah laughed. "Quite soon. But first, Tom is going to let me see his 'books'. We're going to the shop next Friday. I want to see for myself that everything's above board, though I think it is. I hope it is," she sighed.

"I'd like Dad to meet Mike soon. Properly, I mean, Mum. Not just the way it was at the meal the other week, you know, everybody there, Dad more interested in you and Robert, than us. I'd like them to get to know one another a bit. Would that be alright?" she asked as she bit into her toast.

"Don't talk with your mouth full, dear," Sarah said automatically. "Oh, I don't know, Katie," she sighed. "I've not... It's just... Can we hold off a bit on that one?" she asked. "I haven't told your Dad yet about David. He might wonder when he finds out where you met Mike."

"Not necessarily. He might not make the connection. In fact, there's really no reason why he should."

"But I don't want to take the chance. Not yet."

"Don't you think it's time you told him anyway?"

"Probably," Sarah flopped down into the chair in the corner of the kitchen, suddenly deflated. "Probably." She stared into her cup, wishing she never had to tell anyone the truth about David, exposing David's weakness, her failure. She had been grateful for Tom's lack of curiosity, but she knew it couldn't last. Hopefully it would last a little longer. Just till she was ready.

"Let's go to bed, Katie," she sighed. "I've got an early start tomorrow. Have you remembered I'm going through to Glasgow?"

"Yes." Katie stood behind and wrapped her arms round her mother's shoulders. "I'm remembering. But are you sure you wouldn't rather wait till I could come with you?" she asked, bending to kiss Sarah's cheek.

"No, my darling. Thank you, but this is something I want to do by myself."

Chapter 30

The early morning train was busy, filled with business people, students and shoppers, she supposed, people who, for one reason or another, needed an early start to the day. She wondered if any of them felt as small and scared as she did this morning. Not the brash young man sitting opposite, posing, his head held at just the right angle to show off his strong neck and square jaw-line, his hand fingering through his hair from time to time, feathering the highlighted waves perfectly. He had looked appraisingly at each passenger as they entered the carriage, deciding to give the young girl beside Sarah the full benefit of his gleaming, white-toothed smile. She gave him no response, choosing to read her novel rather than study his manly face. Disappointed, he, in turn, drew out a book, a textbook of some kind. 'Ah, a student,' Sarah decided, pleased that she had guessed at once. 'Probably not much older than David,' she thought. Then the pain hit.

David was dead. All the books he'd read, the plans he'd made were useless to him now.

She closed her eyes, shutting out the reminder of young life.

Letting herself rock with the rhythm of the train, she forced her mind back to the conversation she had had with her uncle two days ago. A strange conversation, her uncle curious but cautious, his accent an almost incomprehensible mix of Irish and Glaswegian, not helped by the fact that he was probably the worse for drink... he told her himself that he'd 'had a wee drappie.' A helpful conversation as far as it went, but she wished it had gone further because she had no idea how worthwhile this early morning journey was going to be.

Sarah had decided she had to find her mother's family, guessing they would be her only chance of tracing her father. 'Her father', how strange and new it sounded in her head. 'Her father', not 'Dad'. Not the father she knew, but someone else, someone unknown to her.

What would he be like? Supposing they knew who he was and she could find him, that he was still alive and that he would agree to see her if he was? Such a short time ago, she didn't know of his existence, now, suddenly, it was imperative that she find him. What if he's old and sick, ready to die? She could be too late!

She looked at her watch, willing the train to move faster, longing to be there, knocking her aunt's door, learning the truth, seeking him out. *Oh, hurry! Hurry! Hurry!*

She had used David's method, the telephone directory.

Glasgow seemed the obvious starting point, since her mother's had been a Glasgow family. She reasoned that, surely at least one of her uncles would still be alive and living in Glasgow. The only relative she had any memory of meeting was Auntie Mary, but she had married and Sarah had no knowledge of her married name.

The list for 'Kelly' was long. She had a vague notion that one of her uncles was called Patrick, like her cousin, so she decided to try all the Patrick, Pat or P. Kellys in the list, narrowing the field considerably.

So, what should she say? How could she find out if the person on the line is her uncle? Should she just blurt out who she is and let them make the connection? Would they make the connection? What meaning would 'Martha Kelly's daughter' have for them? How else could she phrase it? I'm looking for Martha Kelly's brother? Do you have a sister, Martha, you've not seen in a while?

How on earth did David ask about his father? Poor David! That could not have been any easier. Once again, she realised what crushing disappointment he must have felt when his enquiries turned out to be fruitless. True, he had found his father, but not by that method. The weeks of working through telephone directories, finding the right things to say to total strangers, holding his breath each time, in case this was the one that would disclose his father. It must have been exhausting and crushing.

She had been more fortunate. Her search had involved only one telephone book, only a comparatively few calls. The trauma of what to say, how to say it, she had found nerve-wracking enough and she had stuttered and stumbled badly, at first. However, she managed to blurt something out each time the phone was answered, her enquiries making more sense as her confidence grew.

'Hello, you're listed as P. Kelly, in the directory. I'm looking for a Mr Patrick Kelly, born in the late 1920s or early 1930s, one of six children, four girls and two boys. One of the girls was called Mary, another, Martha.'

Each time, the person she addressed stopped her at some point in her 'spiel', often before she got past the 'Patrick'.

But then, the call she had prayed for:

'Hello, you're listed as P. Kelly in the directory.'

'Sure that's right, hen. And what of it?'

'I'm looking for Mr Patrick Kelly.'

'Sure an' hiv ye no foun 'im!'

'Mr Kelly? Mr Patrick Kelly?'

'Is that no whit ah sed?'

'I wonder, would you mind giving me your date of birth?'

'Aye an' ah wid min! Wid you gie your age oot tae strangers?'

'I'm sorry, Mr Kelly. I wouldn't ask if it wasn't important. You see, the Mr Kelly I'm looking for would have been born somewhere in the nineteen twenties or thirties, he'd be in his seventies by now, probably.'

'Sure, an' am ah no sivinty-wan masel?'

Her heart fluttered, seemed to skip a beat. With an effort, she managed to keep the tremor from her throat. 'And did you have any brothers and sisters, Mr Kelly?'

'Could ye no call me Patrick, darlin, since we're gettin so frien'ly, like?'

She moistened a smile onto her lips, let it slide into her voice. 'Did you have any brothers, Patrick?'

'Sure an' ah did. A hid jist the yin brither and four sisters. There wis Mary an' John an' Theresa an' Helen an' Martha, bit we canny count her, 'cos she's nae guid.'

No good! But she was my mother! And she was wonderful.

Her heart was beating faster now, too fast. Her mouth was dry. She felt faint, leant her head against the wall beside her, turning her cheek to its cool surface.

She had to make sure. She must make absolutely sure.

She swallowed. 'But it's Martha that I'm interested in. You see, I... I think your sister, Martha, was my mother.'

'Whit'r ye sayin, hen? Ye think Martha wis yir mother? Are ye no sure?'

'Well, yes. I know my mother's name was Martha Kelly. I just don't know if she was your sister.' Sarah held her breath.

'Aye she wis ma sister. Did ah no jist tell ye? Aye, bit dinnae tell ma faither ah sed it! He widdnae own her!'

'Is your father still alive, then?'

'Oh, aye, darlin. Sure'n hiv ah no jist cum back frae the pub wi' him the noo? Ninety-three an' he still can haud a good swallie. Ah've hid a wee drappie masel... ye'll mebies cin tell?'

'Patrick, Uncle Patrick,' she tried it out, liking the sound of it, the first time she'd called anyone 'Uncle'. 'Uncle Patrick, d'you have Auntie Mary's phone number?' Once more, her breath was held captive in her chest, waiting to be released on a sigh.

'An whit wid ah be wantin wi' Mary's phone number? An' her jist nae mair'n a step doon the landin?'

'She lives near you then?'

'Is that no jist whit ah sed?'

'Sorry. Yes, of course.'

'If ah want tae hae wurds wae her, whit fur wid ah no jist walk doon tae her door?'

'I suppose so. But I was wondering, would you mind giving *me* her number?'

'Cin ye no get tae her door, then?'

'Well. No. Or, at least, I'd rather telephone first.'

'Sure an' ah cannae be daein wi a' this waste o' guid drinkin money.'

'If it wouldn't be too much trouble?' *Please... oh please!*

'Trouble? Weel, if it's trouble ye want...'

'No! No, I didn't mean that!"

'Sure, darlin, you jist haud on a wee bittie an' ah'll git ma missus tae deal wi' ye.'

The scuffle that followed was indistinct in the main, but clear enough at times for her to hear her new-found aunt, Patrick's missus, cursing him for his drunkenness and pushing him out of the way to get to the phone.

'Mary's number ye want, is it, dear?'

Sarah's voice was small, forcing its way out of her tight, dry mouth, with little breath to float it on its way. 'Yes, please... if you have it.'

'I have it right here, m'dear. Hiv ye got a pencil? Right,' and she read off the number clearly.

After thanking her, Sarah put the phone down and sank back into the chair, exhausted.

So, that was her Uncle Patrick! A character, to say the least, by the sound of it. Perhaps she should have called sometime other than a Friday night! Never mind, she had got Mary's number. Perhaps she'd be sober and easier to get sense out of.

Sarah made herself a hot drink before she ventured to try.

When she did, Mary turned out to be perfectly coherent and delighted to hear from her long-lost niece.

'My word, so you're Sarah! Sarah! Never thought tae hear frae you! My, my, my! What a lovely surprise. Wee Sarah, Martha's wee Sarah!"

Sarah smiled, warmed by her aunt's pleasure.

"Martha never gi'ed me yer married name nor yer address, so I couldnae ever contact you efter she died. I've often thought o' ye, though," she declared. 'How are ye?'

'I'm fine, Auntie Mary.'

'And that brother o' yourn, Robert?'

'Yes, Robert's fine too.'

'He went off tae Canada, did 'e no? Yer mum fair missed 'im, ah think.'

'Yes, I think she did. Auntie Mary, I was wondering... I'd like very much to come to see you. Would that be possible?'

'Aye, 'course it would, hen. I'd enjoy seein ye after all these years. You come any time you like, hen. H've you got my address?'

And so, here she was, on this early morning train, going to see her Aunt, hoping she'd be able to tell her what she wanted so much to know.

Autumn was once more modelling this season's colours, parading every shade of red and gold you could imagine and the train swung and swaggered through the glorious Scottish countryside showing it to best advantage.

Sarah had always found autumn to be a mellow season, a time for reflection and meditation, and as the train dissected the country, she had time for both. Time, too, to wonder what sort of family hers would turn out to be. They sounded down to earth, kindly, warm people, Mary and Patrick and his 'missus'. Not the sort to throw a pregnant woman onto the street. But what of her grandfather? And her father? That is exactly what they had done all those years ago. Would she meet them? How would they treat her, Martha's child, a child conceived 'in sin'? Would they visit the sins of the mother on the daughter? She shuddered and was glad that it was most unlikely that she would see either of those 'gentlemen' today.

Chapter 31

The address her aunt had given her was not the one where she had visited with her mother all those years ago. This time, instead of the mouth of a 'close' in the Gorbals, the taxi rolled up to a huge tower block of flats, the flat façade reaching for the sky with outstretched fingers.

Sarah paid her fare and watched the taxi negotiate back through the litter of broken glass, abandoned shopping trolleys and heedless children that decorated the forecourt of the flats.

Looking up, it seemed the sky had been obliterated by the sheer mass of grey concrete. She stood in the shadow of a second, identical tower, which stood across the carpark, their forecourts separated by straggling lines of cars and motorcycles.

When she reached the entranceway, she discovered that the intercom that should have serviced the flats was out of commission. That wasn't really a problem, though, because the door was lying open anyway, negating the necessity to 'buzz up' to request admission to the building. Fortunately, as she thought at first, in her innocence, the lifts were working.

She quickly wished she had ventured to walk up the seven flights to Mary's flat. The stench in the lift, as it juddered and ground its way hesitantly upwards, was foul and she was relieved when it finally shuddered to a halt. On the fifth floor. She had stepped gratefully out of its confines before she realised that it should have carried her another two flights, but she decided against entrusting herself to it again and she walked up the stairs, a minimally less disgusting exercise.

In all of this she was not unaccompanied. As she had approached the entranceway, picking her way round puddles and debris, she was accosted by a little boy of seven or eight.

"Whit d'ye want, Missus?"

"You from the Social?" another asked.

"Naw, she's no," the first one replied on her behalf. "You're here tae see mah Auntie Mary, sure ye are?"

"Well, yes…" Sarah turned to look at the child, a scruffy, smiling wee face peering back at her.

"She telt me tae watch fir ye."

"Oh, that was kind."

"Aye, this lift's no wurkin." He had led her towards a row of steel doors, dented and battered and covered in sprayed graffiti. "Nor's this yin, or that yin. But this yin is." He pressed the appropriate button.

"No, it's no," chimed in his companion.

"Aye i'is! Ah came doon on it!"

"Aye bu'll no go the whole way up."

"Disnae maitter! Aun'ie Mary's on seven."

By this time the lift had come and he ushered her into it and pressed the seventh floor button, while denying entry to his companion by means of a well-aimed kick as he tried to squeeze in.

"Thank you," Sarah smiled. "And what's your name?"

"Patrick efter ma granfaither."

"And your uncle."

"Naw. His name's Patrick tae, bu' ah'm no efter him"

"Right, I see."

"Whit's your name?"

"Sarah."

He shrugged, no longer interested in the answer.

"Well, thank you for helping me," she said as the lift stopped.

"Aye," he grunted as the doors closed and he disappeared behind them.

That was when she realised she was not there yet and still had two flights of stairs to negotiate.

'God, am I just a snob, or is this no place to bring up a kid?' she asked as she tried to shut out the stench of things she would not permit herself to imagine. Afraid to touch the iron banister or the walls, she had to climb the stairs without help or support.

When she finally tumbled through the door onto the seventh floor landing, she thought she was prepared for anything it had to offer, but, to her great surprise, she found herself in a clean, tidy vestibule area serving four flats to one side and four to the other. Although bare and grey, with only the dim light that filtered through one wire-meshed window, there was no graffiti, no litter... and no smell.

Someone had even laid a small rectangular rug on the floor at their door, another a scrap of carpet sample.

Sarah checked the address she had copied down. Flat 7/4, the one with the carpet sample. She rang the bell.

Mary was as she remembered her, a tall upright lady with kind, grey eyes and a ready smile. A little older, a little greyer, more wrinkles, less curl in her hair, but still recognisable as the aunt she had visited all those years ago.

"Sarah? Come away in, hen. You found me all right then?"

Mary led her into the house, a smallish hall leading through the rest of the flat to the livingroom.

"Sit yoursel down there." She indicated a chair. "I'll pit the kettle on, shall I, hen?"

Sarah was grateful for the few minutes it took Mary to make a pot of tea, to get her breath back and let her heart rate return to normal, both conditions caused less by the exertion of climbing the stairs than by holding her breath as she did so. Mary had a window open, the curtains billowing in the draught, and Sarah sucked in the cool fresh air with delight.

The room was clean, the furniture modern but well-worn, a red, imitation-leather three-piece suite, an old sideboard... possibly the one she remembered?... and a glass-topped coffee table, the décor plain and sparse, with few pictures or ornamentation of any kind, yet falling short of austere, perhaps because of the profusion of family photographs in little gilt frames that were carefully placed on every surface.

"I hope you didnae take ony o' yon lifts," Mary called through at one point. "I should hiv warnt ye about them. They dinnae always work. Mrs Heatherington, next door, her son Andrew's wee lassie, only six she is an' all, got stuck in yin o' th'm last week. Fire brigade hid tae git her oot. Right state she was in an' all, poor kid. Keep tellin the cooncil, but they dinnae get it sortit prop'ly. Now, whit will it be? Milk an' sugar?" she asked as she came through from the kitchen, carrying a tray, laden with teapot, cups and saucers and all the rest.

"Just milk, please."

"Like your mother."

"Yes."

"You dinnae look like her, mind." Mary scrutinised her as she poured the tea.

"No."

"You're darker." She added the milk.

"Yes."

"And taller." And handed over the welcome refreshment.

"Yes."

"Thought you would be," Mary nodded with satisfaction, offering a plate of biscuits. "Even as a wean ah could see you'd be taller. Mind you, wouldnae be hard, your mum wisnae ower-endowed wi' inches, wis she?"

"No," Sarah smiled. "Not really." Her mother had only been five-foot-one.

"Pretty wee thing, though mind, when she wis younger. She wis always the pretty yin," she recounted, taking her own drink over to the other chair of the three-piece suite. "Helen was the clever yin an' Theresa the 'goody-two-shoes'." She sat down with a sigh. "I wis jist 'good-ol'-Mary', bit ah'm no complainin. Ah did all right for masel. Got masel a guid man, rest his soul.'" She closed her eyes and made the sign of the cross. "Anyways," she said, stirring her tea. "Ah dinnae suppose that's why you're here, tae git a pottit fam'ly history."

"It's a nice idea though. I feel I know so little about Mum's family, *my* family."

"Aye, well. There's a reason for that."

"Yes. I know."

"What d'you know?" asked Mary, not unkindly. "You tell me whit ye think ye know, pet, an' ah'll see whit ah cin fill in fur ye."

"Well, I know you were the oldest."

"Oldest lassie. Patrick wis the oldest o' us all."

"Right. And then?"

"Then me an' yer mum, then John an' Helen. Theresa wis the youngest. Six weans in ten years, ma mither hid!"

"A handful."

Mary shrugged. "They were better used tae big faim'lies in they days. Mum was wan o' fourteen, hersel."

"Goodness!"

"An' they lived in whit wisnae much more nor a room an' kitchen!"

"You wonder how they managed, don't you?"

"Better th'n most these days, ah should think. That many marriages break up, weans runnin wild." She shook her head. "If ye ask me, ah think life's become a sight mair complicatit th'n it used tae be."

"Probably," Sarah agreed.

"But ah doot if ye came here tae chat aboot the difficulties of modrin livin either!"

"No."

"You'll be wanting to know about yer mother?"

Sarah took a deep breath. "Yes," she sighed. "My father, at least, the man I *thought* was my father..."

"Gordon Thompson."

"He died a few weeks ago. When we were going through his things we found letters and things. It seems he was not my father."

"No."

Sarah leant forward, her hand clutching the arm of the chair, her nails leaving an imprint in its smooth covering. "And you knew."

"Aye."

"Because we found your letters to my Mum. You'd helped her, hadn't you?"

Mary nodded.

"Against *your* father's wishes."

"Aye." Mary lapsed into an even broader dialect. "An' he'd no like it ony better if he kent ye wir here the noo. We wir nain o' us tae hiv onythin tae dae wi' her, nor her wean."

"Even after all these years?"

"You'd be surprised how long a man cin haud a grievance."

Sarah shook her head, "No. I know." She forced herself to sit back: relax, be calm, patient.

"Look. If you came here hopin ah wid tell ye yer father's name or such, ah'm sorry. Ah cannie dae that."

Sarah swallowed her disappointment. "But you know?"

"Aye ah know."

"Did you know from the start? When she fell pregnant?"

"No. Jist from efter ma mither died."

"When we came to your house?"

Mary nodded.

"She told you then, didn't she?"

"Aye."

"She was upset, crying. You were shouting," Sarah recalled the scene. She hadn't understood what was being said. They were careful she wouldn't. But she caught the vibes, she knew things were heated between them, that Mary didn't like what Martha told her.

"Aye." Mary shook her head sadly. "It wis hard to hear."

"Why? What made it so hard to hear?"

Mary got up and walked to the window. She closed it, fiddling with the curtains, straightening them and re-arranging them. "Aye, it wis hard to hear," she repeated quietly.

"Because of who my father was? Or because of how it happened?" *Softly, softly.*

"Look, lassie. Ah know it must be hard for you tae find out at this late date, that yer father wisnae yer father, but can ye no jist let it be?" She turned from the window to look straight into Sarah's eyes, straightening her back, refining her accent. "Why rake up the past? It doesn't do any good. Sometimes things are best left alone."

"But don't you think I have a right to know who my father is?"

"Aye, probably," Mary sighed with reluctant agreement. "But sometimes it disnae do tae insist on yer rights. Sometimes ye're best to get on wi' yer life an' let others get on wi' theirs."

Sarah put her cup on the table in front of her and sat at the edge of her chair, leaning forward imploringly. "But I can't 'get on

234

with my life'. I don't know *how to* right now. I don't know what my life *is*! What it's *been*, what it's *about*."

Mary came towards her. "Dinnae git upset, lassie. It's no the end o' the world."

"Yes, it is! It's the end of my world!"

"Because you foun' out Gordon wisnae yer faither?"

"Not just that. There's been so much. David, my son... David died."

Mary sat down on the couch and leant across to take Sarah's hand. "Ye lost yer son? Oh, hen, I didnae know. I didnae know. Whit a terrible thing!" She shook her head sadly. "It's agin the natral order o' things, tae lose yer wean."

"Then I found out that Robert's not my brother either."

"An' it's all just too much, eh? Ye must be hurtin somethin awful." Mary closed her eyes in pain, caressing Sarah's hand, sympathy rocking her body in a gentle rhythm.

Sarah looked up gratefully. "Yes. It's too much. I don't know how to, how I can... "

"But what difference will it make knowin who yer faither was? That's no go'n'tae bring yer boy back."

Sarah nodded. "I know," she agreed. "I don't know why, I just know that I need to find out. I need to find some roots, something to build on, something to make sense of things."

"Even if it meant destroying him?"

Sarah held tightly to the hand that still rested on hers. "He's still alive then?"

"Aye. Ye could say that."

Sarah sat very still while the room spun around. She hadn't dared to hope her father might be alive, that she might one day meet him, talk to him, see for herself what kind of man walked away from the responsibility of a baby. But, there, she was doing it again. She was being judgmental. Until she knew the circumstance she should not assume he was negligent. Perhaps he hadn't known...

"Did my father know? When Mum, Martha, got pregnant. Did he know? Did he know it was his baby?"

"Sarah, Sarah!" Mary took her hand away. She sat back wearily. "These are questions I hiv nae right tae answer."

"But you know?"

"Ah know whit yer mother telt me."

"Then why can't you tell me that much?"

"Because it's no mine tae tell."

"But Mum's dead. I can't ask her!"

Mary shook her head. "It's still no mine tae tell," she said quietly but firmly, fiddling with the teapot, shifting its position on the tray, straightening its cosy.

"But who else can I ask?"

"Ah don't know, hen."

"So, why did you let me come, if you were never going to tell me what you knew I was going to ask?"

Mary looked up at her and smiled. "Because ah wanted tae see ye. Ah wanted tae see how Martha's daughter had turned oot. She wis right proud o' ye."

"Did she say that? In her letters, did she say she was proud of me?"

"Och, aye, hen! She telt me about yer twa bairns, yer fine hoose, everythin. She said ye'd done right well fir yersel. An ah wis pleased fir her. Ah dinnae think her life was easy. Och, on the surface, ah suppose it wis all right. Gordon had his own hoose, a bit o' money from an inheritance, a good investment. But money isn't everythin', is it? It was never a marriage of lovers."

Sarah shook her head in agreement. She was speechless, afraid to speak in case she blew her mother's story apart! Proud of her? Obviously, Mary had no idea that Martha had had no contact with her daughter or her grandchildren, no idea that Sarah had been a single parent, struggling to make ends meet for the past twelve or more years. What was there for her mother to be proud of? But Mary was right, at least, about her parents' marriage. It had certainly not been a marriage of lovers.

"Ah thought you might like some contact wi' us. Faim'ly. Sure'n are we no yer faim'ly, leastwise on yer mother's side?"

"Yes."

"And faim'ly matters, does it no? At the end o' the day, that's all we've goat. Ah never did agree wi' ma faither about this. Ah never thought it was right tae send Martha awa' the way he did, but then, maybe he knew."

"Knew?"

"Aye, well... Would ye like another cup o' tea, hen?"

They talked for more than an hour, about Martha as a girl, her brothers and sisters, their lives as teenagers, their mother and father. Everything, in fact, except what Sarah had come to talk about.

"Aye well, hen, ye must come again," Mary declared when it was time for Sarah to go.

"I'd like that," she replied, not really believing it would happen.

"Ah don't suppose ye've got much faim'ly left, apart frae us."

"No, only Robert and Katie."

"Well, we've plenty tae share!"

"Yes."

"Ah'm sorry, hen. Ah knaw ah've disappointed ye." She looked hard at Sarah, seemed to make a decision. "Look, I dinnae knaw. Mebbe ye should talk tae Father O'Brien," she said. "He was, well, he was the priest at the time. He helped yer Mum get a place."

"Where would I find him?"

"Och, he's retired now. Been livin' wi' his sister these twelve months or more. He's a poor soul, disnae keep sae weel, they tell me, though, to tell ye the truth, ah've no seen him masel' in as mony years," she shook her head. "She's across in yon other flats. Ye'll hiv seen them as ye came in." She led Sarah over to the window, pointing across the way to the other towerblock.

"Yes."

"Well, she's number 12/2."

"Twelfth floor?" Sarah shuddered.

"Aye, but it's okay, hen. Their lifts are workin' better. The janitor ower there disnae drink sae much."

"These buildings have janitors?" Sarah asked with disbelief.

Mary drew herself up to her full height, her accent lifting too. "You must have wondered what you'd come to. This block has been allowed to get in a bit of a mess."

"I'm sorry," Sarah stammered. "I didn't mean…."

"But you mustn't judge us all by the outward appearance of our dwelling."

"Oh, I don't! Really, I don't!"

"Aye, but it's a bit of a hell-hole, isn't it?" Mary relaxed a little. "We moved here when the flats were new-built. Thought they were great. Better th'n whit we had, two rooms, ootside lav. We've even got a view from this window." She drew Sarah into the kitchen and showed her that, by standing to the side and peering out at an angle, you could just see past the other block and catch a glimpse of somewhere green. "Not much, though, is it? Not like your mum's house, out in the countryside…"

"Well, it wasn't really *countryside*, but I suppose, compared to this…"

"An' compared tae where she came from."

"Yes."

"We grew up fast. Had to, runnin wild in the streets."

"Was my Mum wild?"

"No like you're thinkin'" Mary said quickly. "We wisnae promiscuous. No really. Martha was just unfortunate. Fell in love inappropriate, as you might say."

"They were in love, then? My Mum and Dad?"

Mary looked at her kindly. "Aye, hen, they were. You were conceived in love, if that's ony comfort."

"Thank you! Yes, it is. Like you said, there was no love in her marriage. I'm glad she had known love, had been loved."

"Aye, fair broke her heart when she was sent away, disgraced. I thought at the time she wis jist upset at the disgrace. But it wisnae that. There, ah've said enough!"

"Could she not have had me adopted?"

"Aye, she could hiv at that, hen, but she widnae dae it. Telled Faither O'Brien she widnae gie ye up."

Sarah sat down on a nearby kitchen chair.

"Mither said she'd bring the wean up as her own, but *he* widnae allow it."

"Your father?"

"Aye. He leathered Martha, e'en though she was carryin a babby, and telt her tae get oot the hoose. It was terrible. We was all greetin," Mary sniffed. "She could bare walk, he'd hit her sae hard. It wis Faither O'Brien took her away. He found a place for her at St Stephen's, then he got her an interview."

"With my father. Gordon, I mean."

"Aye. She felt she had no choice. There wisnae much you could dae if yer family let ye doon."

"But you didn't let her down, Mary!" Sarah reached a hand out to the older woman as she too sat at the kitchen table. "I know from the letters. You helped her!"

"Ah did ma best."

"Even though it meant going against your father."

"Aye. Och, he wisnae sae bad. But for the drink." She blew her nose on a tissue drawn from the sleeve of her jumper. "He only hit us in drink." She seemed to compose herself, and, once again refined her accent. "And what about you? Was Gordon kind to you?"

Sarah shrugged. "He never hit us, never even spanked us. Mum had to do any disciplining, but I wouldn't exactly say he was kind. Just cold. Gave nothing of himself to us, good or bad."

"Aye. Ah believe he was well cut up when his first wife died. Never got over it, they say."

"Yes."

"Ah b'lieve he could've saved her. If he'd got the doctor quicker. I think he blamed hisself."

"Oh, that's sad." Sarah shook her head. "If only they could have talked about these things, Mum and Dad. If only they could have unburdened themselves, helped us to understand. It might have helped. Things might have been different."

"Folks back then didn't go in a lot for all this 'unburdening'. They just got on wi' things. Locked all their hurt up inside."

"And let it fester there," Sarah added.

"Aye. Maybe. Anyway. Ah really have said enough. You should go see Father O'Brien. 12/2, remember?" Mary asked as she led Sarah to the door.

"Thank you. Yes. You've been so kind."

"Get away wi' ye!" Mary pushed her roughly ahead.

"It's helped."

"Good."

"Bye Auntie Mary." She tried to give the lady a hug, but Mary stood stiffly, surprised at the gesture and unable to respond.

"12/2, remember," her parting words.

Sarah stood on the landing again, loathe to leave its comparative freshness, dreading the stairwell, having decided not to risk the lift. Besides, she had a lot to meditate on and the stairwell was not going to be the place to linger and do it.

After a moment or two, she could hear Mary's voice. She was obviously using the telephone in her hall, not thinking that Sarah might have lingered outside, not heeding the fact that these flats afforded very little privacy. Sarah started to move away.

"Aye, ah think she's on her way ower," Mary was saying. "So ah've left it up tae him. He can tell her as much as he likes, but tell him ah think he should tell her the truth. There's been enough coverin up. Ah think he owes her that. Aye, well, like ah said, that's up tae him."

Good old Mary! Sarah blew her a kiss as she opened the door onto the stairwell. As expected, the stench rose to meet her and she took no further time to digest the information she'd already gleaned before plunging down the stairs as fast as her wobbly legs would carry her.

Once she was outside, she took a deep breath of fresh air and looked around for a wall or somewhere where she could take a moment to store away what she had learned. There was nowhere, so, her head still buzzing with facts and her heart still melting with emotion, she walked slowly across the forecourt, the car park and the opposite forecourt, not knowing what to expect from her meeting with the man who helped her mother keep her baby.

How much would he tell her... how much *could* he tell her?

Chapter 32

"So, what happened?"

"I told you. He refused to see me."

"But you knew he was in?" Kate persisted.

"I'm certain he was in."

"But he refused to see you?"

"Yes."

"And you just walked away! The man could probably tell you who your father was… and you just walked away?"

"What did you want me to do, Katie? Break the door down? Push his sister out of the way and barge into her house? *Demand* to speak to him?"

"Yes!"

"I don't think so!"

"Well, you could've tried."

"I *did* try!" Sarah wailed. "I practically begged the woman to let me in!"

"Bet you didn't. You're far too polite!"

"Katie! I did my best. Don't forget, this really matters to me. I want to know who my father is. If there had been a way to see Father O'Brien, believe me, I would have found it."

"S'pose…" Kate conceded.

"His sister was adamant! She said he was out. I couldn't call her a liar."

"But you're sure he was in?"

"Yes. I think I saw him. I think he was watching me," Sarah explained. "The bedroom door was ajar. Someone was using the mirror in that room to watch what was happening in the hall, at the front door. Watching *me*."

"Yuck!"

"I caught his eye and he jumped back. I couldn't see him any more. Anyway, his sister stepped in and closed over the bedroom door."

"And you think that was this Father O'Brien chappie?"

"Well, he had a dog-collar on. He looked about the right age." Sarah pulled a face. "Seventies, middle seventies, thereabout."

"And your aunt had told you he lived there?"

"Yes."

"So, what are you going to do now?"

"I don't know. Go back, try again, I suppose." Sarah sighed. "I would've gone back over to Mary's but, to be honest, I couldn't face those stairs again. The effort or the smell!"

"You poor thing." Kate put her arm round her mother's shoulders.

"At last!" Sarah exclaimed. "Sympathy!"

"Well, I wanted to make sure you hadn't given in too easily." Kate threw herself along the couch, her head resting on one end, her feet crossed on the other.

"I can assure you I hadn't! And get your feet off the couch," Sarah reprimanded, swatting the offending shoes. "Why haven't you taken your shoes off, anyway?"

"So, will you phone Mary again, or what?" Kate hooked her shoes off and wriggled and stretched her toes. "Before you go back, I mean?"

"That might be a good idea. But first, I think I'll check through all her letters again. See if there are any other clues."

"Meanwhile, Mother." Kate stretched. "I hope you're remembering that we're going out to dinner tonight?" she reminded her.

"Oh, damn, I'd forgotten!"

"Mother!"

"Sorry, dear. It's just that I'm exhausted." Her shoulders slumped. "Must I go?"

"Yes, you promised," Kate replied petulantly, rolling over into a reclining position, her head resting on one elbow. "If you won't let Dad come here, then at least we can get to know him a bit better on neutral ground."

"Okay, I know. I promised." Sarah stretched and yawned, getting up from her chair and making for the door. "I'll just have a half-hour catnap before I get changed."

But, when she lay on her bed, she thought she wouldn't sleep. There was so much to think about, not just today's events, though they had their place in her meditations. So much to digest.

Strange to see Mary after all this time, to hear the Glasgow accent with the hint of Irish, a hint less marked in Mary than in her brother, Patrick, her accent less pronounced when she was on guard, putting on a show for her visitor. Perhaps it would be better next time. Perhaps she'd be less nervous, more relaxed, give more.

She was drifting into a doze, when she saw again a face in a mirror, only it was her own face, then it swam out of focus. An older face, a man's face drifted back, a man's face that was also her face, David's face, her aunt's face. But the door was closing. She craned her neck, trying to catch another glimpse of it. That face... the door...

She snapped awake with that awful feeling that she had missed something... something had eluded her. She looked at her watch. Time yet. Couldn't have been asleep long. Yet, it felt as though she was waking from a deep sleep, a lengthy dream. Her heart was racing, sweat breaking on her forehead. She must leave time for a shower, calm down, freshen up.

She closed her eyes and tried to drift off to sleep again, to catch the dream, to see where it was leading her, but this time she didn't even feel drowsy. As her heart rate slowed and her body relaxed, her mind moved on to other things, things not of today, at least, not yet of today: plans to make, strategies to work out.

She needed to be sure of each stage. So much depended on the timing of everything.

Father O'Brien's refusal to see her had been unfortunate, a setback, but she would cope. Which was more than could be said for tonight's 'extravaganza'! She wished she could refuse to see

Tom! But, for very similar reasons, this was as important to Katie as seeing Father O'Brien was to her. It was all about 'bedding in' some roots.

So she dressed carefully and put on her 'happy' face.

When Mike called for them, she was ready.

Just as she was getting into the car, she said to them both, Katie and Mike, "I hope you two are remembering your part of the deal? No mention of where and how you met. No specific talk of Mike's work." She turned to address Mike particularly. "You're in Social Work, okay? You hate talking about work when you're socialising. Okay?"

They both assured her they had remembered, they would be careful, they got the message...

"I'm just not ready yet, understand?" Sarah needed even more reassurances before she settled into the back seat and let herself be chauffeured to dinner with Tom.

In the event, she needn't have worried. Tom was more interested in 'chatting her up' than getting to know Mike. The dinner went well but Sarah was glad when it was over and she could relax at home with a cup of tea.

"Dad's really got the 'hots' for you, hasn't he?" Kate asked as she took the cup Sarah offered her.

"Kate!"

"Don't you think so?"

"I wish you wouldn't talk like that, dear. It's crude."

"But he has, hasn't he?"

"He was certainly out to impress tonight. Fancy restaurant, best wine, flowers..." She nodded towards the roses she had plunged into a bucket of water when they came in earlier. "But I think he was trying to impress us all."

"So that would be why he sat gazing into your eyes all night?"

"He didn't!" Sarah protested.

"Oh no? Mike and I may as well not have been there!" Kate sulked.

"Well it wasn't my fault! I didn't give him any encouragement. Anyway, It was you who wanted your Dad and I to 'make friends'," Sarah pointed out to her daughter.

"Yeah! But I did think he might like to get to know his future son-in-law a little!"

"Perhaps it's for the best. You know how…"

"Yeah, I know how you worry."

"I know you think I'm being silly."

"Not 'silly', just ridiculous! Dad will have to find out eventually how David died. The longer you put it off…"

"I know, I know. You think it will be harder to tell him."

"Exactly!"

"But I know what I'm doing. Trust me, Kate. Please trust me on this one?"

Kate frowned. "You know, no-one blames you for David, don't you?"

"Do I?"

"There would have been nothing you could do about it, even if you had known…"

Sarah finished her tea and rose to take her cup to the kitchen. "Probably not," she agreed wearily, holding her hand out for Kate's cup too.

Instead of the cup, Kate gave her hand a squeeze. "*Certainly* not," she emphasised softly.

"I know."

Kate held on to her hand. "Do you, Mum?" she asked. "Do you *really* know that? That there was nothing you could have done differently?"

"Oh, there was plenty I could have done differently!" Sarah put the cup down on the floor and tried to pull away from Kate. "If I had my time over…" She sat beside her, anger and frustration making her tense and edgy, "…there would be an awful lot I would do differently."

"But you can't be sure it wouldn't have happened anyway."

"True! But I'd have liked the opportunity to *try* to stop it happening."

Kate drew her back, deeper into the couch, beside her, holding her. "Oh, Mum. I'm sorry. I wish I'd told you. I wish David had told you."

"I wish somebody had."

"Oh, Mum." And they sat holding one another, the old familiar pain throbbing between them.

Sarah drew out of the embrace a little. "I found his diary, you know."

"David's diary?" Kate sat up. "David kept a diary?"

"Yes."

"Have you read it?"

"Do you think I should?"

"Darn right you should!"

"But it's his private diary."

"He's dead, Mum," Kate shrugged. "He has all the privacy he needs right now. I'd read it. No hesitation, I'd read it! In fact, do you want me to read it first, make sure there's nothing that'll upset you?"

"There's plenty that upset me."

Kate, in turn, drew away. "You mean you've already read it?"

"Yes. Or, most of it. There were some parts I just couldn't make out."

"I didn't think you would. Read it, I mean."

"No, neither did I. I couldn't at first, you know how careful I am about respecting your privacy."

"That's why I'm surprised."

"Like yourself, I reasoned eventually, that David's need for privacy was not so great as my need for some answers."

"So? Was it a help?"

"Yes... and no. It helped to know what's been going on in his mind, how he felt about things, why he killed himself."

"Oh no, Mum!" Kate held her hands up. "David didn't kill himself! It was an accident. The inquest..."

Sarah waved her objection away. "David wanted to die."

"No! I don't believe you," Kate shrank back into the couch. "I don't believe you!" she shouted. "It was an accident. Bad dope. Mike said..."

"He says in his diary that he wanted to die."

"No!" Kate shook her head. "No! Stop saying that!"

Sarah tried to hold her but she pushed away roughly. "I'm sorry, Katie, darling. I'm so sorry."

But Katie had her hands over her ears. "No! No!" she kept repeating. "He didn't kill himself. I know he didn't kill himself. He just wouldn't. He wouldn't!" She looked at Sarah, waiting for her to take back the accusation. "Why are you saying that? What gives you the right to judge my brother?"

"His diary, Kate. It's in his diary."

"I want to see it!"

"And you will, my darling, you will. But not tonight."

"Why not tonight? I want to see it right now. I don't believe you! Why are you lying?"

"Oh Katie, my poor Katie," Sarah tried again to comfort her but was once again rebuffed. "I had to tell you. There are things that you're going to need to know."

Katie put her hands over her ears again. "I don't want to hear any more!" she screamed. "I hate you! I hate you!" But she fell, at last, into her mother's arms choking and sobbing. "I don't mean that, Mummy, really I don't."

"I know, love, I know. It's just hard to hear these things."

They were sitting in what was left of the living room. Kate and Mike had decided to redecorate it and the walls were half stripped, the furniture was either piled up or had dust-sheets over it. They had had to move things to make room to sit down when they came in. Sarah looked round it now, as she held Kate's shaking body and wished it looked more like home. She missed the photograph of David that had stood on the sideboard, missed looking into his smiling eyes. "Oh, David," she whispered. "What have you done to us?"

"He didn't do anything to us," Kate sobbed. "Something awful must have happened to him to make him want to die. David had so much to live for. That's why he was trying so hard to come off the drugs. Something must have happened."

"You're right, Katie. Something did happen. Something awful. That's why I need a bit of time. I need to find out exactly what did happen. I'm not ready yet to tell your Dad about David. I want to have the full story first."

"Do you know what happened?" Katie sniffed.

"I think so. More or less. But I need to check out some details."

"From the diary?"

"Yes... and other things. I've asked Mike to read the diary."

"Why Mike? Why not me?"

"I will let you read it... in due time, darling, but there are things in it I hope Mike will be able to shed some light on. Things to do with the drug scene, things I hope will lead us to his main supplier."

"That would be good."

"*If* we can do anything about it," Sarah added ruefully. "Mike assures me these people are notoriously 'slippery' to pin anything on. But we can try." She took a deep breath. "And that's why I need you to trust me, to work along with me. Can you do that, my darling?" She lifted Kate's tear-stained face to look at her.

Kate assured her with a kiss. "If it nails the bas..."

"Kate!"

"If it nails them. Anything, if it nails them!" She dried her tears with the sleeve of her top. "And I don't care what it says in David's diary, I *know* he didn't mean to kill himself!"

"Well, perhaps you're right. But he certainly wanted to die."

"Not the same thing," Kate said desperately. "You can lie in your bed feeling so awful about something that you tell yourself you just want to die. That doesn't mean you'll try to kill yourself."

"True."

"You could even tell a friend, write it in your diary. That doesn't mean you're going to do anything about it."

"Yes. But if you then die that night?" Sarah suggested.

"You could say something like that then step off the pavement under a bus. It doesn't make it suicide!"

"So you think it could just be a coincidence?"

"Why not?"

"Oh, Katie, I'd love to believe that."

"Then do believe it! Why not give David the benefit of the doubt? The inquest did!"

"Yes, oh yes," Sarah sighed, allowing Katie to clutch the straw, all the while knowing she was missing the needle.

Chapter 33

'It was a hard thing to hear what you told me, Martha, and I'm not sure as I'd rather not have heard it. Not that I doubt but what you said was true. Just that it was hard to hear

I knew you were sweet on him... let's face it... who wasn't? But he hid it well that you were his favourite. I find it hard to look at him now and I can't go to confession because it weighs heavy on me, Martha, and I wish you'd kept your secret to yourself. I won't have you speak of it again and I don't want you to visit my home again. I would be feared that he could come while you were here and I don't know what I could do about it.

I'm sorry you don't ever go to mass any more, Martha, but perhaps you're right and your eternal soul is doomed anyway. Maybe Dad was right all along. It was a terrible thing that you did, even if it wasn't just your fault. May God forgive you, Martha, cos I don't know if anyone else will.'

'A terrible thing to hear,' that's what Mary had said when she spoke to her and here it was in her letter, written not long after the visit they'd paid her when she and Robert were children. Sarah hadn't read that bit first time round. They'd been too busy laughing at the notion that Robert was 'a fine wee fellow'.

But, as she read it now, she felt sad for her mother: sad that she'd lived in such an unforgiving time. If a girl got pregnant these days hardly anyone turned a hair. They didn't care who the father was, married or not. It would be a ten-day wonder, a spot of scandal when it first got out, then, so what? He's married, big deal! If the girl decided to keep her baby, then she would get help from all sorts of agencies as well as her family, probably. Sarah knew from first-hand experience that it still wasn't easy being a single parent but at least it was seen as an option nowadays.

Martha had the double misfortune to belong to an unforgiving family too. Surely not everyone would have reacted like Martha's family, even back then?

Sarah knew what the Bible said about fornication and adultery, she knew they were sins and she bitterly regretted that she'd been foolish enough to commit them. But she knew too that there was forgiveness. The Bible says that a repentant sinner can be forgiven and she was sure that her mother would have been as repentant as she was herself. Not just sorry to have been caught, for, in many ways, neither of them were. They both were perceived as respectable, married women in the community in which they lived. The shame was what they felt inside, not something forced on them by anyone else.

Reflecting on these things, Sarah began to understand her mother's unwavering loyalty to her husband. She would have seen that as part of her self-imposed penance. She never went to chapel or church as far as Sarah could remember, but her mother had tried to instil Bible morality in her children. How it must have hurt when she saw her daughter repeating her own mistakes. How she must have worried. But, yet, she chose to inflict the same punishment... banishment.

Sarah turned again to the letters, but there were no further clues for her, only sadness. There were no more letters from Mary after that one, though she knew her mother must have continued to write. How else could she have told Mary how proud she was of her grandchildren?

* * *

"Oh, it's you again, is it?"

"You said I could come again, any time," Sarah reminded her aunt.

"Aye, but ah didnae think ye would."

"But you thought Father O'Brien would see me too, and he wouldn't. So I've come back to ask you again to help me."

"Ah cannie, hen. Ah jist cannie."

"Please, Auntie Mary, may I come in?"

"Well... seen as ye've come all this way." She stood aside and held the door open for Sarah to enter. "But that disnae mean ah'm goanna tell ye onythin'! An' besides, ah've got ma brither here."

"Patrick?"

"Aye, Patrick."

Sarah smiled. "But that's lovely. I'd love to meet him."

"Huh!" Mary seemed to doubt that the meeting would be 'lovely'. "Ye'd better come awa' ben then."

Mary had not been expecting her, yet the flat was impeccably tidy. The same could not be said for Patrick.

He sat by the fire reading a paper, his stockinged feet propped on the fender displaying filthy toenails through the holes at the toes, his fingernails no better and his clothes looking slept in, which it turned out they were.

"Aye. He's ben kippin' here by the fire the past twa nights," Mary explained.

"Till her doon the landin' cools aff," Patrick supplied.

"Or you apologise," Mary suggested.

"Huh! Hell'll freeze ower first!"

"Well yer no bidin' here till it does. Ah've aboot had it wi' you an' yer mess."

Patrick got to his feet. "Ah knaw when ah'm no wantit," he announced haughtily.

"Guid. Ye can pull the door to ahint ye."

"Uncle Patrick," Sarah intervened hastily, holding out her hand for his handshake.

He stepped back and looked at her suspiciously. "Wha's this, cryin me 'Uncle'?"

"I'm Sarah, Martha's daughter."

"Ye don't say, dae ye? Martha's bas...."

"Aye," Mary cut in quickly. "Martha's bairn."

251

"Well, well, well! So you're the wee lassie that wantit Mary's number?"

"Yes."

He stood back to get a good look at her.

"Aye, ah cin see the likeness. Ye've yer faither's nose tae."

"Whit wid you know aboot her faither?" Mary demanded.

Patrick touched his finger to the side of his nose. "Aye, ah knaw mair thin you think. Ah'm no daft."

"You knaw nothin'!"

"Weel now, maybe ah knaw mair thin you think," he repeated. "Ye wur all at it, ye dirty wee bug…"

"That's enough Patrick! You know nothing!"

Patrick chuckled, a deep throaty chuckle, filled with innuendo. "Oh, ah know whit went on ben the room when ye all thought ah wis sleepin'."

"That's enough, ah'm tellin' ye!" Mary started pushing him towards the door.

"Unnat'ral. That's whit it wis. Unnat'ral!"

"Go on. Get out. Ye've said enough. We dinnae need tae hear yer dirty talk. Ye know nothin'. Nothin', ye hear?" She stared him in the face with cold anger before giving the final push that put him out on the landing, shutting the door firmly behind him.

"Bit ah've no got ma shoes," he whimpered from beyond the closed door.

"Ye cin get them later when ye've cleaned oot yer mouth," Mary shouted back. "Pay him no heed," she said to Sarah when she returned to the living room. "He disnae know whit he's on aboot."

"Will he be all right? Will his wife have him back?"

"Dinnae you worry aboot Patrick, hen. He gets thrown out regular. As often as not he sleeps here on ma guid sofa," she said as she plumped up the cushions. "Bit she'll open the door tae him efter a bit o' shoutin' an all. It's jist their way. But noo, ye'll be needin' a wee cuppa afore ye get the train back?" she offered.

"That would be lovely, thank you."

"An' ye'd best take yer wet coat off, hen. Here gie it here. Ah'll pit it on the pulley, ben the kitchen."

"Thank you." Sarah slipped her coat off and handed it to Mary, glad to be out of its cold dampness. The rain had been steady all day, creating deep puddles in the forecourt of the flats. She had been glad too, to take off her wet shoes as she came in the house, though she knew they'd be unpleasant to put back on, cold and wet as they'd still be.

"Here gie us yer shoes too, hen. Ah'll pit them under the boiler. They'll no be sae caul when ye pit th'm on again."

Gratefully, Sarah handed her the shoes. "Thank you."

"Ah'll pit the kettle on," Mary said as she went through to the kitchen.

"What did Patrick mean, he knew what went on when he was asleep?" she called after her.

"Ah telt ye. Pay him nae heed. He knaws nothin," Mary shouted back. "He thinks he dis, bit he disnae. Jist you relax an' get yersel' warmed up by the fire, hen, an' forget Patrick an' his imaginins."

So Sarah put her uncle's crude innuendo out of her mind and, holding her hands to the fire, waited patiently for her cup of tea.

She used the time to catch her breath from the rocky encounter with Patrick after the long, odorous climb up the stairs, worse this time because the dampness added its own distinctive, musty smell to the whole property. Thankfully, Mary's flat smelled of polish and fresh air. Even on a wet, miserable autumn day, Mary had her window open a crack.

Once again, she looked around the tidy room, comparing it to the room remembered from childhood. The walls here were plain, magnolia emulsion; the remembered swirls of bright colour, the paper thick and textured. She remembered being fascinated by it. She had sat in a corner quietly picking away at a loose end, pressing the raised surface flat, watching it recover its bubbled effect. If her mother or Mary had known what she was up to, no doubt there would have been a scolding for her, but, as it was, they were too intent on their quiet, intense conversation. From time to time, their voices would become raised, Mary's in anger, Martha's in anguish. Then Sarah would stop her surreptitious destruction to listen, but she could make little sense of it all.

"You were angry that day, when my mother came to your old house," Sarah stated when Mary came through with the tray.

"Aye, ah wis angry. She shouldnae hae telt me whit she did."

"She told you who my father was."

"Aye. An' fine ah wish she hidnae." Mary put the tray down and, having checked it over, returned to the kitchen for some forgotten item.

"But why did it make you angry?" Sarah called after her.

"Because she had the ruin of a good man on her tongue."

"A married man?"

Mary looked at her cautiously. "Ye could say that."

"A 'pillar of society'? A man with a good reputation?"

"Aye, ye could say that."

"A man who thought more of his 'good name', his 'reputation' than of my mother and his unborn child."

"Ye could say that too, but it widnae be fair. He wis a guid man... jist a weak yin."

"How long had they been lovers?"

"That ah dinnae ken, but ah'm thinkin' it must hae been the best part o' that winter."

"The winter of '54?"

"Aye. '54, '55."

"And on into spring then, because I was born in December '55," Sarah reasoned.

"Aye."

"How did they meet?"

"Och, she'd known him a long time. We all had. He'd growd up in our street and came back efter... efter... Aye, well he came back."

"And?" Sarah prompted.

"She used to help at the youth club. We all did. Those of us as were too old tae be in it, we helped wi' the bairns. Faither O'Brien's idea it wis. He wis all fur the young yins in thae days..." Her voice trailed off. "Look, hen. Ah cannie tell ye whit ye want tae know. Ah jist cannae. Ah telt ye afore, it's no mine tae tell." She picked up her cup and saucer and occupied herself with the business of stirring and drinking her tea.

254

Sarah waited quietly, sensing correctly that Mary more than half wanted to tell her anyway.

"She used to stay back. After the youth club, she would stay back to help with the clearin' up. Wan or twa did."

"And my father was one of those?"

"Ye could say that. Sometimes it would end up wi' jist her an' him. He'd see her safe hame. Or that's whit we were thinkin! We didnae know whit wis goin' on afore they got that length. She says he didnae seduce her, she wis willin'. They were in love, she thought." Mary shook her head. "Playin' wi' fire, she wis. He wis a weak man." She shook her head more sadly and sighed. "Aye, a weak man."

The silence was broken only by the gentle sipping of her tea as she let her mind trail back to those long forgotten days: days she must have thought would stay forgotten.

"He should've known better than tae mess wi' an innocent like yer mother," she tutted. "Claims he never noticed her before. She wis younger than him by eight or nine years. A different generation almost. She wis jist a kid when he went away, a woman when he came back. An' beautiful, an' wi' a nice, trustin nature," she sniffed. "Ah blame *him* masel'. He should hiv known better. She says she wis willin, bit ah say he shouldnae hae taken advantage!"

They sat for a while, the crackle of information between them, both disclosed and expected, like static electricity. Sarah's skin tingled, goosebumps on her arms, prickling at the roots of her hair.

It was Mary who broke the tense silence between them.

"Would you like to see some photographs of your mother?" she asked carefully, her accent gone, her diction perfect.

With a sigh, Sarah realised that Mary's guard was back up, her tongue back in control, her heart being overruled by her head.

"I'd love to. I only have a few. Mum hated getting her photograph taken."

"Did she?" Mary sounded surprised. "Oh, she used tae love it. Look. Ah've got a great bundle o' her." And she pulled out of the sideboard drawer, a chocolate box of photographs.

"Are they all of my Mum?" Sarah asked incredulously.

"Well, o' her and the rest o' us but she's in a lot o' them. These are the old yins. All these..." The sweep of her arm indicated the many little gilt frames around the room. "These are mair o' *my* kids an' *my* man, an' ma gran'children," she added proudly, "but ah dinnae suppose *they*'ll be o' much int'rest tae ye the now."

"I'd noticed them," Sarah said truthfully.

"But these ye'll be interested in!" Mary held the box up, shaking it gently to let her guest hear the rattle of its precious contents.

"Yes," she nodded.

"There's some go right back tae when we were all bairns thegether. Uncle James wis a great one wi' his box-Brownie." She picked out some of the early snap shots.

"Like David," Sarah said without thinking.

"David?"

"My son. He used to love taking photographs. So did my brother, Robert, funnily enough. I used to think David took after Robert. But, of course... of course... they weren't really... Robert wasn't actually..."

Mary patted her hand. "It's okay, hen. You jist enjoy some o' these old photies," she encouraged her, putting a bundle in her lap.

It was a delight to Sarah to see her mother as a young child. None of these photographs had been passed on to Martha, so none of them were among the few she and Robert had found. "Oh, look!" she exclaimed. "Look at her face! Wasn't she sweet? And this one. Is that you with my mum?"

"Aye, it's me, hen," Mary smiled. "We had been on the steamer, sailin doon the Clyde. Uncle James took us for the day. Aye, it wis a braw day," she reminisced. "He used tae dae that frae time tae time. It wis the only chance we had o' a day oot. There wis nae money fur outin's in oor hoose!" She held her hand as though round a glass, supping beer.

"How old were you in this one?"

"Och ah must hae been about eight or nine, yer mither about five or six."

"And this one?"

Mary laughed. "Wid ye jist look at that skirt! An' we thought we were the 'bees' knees'! Yer mother hid jist turned eighteen. That photie was taken at her birthday perty. My, whit a sight we were!" She took the photograph out of Sarah's hands and looked at it fondly. "Made they skirts wersel's, sure we did. All that net. Seven layers yer Mum had in her underskirt. Seven layers! She had tae beg, borrow and steal tae get a' that net. She haggled wi' the man at the 'barras' tae git a good price on it!" She shook her head. "Aye, she could charm her way tae onythin she wanted, that one."

Sarah looked through a few more of the photographs, ranging from Martha's childhood through to her as a young adult. From time to time she'd comment or ask a question or two, but mostly, she just savoured this unexpected treat, the chance to peep into her mother's past.

Mary enjoyed sharing the stories that went with the images, and Sarah encouraged her to tell them. She held up another. "And this one?"

"Aye. The youth club. 1954."

Sarah looked at the photograph closely, studying each face in turn. "That's him," she whispered, pointing. "That's my father, isn't it?"

Mary sighed. "Aye, hen. Ye could say that."

Chapter 34

"And you learn that you really can endure
you really are strong
and you really do have worth
And you learn and you learn
with every goodbye, you learn... "
1971 Veronica A. Shoffstall

David's eyes! David's eyes, David's smile: there was no mistaking them. Her own eyes, her own smile. The same.

"Oh, God, no," Sarah groaned. "Oh no, not that. Oh my poor, poor mother!"

"Aye," intoned Mary. "Ye could say that."

"But how could she let it happen?" She hit the photograph she held in her hand. "How could *he* let it happen?"

"Like ah said," Mary sighed. "He was a guid man, but a weak yin. She was his weakness. She got under his skin, he couldnae let her go."

"But he *did* let her go," Sarah said angrily, throwing down the picture, pushing it from her, not wanting to look into those eyes, eyes so like her own, so like her son's. "He *did* let her go. He let her *and* his baby go!"

"But what was he to do, lassie? He'd made a vow."

"He should have thought of that before he made love to my mother!"

"Aye, ah daresay ye're right there."

"What was he thinking of? How could he let things go that far?"

"Like I say..."

"Weak? 'A weak man', you said," Sarah blazed, reaching for the photograph again, hating it, yet fascinated by it too, wanting to see it but hating to look at it. "Criminal, more like!" she said to him.

"Hardly that, hen!" Mary looked up as Sarah paced around her little livingroom, the photograph in her hand, her agitation not allowing her to settle.

"But he must have known the risks. He of all people! He must have known she could fall pregnant."

"Ah don't suppose that wis in his mind at the time."

"But it should have been!" Sarah declared, sitting down abruptly on the couch. "You said the affair went on for months. He should have guessed at some point that it could only end badly. Why didn't he stop it before it went that far?"

"He wis besotted wi' her. It wis out o' control!"

"*He* was out of control, out of order!" She was up again, pacing again, waving the picture about. "Surely self-control is something that he's supposed to know about?"

"Sure, an' ye're right enough there, hen."

"He must have known that he couldn't take the responsibility, no, *wouldn't* take the responsibility! An honourable man would have! If he'd been an honourable man, he'd have owned up, he'd have sacrificed his position to care for his child!"

"He would have been ruined."

"So? *She* was! He let my mother face the shame, the disgrace, the humiliation, the ruin on her own! He let her be cast out of her family, with nowhere to go, no one to go to."

"He found her a place."

"Oh yes. He found her a place in a convent, then he set her up in a loveless marriage. To... to a man not even of the same faith, a man she'd never seen." Her anger and frustration threw her down onto the sofa again. "He stood back and watched her pain."

"What else was he to do?" Mary pleaded for him.

"He could have left the priesthood and married her! Would that have been so difficult? If he'd loved her, he would have done it!"

"Aye, lass. Daresay, ye're right," Mary sighed heavily. "Ah had the thought masel'. Couldnae go tae confession tae him ever again. Nor mass. Ah couldnae bear tae see the man's face efter yer mither telt me. Fair broke ma hert fur her," Mary sniffed.

"Oh Mary," Sarah sobbed, sliding from her seat and going to kneel by Mary, her arms around her aunt's waist, the embrace tolerated this time. "Oh Mary, my poor, poor mother."

"Aye, lass. Aye, ah knaw." And she held Sarah tightly as they cried together for the shame and suffering of the one they'd both loved.

Chapter 35

"Father O'Brien!" Kate exclaimed. "You're telling me you're father was a priest?"

Sarah nodded. She was exhausted. All she wanted to do was have a long, hot bath and go to bed, but Kate had been waiting for her, desperate to know how she had got on. She hadn't been able to fob her off with 'I'll tell you later.' It wouldn't have been fair.

"So, what are you going to do?"

Sarah shrugged. "Do?"

"Well, are you going to try to see him?"

She shook her head. "No. I doubt it. Certainly not in the foreseeable future."

"No?"

"No," Sarah repeated wearily. "I really have absolutely no desire to see the man."

"Not even out of curiosity?"

She shook her head again. "Not even out of curiosity."

"So what do you feel about him?"

"Nothing but contempt! The man has no honour, no guts! Even my Dad, Gordon, stepfather, I suppose," she mumbled, "had more honour. In fact, for all his faults, he was, at least, an honourable man. He made an honest bargain with my mother, with no pretence, and they both kept to it. I have to respect that." She leant back in her chair and closed her eyes. "It's funny. On the train coming home today, I started to feel, I don't know, a sort of gratitude, I suppose you'd call it, to my dad. He gave Mum what she needed. Respectability." Sarah rubbed her forehead, trying to think as her mother, wanting to understand. "She seemed to need that," she shrugged. "I suppose, in her own way, she was happy. As happy as she was able to be, in her circumstances. She loved Robert and me. We loved her. We were close, the three of us. Perhaps that's as much as she felt she had a right to."

261

"Maybe she loved Grandad?"

"Can't imagine it. He was never easy to love. Anyway, Mary says she told her she still loved Fa... ath... *him*. God," she pleaded. "How can I call my father 'Father', in that way? It's awful! I'm not even a Catholic and it seems sacrilegious!"

"It's weird!" Katie agreed.

"It's hideous! I just keep remembering his face in that mirror, at his sister's. You know, that day?"

Kate nodded.

"I keep remembering how he was watching me." She shivered. "You're right, it's weird."

"D'you think he'll know Mary told you?"

"Mary didn't tell me," Sarah replied quickly. "I knew as soon as I saw the photograph. In fact, I think I knew before that. Maybe when I saw him in the mirror." She shivered again. "There just was something…"

"D'you think she'll tell him you know?"

"Doubt it," Sarah shook her head, shrugging. "She claims she hasn't seen him in years, hasn't spoken to him since Mum told her. D'you know, she really loved my Mum. She really misses her. Grieves for her."

"Will you keep in touch with Mary, d'you think?"

"I really don't know," Sarah answered after a moment or two's thought. "I really don't know. Perhaps. Maybe later, when it's all sunk in. When I've tied together all the other loose ends."

"Other loose ends? What d'you mean? What other loose ends?"

Sarah got up and stretched her weary limbs. "Oh, nothing, nothing. Just this and that. Listen, I'm going to have a really long, lazy bath, so if you need into the loo, now's your chance." She rubbed her aching back. "I don't intend to surface for quite some time."

Chapter 36

"So where shall we go for dinner?"

"I thought we were going to look at your 'books'?"

"Time enough for that." Tom looked at his watch. "It's nearly seven o'clock."

"Twenty past six actually."

"Well, near enough. Anyway, I'm starving. So where shall we go?"

"Anywhere... except that awful dungeon you took me to the first time!"

"Yes, sorry about that. Wasn't exactly cosy, was it?"

"Awful!" Sarah shuddered.

They were sitting in Tom's car outside the house. She'd watched for his arrival and emerged from the front door before he had time to get out of the car, pre-empting any chance of his coming inside.

"Do you still like Italian food?" he asked now.

"Yes, but you don't have to... "

"Armando's. How about 'Armando's'? For old times sake?"

"Goodness! Is 'Armando's' still there?"

"I think so," Tom replied.

"I'm never over that way. Haven't been in years."

"'Armando's' it is then. Let's go!" And he started up the engine and drove off, the decision made.

"You look lovely, Sarah," he whispered as he proudly escorted her into the restaurant a little later. "You've hardly aged at all. You're still beautiful. If anything, the years have only improved your face and figure."

"Flatterer!" she blushed. "You haven't changed much either. You still have a smooth tongue!" But she was pleased with his flattery anyway.

Their banter continued for a time as they were shown to a table and offered the menu. Once they had dispensed with the business of choosing their food, there was an awkward silence for a moment or two.

The following day would be the twenty-fifth year since their 'marriage', when Tom had first taken her to 'Armando's' to celebrate. They had returned for their first anniversary and every anniversary after that... until Tom disappeared. Sitting in the same corner they always sat in all those years ago, looking around at the refurbished but still familiar restaurant, Sarah wondered if Tom remembered it was their anniversary on Saturday.

"D'you remember the first time we came here?" he asked.

"When we decided to live together," she added.

"I hadn't forgotten," he said. "I hoped you'd agree to come today. It's been twenty-four years," he stated proudly.

"Twenty-five actually," she smiled.

"Well, twenty-five today," he shrugged.

"Tomorrow."

"Tomorrow, then! Damn! I thought I'd got it right!"

"Near enough."

"Anyway, I thought we could celebrate."

"Celebrate what? The twelve years we were together? Or the twelve... no, thirteen years we haven't been together?"

"Sarah, you..."

"I said I'd try not to go on about it! I know. Sorry," she shrugged. "Couldn't help it. It's just kind of hard...."

"I know. I'm sorry too. Start again?" he asked, smiling into her eyes.

She nodded. "Start again."

He reached into his pocket. "I got you something," he said, handing her a small package.

"Oh, Tom. You shouldn't... I didn't..."

"Please, Sarah," he pleaded, offering the package again.

"But, I..."

"Let me spoil you a little."

With a smile, she took the gift and opened it. "Thank you, Tom. They're beautiful," she said, genuinely pleased with the present as well as the thought.

Sarah had dressed especially carefully tonight and she knew that the soft creamy blouse she had chosen complimented the golden tones of her skin and the golden flecks in her brown eyes. She felt good. The gold earrings Tom gave her were perfect, the last brush stroke, as Tom lost no time in telling her.

"What a picture. My golden girl."

"Hardly a girl," Sarah giggled.

"My girl," Tom replied.

The warm glow stealing over Sarah felt delicious. She became aware of all the delights around her; the gentle perfume of her own skin, the stronger smell of the food being prepared, the taste of the wine, the soft music playing in the restaurant and the warmth of Tom's hand resting on hers.

She looked at his dark, handsome face. He had matured well. The greying hair at his temples was attractive and his skin was still smooth and soft, clean-shaven and lightly tanned. He had brown eyes, tinged with green and fringed by long dark lashes. A long forgotten feeling stirred in her.

When Armando, *surely not the same Armando?* had realised they were celebrating, he brought them a bottle of champagne. The bubbles made Sarah giggle like a young girl... Tom's girl. When Tom held her hand, the years rolled back and all the old feelings were still there, pushing, surging, rising.

It was happening again! Just like the first time. He was humming the old tune and she could feel herself move to its rhythm. She had tried to resist, but the old, remembered melody drew her to him. As they talked and in their silences, she felt the centre of her being shift and change, the pain floating out as the languorous warmth drifted in. It had taken a long time for the hope within her to die. It had not been long or deeply buried. Now it rose again like a geyser bubbling up within her.

The champagne, the soft music, the aromatic food all conspired to breach her defences. Tom had chosen the restaurant well. Nostalgia played its part in her defeat. As they talked and laughed over shared memories, memories of happy, joyous times, her frustration and anger were quelled. The dreadful anguish of all those lonely years seemed forgotten, as are the pains of labour when a child is born.

The evening lengthened, the 'books' forgotten, the moments savoured.

"Let me take you home, Sarah." His voice was husky, remembered too, his hands lingering on her neck, sliding down her arms as he put her coat around her shoulders and led her to his car.

"The old house still the same?" he asked as he gently roused her when they reached the gate.

"I wasn't really sleeping," she smiled up at him, "only dreaming."

"We had some happy years here, didn't we, doll?"

Sarah leant closer. "Would you like to come in for coffee?" she asked.

* * *

Tom looked around at the old familiar things in the living room while Sarah put the kettle on.

"We had some good times in this house, didn't we, doll?" he called through softly. "It hasn't changed much, new cushions, different wallpaper, but still the same." He picked up a book from the sideboard and pulled a face at the title. "'Holding on'. Sounds cheery," he muttered, putting it back, scanning a few more titles, prowling round the once-familiar room, a room that contained nothing of him, a room that never had. It had been Sarah who fashioned its original style, its colours, its comfort. He had merely lived in it. "I always liked this room," he called through again. "Your taste always was classy."

"Thank you," Sarah smiled, setting down the two cups on the table beside the couch.

"Katie out?" Tom enquired sipping his coffee. "Hey, this is good!"

"Don't sound so surprised."

"Well! Coffee didn't used to be your strong point, as I remember."

"Only because you used to bring home that ghastly, cheap stuff you got from one of your customers!"

"Cheap! That wasn't cheap! Those were the best Chilean coffee beans you could get..."

"As a freebie!"

"Well, at least there was plenty of it."

"You never could resist a bargain, could you? Even if it was rubbish."

"Anyway," he raised his cup to her. "This is okay."

"Thank you," she said again.

"Katie?"

"Out with Mike."

"The boy of the blushes," Tom mumbled with a grin.

Sarah smiled a question.

"When I teased her, about boyfriends, she blushed," he explained with a shrug. "Mike." He shook his head. "My little girl is getting married. A Social Worker or something, isn't he?"

"Yes, and he does voluntary work in the evenings."

"Busy man."

"She wants you to get to know him."

"That would be nice. He seemed a genuine sorta fella."

"Yes," she agreed, crossing to the window to close the curtains, shutting out the wintry chill that was creeping into her bones. Shivering slightly, she closed her eyes for a moment and wrapped her arms around herself. "God, I hate this time of year," she muttered. "Such a waste."

"Sorry?"

Instead of an explanation, Sarah turned to him with a smile, then, switching one of the little table lamps on, "there, that's cosier, isn't it?" she said.

"No, don't sit over there, Sarah. Come. Sit beside me here." He patted the couch beside him. "Please."

Sarah hesitated for a moment.

"Please," he repeated softly.

267

Chapter 37

The evening air was cool and Mike put his arm round Katie's shoulders as they walked from the community centre to the car across the road. Mike had been leading a question and answer discussion about drug addiction among young people, aimed at helping the local community become better informed and therefore better able to help their friends or relatives involved with the problem.

"You were a great help. That was a good session," he said to Kate, giving her a squeeze as he spoke.

"Thank you. I enjoyed it. It's good to be able to help." And it was good. To feel that perhaps her experience could help someone else, that it hadn't been for nothing.

"Listen Katie," Mike said as he opened the car door for her. "I need to talk with you. Can we go somewhere for coffee or something?"

"Sure. Your place or mine?" Katie quipped.

"Yours, if that's okay." Mike ignored her flippancy. "I'd like to talk to your Mum too."

"Sounds serious," Katie dropped her voice to a husky baritone. "You'd better tell me now, Bluey. I can take it!"

Mike shook his head and gave her a rueful grin. "I'm afraid it is serious, and I'm not sure that you can take it, you or your mother," he added with a deep sigh, as he pulled out into the traffic.

"But you said yourself that I can take anything since David."

"She's seeing a lot or your father again, isn't she?"

"Who?"

"Your Mum."

"Yep, it's great. Really perked her up. But you've seen that for yourself!"

"Yes."

"You don't sound too happy about it, Mike. I thought we agreed to encourage her to get out more."

"Don't remind me!"

"What d'you mean? What's wrong? You've been quiet all evening. In fact you've not been right since, I don't know, for ages, weeks. What's on your mind? Is it us? D'you want…"

"No… no," he reassured her quickly, putting his hand on her knee, pulling it towards him. "We're cool," he grinned at her. "Cool."

"Good," she smiled back at him. "You had me worried for a bit there." She let her breath out again. "So, what's wrong then? What's so serious?"

Mike didn't reply at once. He waited until they were clear of the traffic. "Katie. Did your Mum tell you she let me read David's diary?"

"Yes, she did. I was a bit miffed, actually. I thought she should have let me see it first."

"There was a reason she gave it to me first. You see, she thought some of the entries threw some light on …"

"…David's supplier. I know. She told me."

"Well, it did."

"And?"

"I made some more enquiries, did a bit of snooping, got a bit of help from a pal in the drug squad…"

"And?"

"And that's what I need to discuss with you and your Mum."

They were turning into the street where Kate and Sarah lived, where he would soon join them after he and Kate got married. A nice enough street: ordinary, council house estate, pleasant houses, neat gardens. Tonight it felt like a war zone to Mike. He was tense and anxious, filled with apprehension.

"I'm not sure she'll be home yet. She and Dad went out for a meal."

"I was afraid you would say that," he sighed as he drew up outside the house.

"Why?" she asked. "Oh, that's Dad's car over there." She pointed it out to Mike. "Mum must have let him bring her home. Progress!"

Mike groaned.

"What's wrong? I thought you'd be pleased. Now you'll get the chance to chat with him, get to know him, like we wanted."

"A problem! A big problem! No, don't get out." He reached across to stop her opening the door. "I think we need to talk before you go in."

"I'm listening," she said, frowning, frightened.

"Does the name Harry Fame mean anything to you?"

"Harry Fame?" Katie shrugged. "Don't think so. Fame. Isn't that the name on Dad's shop?"

"Yes. He sometimes uses the name Harry Fame."

"Harry? Harry!" Memory stirred in Kate.

Chapter 38

Sarah and Tom didn't hear Katie until she was pounding up the stairs. She burst into the room before they had time to do more than straighten their clothes.

"Katie!" Sarah prepared to scold her daughter for her rudeness but was shocked at the whiteness of her face, the tears, the wildness in her eyes.

"No! Oh no," Katie groaned.

"Katie dear..." Tom began.

"No!" she screamed. "No!" She threw herself across his legs punching wildly at his body. "No! No! NO!"

"Stop it Katie! You're hysterical! Stop it!" Sarah was scrabbling, straightening her clothes, trying to pull Katie off of Tom.

"It's all right. It's all right," Tom soothed, stroking Katie's hair, warding off her ineffectual blows. "Your mother and I are not doing anything wrong."

"But I know who you are. I know who you are," she sobbed.

"Of course you do, doll."

"I know *what* you are!" She pushed his hand away.

Sarah tried to lift Katie off the bed. "Come on Katie. It's all right. I know."

"No, Mum," she sobbed, clinging on to Sarah. "You don't! He's... he's..."

"I'm your father," Tom said firmly, disentangling himself and sitting on the edge of the bed.

Kate pushed herself up from the bed. She faced Tom.

"Do you want to know how David died?" she spat at him.

"No Katie, not this way!" Sarah said. "It's all right. I know."

"Oh yes, Mother. Yes! It's time *he* knew! It's time he found out what happens to nice young boys who meet up with pigs like him!"

"Katie!"

"David died of a drugs overdose, Father dear. He was a drug addict!"

"Stop it Katie," Sarah said firmly, holding her arms. "Stop it!" But Katie wasn't finished.

Facing her father scornfully she demanded, "Well, Father, what do you say to that? Your own son, a junkie! And you, and you, dear father, a pusher! A drug peddler. Someone who sells drugs. To young boys." She brushed the tears from her eyes with an angry, impatient gesture. "Like David!"

"Sarah?" He turned to her.

Sarah squared up to him. "Yes, Tom?"

"Sarah, I…"

"Don't waste your breath, Tom. She's right. Except that you don't just sell drugs to boys *like* David. You *did* sell them to David."

"But, Mum." Kate stared at her mother in horror. "You just… you…" She looked towards the bed. "How could you?"

"It's okay, Katie." She held her by both arms and forced her to look straight at her. "Trust me, just trust me. I knew what I was doing."

"What d'you mean?" Tom asked, standing up, looking foolish, his hair tousled, his face flushed with their love-making, his clothes in disarray, no dignity. "What d'you mean 'you knew what you were doing'?"

Sarah drew Kate close to her for a moment. Her voice was cold and calm. "I had a plan, you see." She looked down at Katie. "You've pre-empted it a little, Katie love, but I don't think it'll matter."

"But…"

"David found you, Tom. As Harry Fame, small-time crook, big-time drug dealer. He came to you, as recommended by one of his fellow druggies. Came with what he thought were his valuables to trade for drugs."

"This is nonsense!" Tom ran his fingers through his hair, trying to tidy up, feel more in control.

"He wrote it all down in his diary. Took me a while to read it all, to get to the nasty ending."

"This is nonsense, a fairy story. It's not true!"

"No? What about his watch? The one I bought back from you, the one he gave you in exchange for drugs? And his ring? He gave you his CD player as well, but I didn't see that in the shop. Sold it on, had you? Plenty buyers for that sort of thing, eh? Not so easy with old watches and rings, especially if they were never too valuable in the first place. But you took them anyway. Just to keep him hooked, eh Tom? You knew he'd have to come up with real money soon. They always do, don't they. As long as you keep them hooked."

"I don't know what you're talking about. If I had anything of David's in the shop, then he must have sold them to me as second hand."

"No. No receipts. He always kept receipts. I found all the others. For his camera, his binoculars. He'd kept the receipts when he pawned them. But he didn't need to pawn things after he found you, did he Tom? You set up a barter system for young lads like David!"

"Fantasy!"

"He wrote it all down in his diary. How he came to you, looking for something to 'pep up a party', not knowing who 'Harry Fame' would turn out to be!"

"What diary?"

"David's diary. The one I've given to the police. Once Mike had read it and agreed with me about what it said, I handed it over to the police. They should search you out pretty soon," she said to Tom.

"They're at the shop now," Mike interjected.

"It won't hold up..."

"I think you'll find it will," Mike said from the doorway. "Especially when you add it to the evidence we already have from our surveillance."

"And my testimony that a well-known drug addict frequents your shop."

"I don't know what you're talking about."

"I thought I recognised that customer who changed his mind. You remember? It was the first, or was it the second time I came down to the shop? He called you Harry, then made a quick exit when he saw me. I realised later who it was, the un-cooperative guy from Omega House, Alan Hoddle. Name mean anything to you? Eh, 'Harry'?" She sneered the question, her mouth contorted with disgust. "I watched him even more closely after that. Followed him to your shop one night. Realised he was the one in the diary, the one who pointed David in your direction."

"This is all circumstantial evidence! You've built a case on fantasy. The angry scribbling of a teenage boy, the imaginings of a distraught mother, getting revenge on an old boyfriend."

Sarah reached into the bedside drawer. "Distraught mother, you say. Well, you're his father! Let's see how it feels! Remember him?" She pushed a photograph into Tom's hands, making him look into the eyes of his son. David smiled up at him. "Remember him now, do you Tom? He came into the shop one night, gave you his treasure, left in shock! Looks like you, doesn't he?"

Tom was pale, the photograph dropped from his trembling hands.

Sarah picked it up and held it out for him to see again. "How does it feel to look at the son you killed, Tom?" she said quietly. "How does it feel?"

He sat down on the bed, his head in his hands.

"Bit AC/DC in prison, eh Tom? Even tried it with your own son! His watch, his ring, they didn't amount to much, did they? You told him they weren't enough for what he wanted. You knew these young lads would do anything for drugs... anything!" Bile rose to her throat. "But not David, eh Tom? Not David! That's what made him want to die. He took your filthy drugs and ran home to die because his own father tried to..."

"That's enough!" Tom shouted. "None of this is true! None of it!"

"He wrote it all down Tom. Everything! It's all in his diary."

"But you were letting him make love to you, Mum. You knew and you let him touch you," Kate wailed, her face twisted in disgust. "You were going to... going to..."

Sarah held her again, making her look into her eyes. "Look at me Katie." She smiled at her, her voice softening. "It's all right, my precious. I would never sleep with scum like that. You do believe me, don't you, Katie?"

Katie nodded.

"Good! You see, I had a plan. I had no intention of letting it get that far. He's a rotten lover, selfish, always was." She turned maliciously on Tom. "But I'd remembered all the moves, hadn't I, Tom? *I* always knew how to please *you*, didn't I? Blew your mind, didn't it? You told me there'd never been anyone else like me. Well there never was. And there never will be."

Tom was still sitting on the bed, his head in his hands, the photograph on the floor in front of him.

Sarah turned back to Katie. "I was waiting for the right moment. Leading him on, making him vulnerable. Then, when he thought I was reaching into the drawer for something else, I was going to produce the photograph." She lifted it up, smiling back to the smiling boy.

"Let you see how your son had grown up," she said to Tom. "See if that cooled your ardour. Better than any known method of birth control, I'd think, wouldn't you?" she asked maliciously. "They'll lock you up for a very long time this time, Tom. I thought I'd make sure you knew what you were missing. I should think you'll be a very old man when, *if,* you ever get out. Past it, I should think, don't you?"

"You bitch!"

She shook her head. "Language, Tom. Not in front of the children. Oops, I forgot, we only have one now! You killed our boy, didn't you? You gave him the filth that killed him. He can't hear you now, Tom. But *I* can hear *him*. Can you hear him? His pain, crying out from his diary. Can you hear it?" She pushed her face close to his. "You will, Tom. Yes, you'll hear it. I'll make sure you do. When they read it out in court, you'll hear it. You'll hear how he found you, not through all his efforts to trace you, not because you came looking for your children. But because he was introduced to you by another druggie. As a source, a supplier. He didn't find his father, he found his seducer... his murderer!"

275

Tom pushed her out of the way and headed for the door. Mike stood in his way. "Don't think so, chum," he said, barring his flight.

"Let him go, Mike," Sarah said. "He's got nowhere to hide. The Police'll pick him up. They've probably been looking for him all afternoon. Could be right outside our door. Let him run! Let him run. Like the rat he is."

Chapter 39

The morning of Kate's wedding dawned bright and clear, a perfect spring morning.

"Not a cloud in the sky," Sarah observed, looking from the bedroom window, taking a deep breath of the fresh, sweet air, before closing it. "Don't you just love spring? Everything feels so clean and good. A new beginning! A new year growing into itself, sheltering hope in its cusp."

"Mmm, very poetic!"

"Well. I feel so good," Sarah laughed. "And you look absolutely radiant, my darling."

"And so do you, Mum." Kate's tone was tender as she smiled back. "And younger than I can ever remember. A new beginning," she agreed, taking her mother's hands in her own.

They stood gazing at one another for some minutes, words not needed to express the love, the hope, the relief they both shared, the happiness they had fought for.

"Are you all packed?" Kate asked at last.

"Yes. And you?"

"Yes." Kate scooped up the fullness of her skirts and did a pirouette of delight. "Isn't it exciting?"

"Very," Sarah agreed with a laugh. "Who'd have thought you'd be honeymooning in Barbados?"

"And you'd be jetting off to Canada?"

"I know. Isn't it fun?"

"Good old Uncle Robert."

"Did I hear my name?" Robert said, poking his head round the bedroom door seconds before knocking on it.

"Hey, we usually knock *first*," Sarah remonstrated. "Good job the bride's ready."

"And so she should be! The car's due in five minutes. Since I have to give this gorgeous creature away, we'll do it right. We'll be on time. Not keep that poor lad waiting for his blushing bride. He's been patient enough."

"Yes, he has, hasn't he? He's a good sort."

"Sound!" Robert pronounced. "And you look like a princess. And what about my sister?" He turned to admire Sarah. "You look terrific. More like the bride's sister than her mother."

"Flatterer!"

"I only call things as I see them. I'm so proud of you, Sis."

"David would be so proud of you too," Kate added.

"Yes, I think he would." She looked at his photograph on the dressing table.

"He always used to say, 'Mum'll know what to do.' And you did. If only…"

Sarah took her daughter's face in her hands. "Don't look back, Katie. What happened, happened. We can't change it. We have to move on now. We have to grow. Say goodbye to the past."

"I know. I know, Mum."

"We have to learn from it. Learn that we *are* strong, that we really do have worth. As a family. But as individuals too."

Kate nodded.

"I've learned that. I know now who I am. That my identity doesn't depend on anyone else. I'm me… and I'm proud of me!" She stood tall. "Who can say what's in front of us? I can't! But I'm ready for it… whatever it is!"

"That'a girl, Sis!"

"Canada won't know what's hit it, when I get there. I thank you for the sister-flat, Robert, but, you know, I don't intend to be semi-detached to anyone, ever again. I'll use your extension as a base, but I'm going exploring!"

"Great," Robert applauded.

"What if you meet someone?" Kate asked.

"Lovely! I hope I do," Sarah laughed. "But, he'll have to be willing to put up with the new, self-sufficient me!"

"Formidable!" Robert declared.

"Scary!" Kate decided.

"And proud of it!" Sarah announced.

"I wish David could see you now, Mum. Apart from anything else, he'd want to go with you. Canada, Alaska, everywhere!"

They laughed.

"But that would defeat the purpose," Sarah explained. "The point is that I'm learning to live for *me*. Not for you, or David, or anyone else. For *me!* I've got to go it alone for a while, stop leaning on everyone else. Stand up and be *me...* and all the other clichés."

"Car's here!" shouted Robert from the window.

Sarah held her daughter close, then, stepping back a little, she took Katie's face in her hands and looked lovingly into her eyes.

"Remember David as he was, my love. We'll see him again, in God's due time. And we'll be here to greet him, as family... *his* family. That's what matters."

She kissed her daughter tenderly. "Have a good life, my Katie," she whispered. "David would have wished that for you."

End.

Printed in the United Kingdom by
Lightning Source UK Ltd., Milton Keynes
140275UK00001BB/103/P